TRACKER

A Fox Walker Novel

Indy Quillen

TRACKER

Copyright © 2016 by Indy Quillen

Cover design by James T. Egan, Bookfly Design

All Rights Reserved

For information address Treeline Press, 1106 Second Street, Encinitas, CA 92024

Library of Congress Catalog Number: 2016911496

Treeline Press, Encinitas, CA

ISBN: 0997777702

ISBN: 9780997777703

Treeline Press paperback edition / October 2016

Kindle edition / October 2016

To Michael, my best friend and husband
To my sons, Scott and Andrew, who share my love of writing
To you, Mom, for supporting my dreams

AUTHOR'S NOTE

The Fox Walker stories are based on real locations in and around the Rocky Mountains and San Juan Mountain Range in Colorado, but please know that many of the names of places are as fictionalized as the characters that inhabit them. Also, although much research went into the understanding of the Ute nation and its culture, as well as their use of the Shoshone language, the Fox Walker character is a creation of my imagination and a work of fiction based on my life-long fascination with the Native American culture. Thus, I did take certain liberties in that creation and use of the language. As for the tracking and wilderness survival skills Walker possesses, these are based on real skills and knowledge many dedicated survivalists use and have shared with others.

A special thanks to Gabe Waite, a student in Forensic Science, and Patrick O'Donald, who was the head of Forensics in a San Diego County Police Department at the time I wrote this novel. I appreciate their expertise. Any mistakes regarding forensic terms or information in this book is totally on me.

CHAPTER ONE

Elk Meadow, Colorado

Grandfather had taught him to consider his instincts as real entities, to trust in their message. And intuition told Fox Walker to stay close to his cabin today.

Still, on a cloudless late-summer day, he struggled with his restless mood. He stood on the front porch of his log cabin looking out over the sleek waters of the lake, and the snow crowned peaks of the San Juan Mountains beyond. He longed to roam the woods, not stand around waiting…for what?

He stepped off the porch into the cover of the trees behind his cabin, walking amid the fallen leaves, scarlet and gold against the grass. His moccasin boots rustled their scent into the air as he made his way to a worn grassy spot. Pulling his knife from its sheath on his belt, he concentrated on the practice target before him. The woodland sounds and pungent scent of evergreens surrounding him faded into the background. Soon nothing existed for him except the center of the round slab of pine, twenty-five feet away.

For a moment, his compact body tensed—prepared to strike. A second later, muscles relaxed to allow quick action. In one fluid movement, he propelled the knife through the air. It sailed end over end in perfect rhythm, until the tip embedded itself with a solid *thunk* into the center of the target.

Walker strode to the target board and pulled the knife out, looked up to see a small dust cloud rising a half mile away. The long gravel driveway leading to his cabin gave him ample warning if anyone approached. This design had been no accident.

Maybe the approaching vehicle held a clue to his instincts to stay put, maybe not. He returned to the worn spot and took up his practice again.

He had thrown two more bulls-eyes when the sound of tires crunching over gravel made him look up. He stepped behind a tree and watched as a Colorado Sheriff's Department cruiser pulled up alongside his cabin and parked. The back of his neck prickled.

A lone officer stepped out of the vehicle. Walker knew quite a few deputies, but didn't recognize this one. When the man hesitated at the car and scanned the area instead of walking directly to the cabin, Walker stepped into view. This one didn't assume he would be indoors. It gave Walker considerable insight into the deputy's thought process.

The thick-bodied officer walked toward him with a loose, loping gait. Either the man felt at ease in the outdoors, or wanted time to observe his quarry, or both.

The deputy stopped next to the target, glanced at the knife and looked back to Walker.

"Nice throw."

Walker stepped forward, focused on the deputy's eyes and watched the man scrutinize him in the same way, checking out his shoulder length jet black hair, lynx claw necklace and beaded knife sheath. But to the officer's credit, whatever his deduction, he kept it well guarded.

"Name's Deputy Harris," he said, sticking out a beefy hand. "Fox Walker?"

Walker nodded, shaking the offered hand. "That's right."

Walker turned to pull the knife from the target and ran his fingers over the symbols carved on the deer antler handle. Looked up to see the deputy eyeing it.

"That's a handsome blade...looks handmade."

"Grandfather carved the handle from the antlers of the first deer I stalked and killed." He didn't add it had been a gift of initiation—a reminder all life is sacred.

"So, you teach people to throw like that?"

"A few." Walker studied the man. "I might teach someone like you...you being a hunter." He caught the flick of surprise in the deputy's eyes. Watched the veil drop again.

"I've heard people say good things about your wilderness school," Harris said. "Sounds intriguing."

"Is that why you volunteered to come out here?"

The deputy's eyes grew round. "How'd you—?"

Walker slid the knife into the sheath at his side. "Maybe you guys have a missing person, and this visit is for official business. But curiosity is what brought *you* here."

Harris stared a moment longer, then gave a short laugh. "Okay, it's true. Chief Deputy Morgan asked for a volunteer to contact you, and you're right, my curiosity got the better of me. I'm sure I don't need to tell you there are some wild-ass stories out there about you."

Walker gave a wry smile. "So, you came to check out the crazy Indian?"

Harris grinned. "Guess you could say that. Seems only fair that I meet you and decide for myself."

"I will try not to disappoint you." Walker motioned Harris to follow him toward the cabin. "You mentioned Morgan sent you."

"Well, yes...and no. It's really Sheriff Kimball. He's insisting Morgan must conduct a search of Gray's Forest."

"So, you *do* have a missing person."

"Not exactly. I guess you could say this search is more about proving there *isn't* a person out there."

Walker stopped mid-stride and stared at Harris. "The Sheriff wants to search the woods, to prove no one is there?"

"Yeah. He figures if they do a search and don't find anyone, the local paper will stop harassing him."

"So this has to do with those newspaper stories they've run all summer?"

"You heard about 'em?"

Walker's mouth twitched. "I even heard we landed a man on the moon."

"Sorry. Anyways, yeah, the media won't give Sheriff Kimball any rest over the unsolved murder last spring. *The Elk Meadow Bugle* may be a small rag, but it has half the town convinced that a killer, or worse, is hiding out there in Gray's Forest."

"Or worse?"

"Hell, I'm sure you know the reputation of that part of the wilderness as well as anybody, and now the people who own the land are saying they've seen a spirit out there wandering around. Sheriff Kimball wants Morgan to make this go away, once and for all. I got the impression from Morgan you've worked for the Sheriff before."

"I have. Never personally met Morgan, though."

"Yeah, well I suppose the fact Morgan's not thrilled about your search and rescue success rate compared to ours, has something to do with that. But he's not calling the shots on this one."

Walker didn't reply. Instead, he gazed up through the treetops. Inhaling deeply, he savored the smell of crisp air scented with smoke from his wood-burning stove.

What an odd request, trying to prove there was no one hiding in Gray's Forest. The wooded area was considered *mukua sogope* by his people—sacred ground. He searched his feelings, realized his earlier mood had lifted. He turned to the deputy.

"Tell the Sheriff and Morgan I will help."

Harris gave him a thumbs up. "Good. I'm sure Sheriff Kimball will be happy to hear it."

Walker noticed Harris didn't say the same for Morgan. They walked to the patrol car while Harris gave him instructions for meeting the search party in the morning. Harris opened the car door, but didn't get in yet. Walker saw the man gaze out over the meadows and lake in front of the cabin, the dark mountains rising up beyond.

"Quite a view you have here, Walker."

"Thanks. You are welcome to come check out my classes, anytime you want."

"I just might do that."

Walker watched the patrol car pull away, picked up an armload of wood and headed inside. The temperature would soon drop with the setting sun, but his cabin of thick logs would keep out the cold.

Crossing over the boards of the porch, he stepped through the door into a large open-beamed common room, which comprised the kitchen and living area. Warmth radiated from the centrally located cast iron wood burning stove.

Walker carried the wood to the stove and opened the door. Heat rolled over him as he laid a few logs onto the glowing coals. Setting aside the rest for later, he moved to a wire cage sitting next to the window. Inside the cage a Red-shafted Flicker watched him, her wings quivering. He smiled at the woodpeckers' now familiar *wik-wik-wik* call.

"You know it is time, don't you?" Walker picked up the cage and carried it outside.

He sat the cage on the porch railing and unlatched the door. Reaching inside, he gently wrapped his hand around the bird and lifted her out through the opening, placing her on the wood railing.

She cocked her head, looking at him for a long moment.

"Time to test your mended wing, *kwinaa*, so it can be made strong again—go on."

The bird burst into the air, wings fluttering unsteadily, then slowing into sure beats. She made her way to a nearby stand of trees, where she clung to the side of an evergreen.

She let out a single, loud *klee-yer* and seconds later disappeared into the woods.

Walker stepped off the porch, reached down and plucked a single feather from the grass. He held the Flicker feather in his fingers, silently thanking the bird for the sacred gift.

He remained standing in the grass, looking out over the waters of the lake. In moments like this, the absent companionship of Grandfather felt especially poignant. It had been a year now, but still he expected to see the old man out there, walking along the shore.

He sighed.

The last rays of sunlight streamed upward from behind the mountains in a performance of brilliant color, as if the sun, reluctant to depart for the night, could keep center stage a moment longer. He could feel the warmth of the sunbeams as they splashed across his face.

In his mind, he could see Grandfather nodding in agreement with his decision to help the Sheriff and Morgan. But as always, there would be something more to contemplate, for Walker also heard the old man's patient voice. *Expect the unexpected.*

CHAPTER TWO

Gray's Forest, Colorado

The next morning broke cloudless and bright. The aspen trees were at the height of their glorious transformation, golden leaves quivering against the dark evergreen backdrop. Above the tree line, the San Juan Mountains filled Fox Walker's vision as they marched along the southwestern edge of the Rockies.

Bumping along the road in his truck and heading into a wooded area rumored to be harboring a fugitive—or worse—it never occurred to Walker to feel apprehensive. This mystery needed an answer and he meant to find it. If someone really were hiding in the woods, there would be fresh tracks somewhere, and he would find them and after finding the prints, he would find who made them. This wasn't an arrogant thought, just a simple truth. He was a tracker. It's what he did.

Although the local townspeople viewed this particular section of the wilderness as eerie, giving it a dark reputation, Walker's ancestors had for centuries considered *mukua sogope* a place of mystery and spiritual power. They mourned its loss when it became privately owned by the Gray family, and had to resort to secret journeys there. Over the years, the treks into the forest dropped in number, until Grandfather and Walker alone made visits to the area.

When his truck rolled up behind a line of vehicles parked at the edge of the woods, where Harris had asked him to meet, his eyebrows rose.

"Damn, enough people here to hold a Tribal Council," he muttered.

He opened the truck door, stepped out and strode over to a group of deputies gathered around a lanky, middle-aged man and listened in on the conversation. He saw a few faces he recognized, including Harris. He ignored the puzzled glances from the men he didn't know.

"Have your teams report in on the hour," the chief deputy ordered. "Remember, the Search and Rescue Team is working a section of the woods directly north of us. Unless you hear differently, return to this point by dusk. That should give you enough time to penetrate the forest to the center and back, on the west side only." The chief deputy looked up, made eye contact with Walker, turned his attention back to his men. "Depending on what we find today, we will begin searching tomorrow from the opposite side of the forest."

Walker watched in silence. He already knew that calling him in on this search had been the Sheriff's idea, not Morgan's. Being told a meeting time later than everyone else confirmed how Morgan felt about it.

The chief deputy approached him as the other men made ready to begin the search.

"Fox Walker?"

"Yes." Walker extended his hand.

The man gave a quick obligatory handshake. "Chief Deputy Morgan. I realize you've conducted independent search and rescues for Sheriff Kimball in the past, and you're used to working alone."

Walker nodded.

"That's all fine and dandy, but this time you'll be doing this directly under my leadership. You're here because the *Sheriff* wants you here. You have a problem with that?"

Walker met Morgan's defiant glare without blinking. "I'm here to honor the Sheriff's request."

The moment lasted a heartbeat longer, before Morgan looked away, toward his officers.

"So, you know the situation. We don't know if someone really is out there or not. But, in the unlikely event there *is* a fugitive out there, we need to find him and bring him in." He looked straight at Walker again. "The sheriff is anxious to clear up the mystery, and put it to bed."

"I understand."

"You carrying?" Morgan asked, his hand going to his gun.

"Just this." Walker indicated the knife sheathed at his side.

Morgan looked at it and shrugged, not hiding his smirk. "Whatever works. I don't suppose you have a cell phone with you, something to check in with us?"

"No."

"Figures," Morgan mumbled.

"I prefer smoke signals," Walker said.

Morgan eyed him, then continued. "Well, if we miss seeing you back here end of day, I'll ask that you check in at our office and file a report."

"No problem."

Morgan jammed his hands into his pockets, looked away a moment, then faced Walker again. "You and I've never worked together before, and this search could take days in order to cover the entire forest, so I need you to understand one thing. We'll get along *just fine* as long as you take care you don't get in the way of my men out there, you understand?"

"You can be sure of that," Walker said without smiling.

Morgan turned and strode away.

"*Hunan,*" Walker muttered to himself. The man acted like a young badger, full of aggression, but with no understanding of the true power he possessed.

Walker looked over toward a group of deputies standing within hearing distance of the conversation. He saw Deputy Harris among the men.

"Good to see you again, Walker," Harris said as he stepped closer. "Sorry about the mix-up on the meeting time. I didn't know until too late that Morgan moved it up. Don't mind him. He's just marking his territory."

Yeah, that's what badgers do.

Walker nodded.

"Me," Harris said, "I'm glad to have you aboard."

⟞⟞ ⟝⟝

Leaning against his truck, Walker watched the deputies scatter into the trees and undergrowth, equally spaced and heading in an easterly direction. He reviewed what he remembered of this portion of the forest. Foothills bordered the vast tracts to the east, desert-like plains to the west. Because of this, the area contained a wide variety of vegetation.

Walker listened to the noisy passage of the deputies drift farther away. Deep within *mukua sogope*, south of this position, there were many streams and a few small lakes. If someone were indeed hiding out here, that region would have the most resources, and a fugitive would have ample warning if a search party were moving through, especially this group.

The deputies were searching the wrong area. He was sure of it. Well, Morgan *did* ask him to stay out of his men's way.

He opened the door of his truck, reached in and brought out a pair of moccasin boots and an ankle sheath containing a knife, one smaller than the hunting knife at his waist. He removed the worn, leather cowboy boots and stowed them in the truck. Once he'd strapped on the ankle sheath, he slipped on the deerskin moccasin boots. One last check to make sure the pocket of his jeans held his flint, and he headed south into the trees.

He always traveled light when tracking. He could move faster and with more stealth. Nature would provide him with everything he needed.

He passed through the outer edge of the woods, breathing in the heavy scent of evergreens and fallen leaves. The aroma triggered a memory of long ago, the day when Grandfather first took him to *mukua sogope*. Even at the age of eight he understood the visit would be one of significance. He and Grandfather had stood at the edge of the dense woods, the smell of damp earth, leaves and pine filling their senses.

He remembered his excitement being tempered with his apprehension of the unknown. He could hear the white boys at school chanting their favorite rhyme:

"If you walk beneath the trees, watch out for the ghosts of the dead.
Your soul they will surely steal and the forest floor will be your bed."

Grandfather had said only, "Knowing a fact is not the same as experiencing it," and stepped into the woods, leaving him to decide whether to follow, or not.

A lifetime later, he didn't regret his decision. Grandfather had taught by experience. Every spare moment of his youth had been spent discovering the secrets of the natural world. The teachings gave him roots of stability, to counter-balance his struggles in the white man schools.

As he matured, the lessons went beyond awareness and wilderness survival, and delved into the deep realm of the spiritual connectivity of all things.

That's why he inherently understood this search today had purpose. His intuition confirmed it.

⇥ ⇤

The sun sat high in the midday sky when he found the first sign that someone did indeed wander *mukua sogope,* and not a ghost.

The markings in the dirt indicated a digging stick had been used to gather some Sweet Cicely plants. He could tell by the traces of charcoal left in the dirt. The person would have chosen a sturdy sapling, and beveled and fire-hardened one end. Pushing the stick into the ground next to the plant, they would then pry upward, at the same time pulling on the plant from above. An effective technique for collecting the entire plant, and all parts of the Sweet Cicely were edible.

The fact the stick had been fire-hardened and used this way told Walker the person knew something about wilderness survival, or at least about edible wild plants and how to gather them. It made him re-evaluate his notion that if someone was hiding out here, he might have an accomplice bringing food to him.

Could it be one of his people? As far as he knew, no Ute, apart from Grandfather and he, had bothered to come here for many years. Maybe the fugitive story was true, then.

A murderer—at home in the wilderness?

A shiver ran over his skin at the idea. And the sheriff wouldn't be happy with the news.

Walker searched the ground for footprints, but found nothing clean enough to read. Still, he did have a trail to follow, for even without prints he could see where someone had passed through the area. Years of observation had trained him to read signs in nature as easily as most people read street signs. Disturbed soil, broken twigs and overturned pebbles on the forest floor became a marked path for him.

He moved forward with added caution, and within an hour came upon his first set of clear footprints. Judging from the moisture content of the compressed soil, these were fresh tracks, made within a few hours' time. Even at first glance he knew something looked different from what he expected to find. He squatted next to the prints for a closer look, then sat back on his heels.

"A barefoot woman?" he muttered. The size and depth of the depression indicated the prints belonged to a small-framed female. A woman. Out here, shoeless and alone?

What the hell.

Did she have a companion elsewhere? His mind buzzed with questions, but no answers. The news stories he'd seen all summer came to mind. Could she be the elusive *ghost* no one had been able to get close to? Or the perpetrator of the unsolved murder? Or both?

Walker shook off his initial surprise. He needed to concentrate, and use the lessons Grandfather had taught him. To see the details others missed.

The length of the woman's strides told him she traveled in a calm, deliberate fashion. He also noticed the right foot left a slightly deeper depression in the soil. She might be carrying something on her right side, to hold the gathered food. The prints also revealed that she walked heel to toe—white man's way. But, he had to admit that in today's world not many Ute's walked the traditional toe to heel way anymore. He happened to be one of the few who did.

All afternoon he followed the woman. Not a difficult job since she wasn't hiding her tracks. Nothing indicated she felt hunted, or in danger, which he found strange. Nothing here added up, and it annoyed him the puzzle pieces wouldn't fit together yet.

*Patience...*he heard Grandfather's voice say. It had been his hardest lesson to learn from the old man. How many times had Grandfather reminded him "Take time to understand *who* you track, only then will you know their next move—even before they know it themselves."

The woman's path did at first appear random, but it soon became apparent she knew where to find different varieties of food to gather, for each area had been visited multiple times. Even in late summer there were still many berries clinging to the vines. She led him to wild currants, gooseberries, chokecherries and even a small stand of hazelnut trees. A wet area offered up some watercress and purslane for some greens.

By midday, the tracks had taken him well past the center of the forest. He would not be able to return before dark, so he began to gather some of the same food and make plans to spend the night here. Good. He wanted time to observe her anyway, once he found her.

He did not believe in coincidence. Grandfather's lessons over the years had proven to him that life holds more complex workings than most believe. Finding the woman's trail convinced him that accepting the sheriff's request had been the correct move. He had been *led* here. Why, he didn't know yet. But from what he had seen so far, this woman didn't need an immediate rescue. It would be his job to discover what part he played in this scenario.

The tracks headed toward a small creek he knew well. The San Juan foothills were nearby now, with some rather impressive cliffs farther up the creek, cliffs holding many indentations and small caves. It made sense someone would choose this area for shelter.

Hours marched by as Walker picked his way along the rocks and boulders at the creek edge, careful not to make any noise as he neared the cliffs. The woman could be anywhere in the recesses and caves.

He focused on a sound barely audible over the gurgling water of the creek. *Singing?* Nearing the source, he heard a woman's voice. He couldn't make out the words, but the tone and rhythm reminded him of the native Ute songs of his childhood. So she *was* one of his people. He followed the sound of her voice until it stopped. But by now he could smell smoke from a live campfire.

The shallow creek made it easy to cross over closer to the cliffs. He crept forward, hidden by foliage, until he spotted movement in front of a small cave entrance, positioned mid-way up the incline of the cliff. Anyone up there would have an excellent view of the area below, so Walker crouched and watched.

A woman stood up before a campfire, her back to him. It surprised him to see long blonde hair, which fell to her waist. Her skin, although deeply tanned, was not that of a Native American, as he had envisioned.

She turned then, and Walker felt a quiet gasp escape his lips. The woman wore only a pair of shorts, leaving her upper torso bare, with streams of hair flowing around her breasts.

He couldn't help but stare as she added wood to the fire and sat down, facing him. She began to weave her straw-colored hair into long braids that fell over her shoulders. Although petite in statue, her body had the curves of a woman. She reminded him of a painting he once saw of a forest nymph playing among giant ferns. Her delicate features were in contrast to the surrounding wilderness, and yet everything about her gave him the impression he was watching a primordial scene.

Could it be possible this woman lived here alone—surviving as his ancestors had? And if so, why?

What of the newspaper stories about the unsolved murder? Could she have been involved in some way? A man had been murdered, his throat slit, his body wrapped in plastic and dumped in Eagle Lake. The body had been discovered by accident when the lake was dredged in May, to remove silt from the narrow channels feeding it.

He couldn't imagine this slight woman having the strength to handle a man in that fashion. Maybe she had been an accomplice.

Walker looked up through the trees to check the position of the sun—already afternoon. Morgan had mentioned the teams would start the search again the next day from this side of the forest. But that would still put them north of this region. It might give him time to figure out what he had discovered here, before someone else stumbled upon it.

Proceed with caution...his instincts warned.

Movement at the cave caught his attention. The woman gathered up a sharp pointed wooden spear and a small bark container, made her way down the incline and headed into the woods.

She walked along a narrow deer run, with Walker in silent pursuit off trail, in the trees. He kept his distance, for every so often she stopped and turned to look behind her. Habit? Paranoia? Or did she sense his presence?

He followed her until she came to a small stream, fed by the snowmelt of the mountains. The water would be icy cold, but not too deep or swift to wade into.

Walker lowered himself to the ground, camouflaged by leaves and shrubs. The woman stepped into the stream, holding her handmade spear. She reminded him of the great hunting birds, the heron and egret, as they gracefully lift and lower their long legs into the water. Her spear was poised and ready to strike, just like the long bill of the heron.

Even though her movements were fluid and smooth, he could tell from the awkward angle she thrust the spear into the water that she lacked experience. She certainly hadn't been doing this for years, as he had. Still, she eventually caught a medium-sized trout. Pulling it from her spear, she placed it in her hand-woven bark container positioned in the edge of the stream, and returned to her fishing.

When she turned, he could see a knife at her side, hanging from a rope loop, attached to the leather belt at her waist. The long, narrow shape didn't look familiar. Certainly not a typical hunting knife. Other than the blade, and the loop of rope, he hadn't noticed any other modern tools.

Long minutes flowed by until she speared a second fish. Dropping it into her container, she left the stream and began to head back with her catch.

With no reason to keep up with her, he bided his time, contemplating what course of action to take next. An overpowering urge to make contact filled his thoughts and he decided, as usual, to follow his instincts.

The woman would most likely stop at the creek, downstream of her cave, to clean the fish. Perhaps it would be the best time to make his appearance, just in case she did become frightened. If occupied with the food, she might be more reluctant to flee and leave her prize behind.

Crossing over the creek downstream of her, he made his way toward her from the opposite side. She might perceive him less of a threat with a body of water between them. He employed a hunting technique he used when stalking a herd of animals in the wild, moving forward in a relaxed manner, making no eye contact, as if he too, were there simply to gather food. Hopefully this would allow him to work his way closer.

Walker could tell the moment she caught sight of him, for in his peripheral vision she froze in position and stared. He continued to wander along the edge of the water, gathering edible plants as he walked. She now crouched lower to the ground, watching, like the big cats do.

His path took him behind a small stand of trees and he lost sight of her for a brief moment. When he rounded them she had disappeared.

Damn! He hadn't expected her to bolt like that. He scanned the tree line and caught sight of her slipping into the woods. He also hadn't expected her to be so fast on her feet.

Stepping on the larger stones in the creek, he crossed the water and noticed one of the fish, partially cleaned, still lay on the rock where she had worked. He sat down beside the abandoned catch and took up cleaning it. He wanted her to have time to arrive back at her cave, where she would feel safer. Besides, the left-behind fish gave him a new plan.

When done, he gathered up the fish and made his way back up the creek toward the cave. He crept forward into the brush to watch. The woman sat by the fire, furtively following any movement around her. He waited until her body language told him that she had relaxed her vigil, and her breathing returned to normal.

Then, quietly, he stood. To the woman he must have appeared to rise up from the very earth. He didn't make eye contact, but could tell she sat stone still. Whether fear or curiosity held her captive, she followed his every move.

Walker made his way closer until the woman stood, ready to flee. He stopped and made eye contact with her for the first time, holding the fish out at arm's length for her to see. Her eyes grew wide, but she held her position. Laying the fish on a large rock at the water's edge, he stepped backward, turned, and without looking behind, walked into the woods. But he sensed her stare the entire time.

A slow smile spread across his face. It had been a good interaction. He headed back to the stream to catch some fish for himself. With no reason to hide his presence, he would have a fire tonight, and a hot meal.

A quiet thought skittered through his mind, then remained to nag at him until he acknowledged it. He had to believe the woman had avoided human contact more than once before today. Would his presence cause her to leave her home, to hide elsewhere?

CHAPTER THREE

Gray's Forest, Colorado

Walker picked up his spear from the riverbank and made sure the fish were secure. He turned in time to catch a glimpse of the woman scurrying away through the trees. He had heard her follow him to the stream, and guessed she watched from her hiding place as he carved his spear and began fishing. Her curiosity must have won out over her fear. A good sign she might not flee this immediate area and hide elsewhere. But the sun would soon drop behind the mountains, causing the temperature to fall, so the woman must be returning to her cave home.

Walker gathered some dry leaves from the ground and stuffed them inside his shirt and down the sleeves as insulation to keep the cool air away from his skin. He needed time to set up a shelter before dark. As he hurried through the woods, Morgan's instructions came to mind, to stop by and fill out a report when he returned at end of day. He could only guess what might happen back in town when he didn't show up. Maybe nothing. Maybe the searches would be halted.

On the other hand, he knew how much the small newspaper in town, *The Elk Meadow Bugle,* loved drama. If they caught wind his truck still sat at the forest edge, and he hadn't reported back in to the sheriff, they might do something with that bit of information. They would most likely link his *disappearance* in some way with the *supposed murderer* hiding out here. Tomorrow might bring the search to a fever pitch.

The idea of the woman being confronted by a group of deputies brought a distasteful vision to his mind. He couldn't imagine how she might react. Would she panic—or attack? How might *they* bungle the situation? He wanted to make sure it didn't happen.

Walker stepped into the small open space he remembered from earlier in the day and began to gather up the materials needed to make a simple debris shelter. Using a tree stump as the base, he propped one end of a large branch on it, the other end on the ground. Then he leaned sticks and limbs against the center pole, creating a wedge-shaped hut. Covering the form with evergreen boughs and thick layers of leaves, grasses and moss made it more than capable of keeping out the night chill. The thick mat of evergreen needles he piled inside created a comfortable bed to lie on, and would keep away insects and the dampness of the earth.

Using his steel knife to strike the piece of flint he carried, he threw a spark onto a pile of tinder and blew it to flames. Adding small sticks, he would soon have a fire to cook the fish. As he worked he reflected upon what he had learned during this short time observing the woman.

The woman appeared as a creature of the forest, distrustful of man, like any wild being. Until he could talk with her he had no real idea of her state of mind.

If only he could take his time and watch her...get to know her... gain her confidence. He had to admit it. He no longer followed the woman out of curiosity. He acknowledged, with surprise, he felt responsible for her safety. *Why?*

He wished to ask Grandfather. *Have the spirits led me here to serve as her protector?*

He reviewed all the possibilities as he pulled the tender meat from the cooked fish. More search parties might arrive tomorrow. He couldn't count on an unlimited time frame within which to observe the woman.

I must make the effort to speak with her tomorrow—even if from a distance.

Revived from the hot meal, he laid another log on the fire. Not wanting to take time to create a container to boil water, he sliced a nearby grapevine. It gave him all the fluid he needed to quench his thirst for tonight. But he tied the ends of a clean handkerchief to twigs on a nearby shrub, as a collector for the morning dew.

Shaking the leaves from his shirt, he crawled into his shelter as dark descended. Inside the insulated debris hut his body heat would keep him comfortably warm. He inhaled the fresh scent of the evergreen boughs surrounding him. Nearby, an owl greeted the darkness with his haunting call and cricket song filled the air. Sleep came, with the night noises of the forest surrounding him in peace.

But his dreams were filled with images of a strange woman who sang hauntingly familiar melodies and rhythmically swayed to the dancing flames of a fire…as he approached, she moved ever beyond his reach.

CHAPTER FOUR

Gray's Forest, Colorado

A haze lay all around when Walker awoke, the trees appearing and disappearing within the swirling mist. The night noises had ceased, replaced by birdcalls anticipating the first rays of sunshine, soon to burst free over the mountaintops.

Walker crawled from the debris shelter and stood, stretching. He drank in the fresh, clean air, filling his lungs and charging his body with its energy, nourishing his very soul. A song came to his mind, one Grandfather had taught him for giving thanks for another day, for the warmth the sunlight would bring. He softly hummed the melody.

After eating a few berries left from the previous night, he untied the handkerchief, now heavy with dew, and squeezed the water into his mouth.

＝┿ ┿＝

The morning mist turned to wisps and dissipated in the sunlight as Walker stepped within sight of the woman's cave. He sat down and leaned back against a tree to watch for her, shrubs camouflaging him from her view.

Before long he saw movement at the cave entrance. The woman emerged, but stood at the opening and looked all around before stepping out into the open. She crouched next to the fire pit and began to blow on the smoldering coals of the previous night, to re-kindle the flames. She fed the tiny flames small twigs and then larger sticks, humming as she worked. Sitting down on one of the logs by her fire, she began to sing as she unbraided her plaits of hair and ran her fingers through it to loosen it, shaking it to fall freely over her shoulders.

The words of the song were Shoshone, a language used by his people, along with other tribes in the area long ago. The melody transported Walker back to childhood memories of his mother singing as she worked. How this woman knew the song he couldn't guess, but it gave him inspiration about how to approach her.

He rose from his hiding spot and walked toward the incline to the cave, watching for any reaction from the woman. The moment she noticed him she froze. He stopped, stretched out his arms and hands, palms turned upward, showing they were empty. He spoke, using his native language.

"Don't be afraid. I come as a friend."

She studied him, ready to flee.

Thinking she didn't understand, he repeated the phrase, this time in English.

The expression on her face changed to one of surprise, as if startled to hear the words, or perhaps that she understood them.

"I was sent to find you," Walker said in Shoshone. The words spilled out before he thought them. But with the words came the realization, once again, of why he had felt compelled to join in the search. He *had* been sent to find her—and not really by the law. He watched for her reaction.

She motioned him to the fire.

Walker scrambled up the incline. The woman stood off to the side, poised for a quick retreat, never letting him leave her sight, her eyelids lowered. Her tensed body and untamed manner made him wonder whether she might attack him, but her hand did not stray to the knife at her side. When she stepped out of a shadow and into the sunshine, a glint of silvery lines against bronzed skin caught his eye. There were markings of some sort on her torso.

He approached the fire and sat down on one of the logs. With slow, calm movements, he withdrew his hunting knife from its sheath and laid it on the ground in front of him.

A quick look of uncertainty crossed her face. Then, without breaking eye contact with him, she walked over and slid down opposite him, the fire between them. She mimicked his actions of laying her knife on the ground before her.

They sat across from each other in silence, each studying the other. Gray-blue eyes stared at his long, black hair, and then lingered on his turquoise and lynx-claw necklace hanging in his open shirt. When she spied his moccasin boots, her expression changed to one of admiration...and yearning?

He gazed into the eyes of someone long removed from the modern world, and the untamed spirit touched his soul in a way that surprised him. He returned her look, open and honest, fearing any moment she would sense his amazement, and flee.

He studied her as she watched him. Her smooth skin still held a youthful suppleness, but her body was that of a full-grown woman. She wore a necklace, fashioned from braided plant fibers. Small shells from the stream beds and colorful little pebbles with holes were strung on the fibers. It lay just above her bare breasts, which were partially hidden by the long waves of hair.

Trying not to stare, he studied the shiny lines on her torso he had noticed. They looked to be scars, and filled an area the size of the width of his open hand. They were taller than wide, running from just below her breasts and continuing under the waistband of her shorts. The scars crisscrossed her torso in a series of straight lines, some horizontal and some vertical. Within these lines were spirals, curving in different directions. But because of the way she sat, he couldn't see it clearly.

What happened to this woman?

Her cotton twill shorts were cut off at the knee, frayed from use, and showing both stains and fading from repeated washings. The simple leather belt had a worn spot, where it had recently been notched up a hole, showing a loss of weight. The woman also wore an anklet fashioned like her necklace. Her bare feet were heavily callused.

He glanced at the strange knife. The straight blade ended in a black handle, with swirling carvings that suggested dragons. Could it be Asian in origin?

It took all his concentration to keep his expression from revealing his astonishment.

He looked back up to her face and waited, hoping she would speak first. When she did, it was in English mixed with Shoshone words.

"The *mukua* sent you?"

Taken back by the straightforwardness of her question, he nonetheless understood what she asked.

"Yes, the Spirits wanted me to find you."

She blinked. "I have been *told* someone was coming. But I don't know why."

"Perhaps I am to help you."

"Help me? Why?"

"I am not sure," he said.

The fire crackled in the silence that followed. Walker struggled with what to say next. His instincts warned him to be patient and honest. But she spoke before he could form the next question.

"The birds and animals did not warn me that you were near. You are *daga sogope*?"

"Yes, I am a friend with nature…as you are."

She nodded, and Walker watched her body relax ever so slightly.

"I would like to know your name," Walker said.

"My name?" She looked puzzled.

"Yes, what are you called?"

For a moment bewilderment flitted across her face, then her brows furrowed in concentration. She looked up at the trees and the sky. Just as suddenly her expression brightened. She waved her arms to encompass all the surrounding nature and said, "*They* call me Nataya."

"Nataya—a beautiful Shoshone word. You use Shoshone as you speak, but most of your words are English. You know both languages?"

Nataya cocked her head sideways. "I don't know about *lan-gua-ges*. This is the easy way for me."

"Easy?"

"Yes, I don't have to think so hard."

Walker tried to place why her Shoshone words sounded odd to his ear—realized her pronunciations were off, as if she learned them from a book, or from a non-native. He smiled. "That's fine, we can speak this way. You can call me Walker. But my name in Shoshone is *Waahi Mia*."

Nataya laughed, a lilting melody, surprising Walker with the spontaneity of it.

"*Waahi Mia*. You walk smart like the fox. This is how you found me."

"Yes, people call me Fox Walker."

"*Waahi* told me someone would come."

Now he understood her laughter. To her, his name was an in-side joke from the spirits. He saw a piece of her reserve fall away, a hint of trust appear. He looked around at the cave entrance and back to her.

"You live here alone?"

Again she looked confused. "I live here with all creatures of *sogope*."

Her answer revealed how in tune with nature this woman was. She didn't even understand the concept of being alone. He tried another approach. "Yes, but do others like you live here too?"

She shook her head. "I have seen others, *diaboo*, not like you. They frightened me and I hid from them."

"White men. Why were you afraid?"

"I followed what *pihyen* told me to do."

"Your heart told you to hide from them?"

She nodded.

"Did you also listen to your heart to know how to live here, to make fire and gather plants?"

She nodded. "Sometimes...when I ask...the *mukua* help me."

Walker caught his breath. "The Ancient Ones—Spirits from the Past—they help you?"

"Yes. Sometimes."

"They give you guidance?"

"Yes, they tell me what to do. They were with me when I awoke from *pohanapusa*."

How intriguing that she spoke using simple words, substituting Shoshone nouns in places, but when he answered in English and used more difficult words, she understood him. Then it registered in his mind what else she had just said.

"So, the spirits were with you when you awoke from a dream of power? When was this dreamtime?"

She frowned.

"Do you remember?"

"I don't want to remember...the beginning."

"Why?"

"It hurts when I try."

In the quiet that followed, Walker attempted to make sense of this information. The direct route didn't work. Maybe he could prompt some sort of memory if he asked the right leading questions.

"When you awoke—what kind of weather do you remember?"

"The smell of rain…and flowers…*dahwaa'ai*."

"Springtime. Many moons have passed since then. Do you remember how many?"

She looked up at him, pleased. "After *pohanapusa*, I watched for Father *Muh* to become round. I have counted *naafaite* moon times."

Six months ago. What had happened to her? And what about this dreamtime she referred to? Did she just awaken one day with no memories? And where did she really come from?

"Why *do* you live here—in the forest?"

She glanced at him sideways, as if he teased her. "I live here because it is my home."

"Where did you live before you came to the forest?"

"This has always been my home."

Baffled, he looked down at the fire and picked up a stick to move some coals around. He didn't want her to read the emotions in his expression. He breathed in the smell of wood smoke and listened to the crackling fire while he gathered his thoughts. Although he could tell that she could have spent months here, what clothes she wore did not have the tattered look from years of wear. Her skin and hair didn't have the appearance of someone who had lived her entire life in the wilderness. Nothing added up here.

Walker looked up. They were no longer alone in the area. It wasn't an actual sound yet, just the way nature reacted off in the distance. He looked at her and could tell she sensed it also. As she stared in the direction of the creek, he slipped his knife back into its sheath and began to cover the fire with dirt, putting out the flames with no telltale smoke.

When she looked back to him, he motioned for her to join him as they made their way to the cave and crouched at the entrance, listening.

They heard the commotion at the same time, still off in the distance, but loud enough to know it was human. It sounded like a group of people coming toward them along the creek, perhaps some deputies. Whoever it might be, he felt confident that he and Nataya could hide in the cave and not be discovered.

Then he heard something else. Dogs barking. It had to be a search party. Who else would bring in dogs?

Damn! It would be just like Morgan to panic and think the worse when he didn't show up to file that report last night. Hell, Morgan might even now believe there *was* a fugitive, and the killer had got to him first. They must've brought the dogs to his parked truck and followed his scent through the woods. It would have been easy. He hadn't been hiding his trail. And it would lead them straight here.

Now what to do?

The barking turned to baying. He sensed the woman's fear, and reached out to touch her, to reassure her, but his hand found only open air. He turned, and saw her scrambling down from the cave. She bounded through the trees like a young doe fleeing a hunter, never hearing him call to her.

He hesitated. Should he head off the search party, or pursue her?

The yipping and howling of the dogs grew into a tumult as the scent became stronger. They knew their quarry was near. It would only be moments before they tracked him to this cave.

Damn it! He didn't want them to discover her cave home. He had to head off the search party. By now she had a good lead on him anyway.

But as he watched her through the trees he caught sight of some uniforms coming toward her from the left side.

There's more than one search party.

She wouldn't be able to see them yet. And the noise of the dogs kept her from hearing them. He scrambled down from the cave and headed uphill toward her, the branches and undergrowth ripped at him as he struggled to get near enough for her to hear him.

"Nataya!" he yelled.

She halted, and turned to look at him. He motioned to her to come back toward him, but she must have thought he wanted her to wait. She hesitated, allowing the men to come crashing in toward her. They didn't even realize she was there at first, but the noise and ensuing chaos terrified her. She fled in the opposite direction. The men took pursuit.

He knew at the top of this hill the terrain leveled out and quickly came to the edge of a large clearing. Clearly Nataya hadn't explored beyond her cave and didn't realize she headed for the edge of the forest. He yelled to warn her, but she was beyond hearing him. She raced through the woods, the shouts of the men behind her, and the howling of the dogs, spurring her on.

Tree limbs and forest undergrowth impeded his progress as he rushed through the forest, trying to stay ahead of the dogs in pursuit behind him and close the distance between him and the uniforms chasing Nataya.

The baying of the hounds behind him grew fainter as the noise of the men ahead of him gained in volume. He had to be getting closer to them.

As they neared the edge of the forest and the trees thinned, he could see the group before him, and hear them yelling.

He watched, helpless, as the men chased her out into the clearing like an animal, right into the surprised arms of another group of several deputies, who instinctively grabbed her. This started her fighting, kicking and biting. She fought hard with fear, but by then the officers following had joined in the struggle.

Walker emerged from the trees, raced across the open area and began to push his way through the crowd. He glimpsed Morgan among the deputies, shouting orders. As Nataya fought, she scratched and drew blood of more than a few deputies, and Walker didn't like the stony expression of determination he saw on their faces. He yelled over the top of the crowd.

"Stop! Dammit—leave her alone!"

But now the dogs joined the fray and no one could hear him over the uproar. Over the tops of bobbing and weaving heads, he could see a Rescue Unit parked among the officers' cars along the dirt road.

Morgan definitely thought the worst when I didn't report in.

He worked his way through the crowd until he saw Nataya, surrounded by the officers. They had overpowered her and managed to get her on a gurney, where they held her down. Her lack of clothing, which seemed natural in the wilderness, bothered him here among the strangers. He watched gratefully as a paramedic grabbed a blanket and draped it over her.

Nataya saw him then, among the others, and glared at him, her eyes full of betrayal.

The venomous glance hit him like a blow to the gut and he almost missed the fact one of the paramedics was about to inject her with something. "No!" he shouted, too late.

Nataya's eyes grew wide before she lost consciousness, and her head lolled to the side. The orderlies began to load the gurney into the back of the vehicle.

I've got to do something.

Shoving the others aside, he climbed up into the rescue truck and sat down next to her. Chief Deputy Morgan appeared at the open doors, his face dark from exertion.

"So, I see you're still among the living, Walker. I suppose you'll want credit for helping us flush our elusive *ghost* out of hiding."

"No. Your men did that, not me."

"Figures. I can take over now. You're free to leave."

"I'm not leaving." He tossed his truck keys to the chief. "Have someone take my truck over to the hospital."

Walker watched the quick moment of surprise on Morgan's face dissolve into indignation, but he seemed to think better of saying anything. Motioning to close the doors to the rescue truck, Morgan turned toward his patrol car.

Walker leaned over the quiet figure and straightened the blanket covering her. While the paramedic had his back turned, Walker checked under the blanket for her knife and found it missing from the belt. Did one of the deputies take it? Then he remembered. She had not picked it up from the ground by the campfire. It still lay back at her cave.

Good. No need for the diaboos to know about it.

CHAPTER FIVE

Elk Meadow, Colorado

The high ceiling and bright lights of the emergency ward dwarfed Nataya's unconscious body as Walker followed the gurney to an examining room. Her long hair, now tangled with twigs and leaves, tumbled about her. The blanket lay draped over her, making her appear even more fragile and…lost.

A scene flashed through his mind of a strong bird in flight, the Flicker he had later discovered lying hurt among the leaves and grass.

Chief Deputy Morgan walked into the room, leaving his men to loiter in the doorway. They were still hyped-up with curiosity, even as they strove to act cool and nonchalant. Things like this didn't happen in such a quiet community.

A doctor charged into the room, addressing Morgan as he walked across the room toward the gurney. "Fill me in on what we've got here. You found her where?"

Morgan followed the doctor into the room, leaving his deputies to hang around at the door. "Like I said, we found her running around out in Gray's Forest. No idea how long she's been out there."

The doctor bent over the still figure. Behind glasses, serious hazel eyes scrutinized the scene. Then he looked up at Walker, noticing him for the first time.

"Who're you?"

Morgan started to answer, but the doctor put a restraining hand on his arm, and waited for a response to his question.

"Fox Walker."

"Of Walker Wilderness School?"

"Yeah."

The doctor offered his hand. "Glad to meet you. Dr. Roy Baker. Everyone calls me Doc—I know—people don't have much imagination when it comes to names around here. Are you the one who found her?"

Walker nodded.

Morgan fidgeted at Doc's side. Walker recognized the symptoms. Being ignored didn't sit well with him. Doc turned to Morgan with a question.

"The paramedics say you insisted they knock her out. Why the hell did you have to drug her like this?"

"Had to Doc. She fought like a wildcat. Took all of us to hold her down. We had to sedate her before she got injured."

Doc looked at Morgan over the rim of his glasses.

Walker spoke up. "She spooked when the searchers rushed in like a damn SWAT team."

Morgan's face turned red, but he ignored Walker. "I know it's hard to believe looking at her now, but she acted like a crazy person, I tell you."

"Maybe she *is* crazy," muttered one of the deputies from the doorway.

"Yeah—what the hell was she doing out there in the forest, half naked and living like some wild animal, anyway?" added a second deputy.

"You should see the bites and bruises some of the guys got from her," grumbled another.

Walker's voice cut through the mumbling. "She thought she was fighting for her life."

Doc held up his hands. "Look, enough. I need to do a preliminary exam while she's still sedated. Let's clear the room now."

The nurse picked up the cue and began ushering the men away from the doorway. The deputies wandered down the hallway, muttering amongst themselves, and Walker thought he heard the word "crazy" more than once. He saw Doc glance his way as he stood aside from all the others, his arms folded over his chest.

"Walker. When you found her, were you able to communicate?"

Walker nodded.

"I may need your help. I'd like you to stay put, if you can?"

Morgan jerked his head around to stare at the doctor. "You can't do that, Doc. I'm the law around here, and I've got questions to—"

"And I'm the doctor around here. And this is my patient. You'll get to ask your questions. She's not going anywhere for a while."

"Okay Doc, I'll trust you on this one, but I want to know the moment I can talk to her." He turned and stormed out of the room.

Doc Baker turned to Walker and motioned him to some chairs just outside the emergency room. "I appreciate your help on this, Walker."

"No problem."

Doc started to go back into the room, but turned around.

"You didn't happen to get her name, did you?"

"She calls herself Nataya."

"Nataya. Never heard that before."

"It's a Shoshone word—means 'dance the woman's dance'."

"She doesn't look Native American."

"No, but I found her living like the old ones did, long ago. Seems she doesn't remember anything further back than this last spring."

Doc stared at Walker with disbelief in his eyes. "Shit, none of this makes any sense," he said and returned to the examination room, where the nurse stood waiting.

Walker didn't sit long before Doc came to the door, shaking his head. He motioned for Walker to follow him back into the room. They stood by the gurney looking down upon the quiet figure. Someone had pulled the twigs and leaves from her hair and slipped a hospital gown on her. She still wore the shorts.

Doc looked at Walker. "I take it by her tan lines, that the clothing she has on is all she owns?"

"Not sure, that's all I saw, just the khaki shorts."

"I'm sure you noticed that the bottoms of the pant legs are cut, not hemmed, like they were once long. The lack of clothing, along with those scars, makes me think someone attacked her."

"My thoughts too, especially since she doesn't want to remember her past. Maybe she was left in the forest to die."

"Could be. These superficial scratches and scrapes are fresh, probably from being chased through the woods today—damn shame about that. But these scars are different."

"They were made by a knife."

"I agree, Walker. Medically they would be considered superficial, too, but nonetheless, deep cuts made these scars, even though they aren't stab wounds. The manner of them has me puzzled. It could be scarification, I suppose. But one thing is clear, if someone else did this to her, they wanted to torture her—not kill her."

Doc lifted the gown and bent closer to study the healed wounds, mumbling to himself, "You know, if you look at them long enough, there's a pattern to the marks…"

Walker leaned over for a better view. "I thought so too. These curvy lines kind of look like two number threes, facing each other. Maybe these marks are supposed to represent something."

"Could be. If the cuts weren't so jagged and crude maybe we could tell."

"How old do you think they are?"

"Good question. If these were recently made, they should still have a slight pinkish to brownish-red look to them. But see here, how the scars have healed to the point that the collagen has faded. The scar has shrunk considerably. I'd say they're over four months old. He looked up at Walker. "You don't suppose she spent that much time out there alone?"

"She remembers six full moon times, so that fits."

"But, if the scars are from an attack, she would have needed medical help, let alone having to survive alone in the wilderness for that length of time."

Walker shrugged. "I teach others how to do it."

"Yeah, you're right. But what about her—being wounded like that?" The doctor gazed down at the petite, tanned figure, her long, sun-bleached hair tangled and tousled. "Did you notice the one earring?"

"Yeah, while I was in the rescue unit. I checked for the matching one, but her other earlobe isn't pierced."

"Yeah, I noticed that too." Doc studied the piece of jewelry. "Looks like some kind of Japanese symbol. Not anything I recognize, but maybe it will help the sheriff find a clue to her past. I have to wonder what kind of nightmare this poor young woman was subjected to."

Nataya moved her head and moaned.

"Okay, Walker. If she's been living as you say, let's get her to a regular room. Maybe it won't be as frightening when she wakes up." He began to put restraints on her arms, and then her legs.

"Does she have to be strapped down like that?"

"At least until we see how she's going to react. It's for her own protection as much as anything else."

They rolled the gurney into a room, and Walker pulled a chair up as Doc turned to leave.

"I'll give you some time to talk with her while I make rounds. I'll check back soon."

The young woman again stirred. Walker leaned in close.

"Nataya."

Her eyelids fluttered open. She focused on Walker's face and her eyes filled with fury.

"You—*koihkwa*!" She tried to pull back from him, only to discover that her arms were in restraints. She attempted to raise her head and shoulders, to see the rest of her body. She began to turn her shoulders, first one way and then the other. "Let me go!"

Walker stood. "Nataya, stop! You can't get free like this. Listen to me. The spirits *did* send me to find you. I am here to help you."

"You are *isapaippeh natesu'un*. You tricked me!"

"No, I am not coyote medicine. I tried to help you, but you ran away."

"I don't believe you." She twisted in the restraints. "Why am I tied?"

"You fought with the others."

She glared at him, and resumed her struggles, her voice rising in anger, her attempts growing more desperate. "You can't keep me here—let me go!" She thrashed against the straps and attempted to turn her entire body in the restraints, but yelped in pain.

"What is it? What hurts, Nataya?"

"*Da'winja*."

Walker leaned over the gurney to look closely at her ankles. He hadn't noticed anything earlier, but now he could see that her left ankle appeared puffy compared to the other one.

"This one?" He touched it and she reacted with a jerk.

She nodded.

"I'll have the doctor look at it when he gets here. Maybe you sprained it when you were running through the woods."

"Doctor?"

"Yes, the doc—the *pohakanten*. The Shaman."

She looked around at the room then, fear showing for the first time in her eyes. "What is this place?"

"It's a medicine lodge—*natesu'ungahni*."

"So bright!" She turned her head away from the overhead fluorescent lamps

Walker strode over to the light switch and dimmed the lights.

"Why am I here?" She called out, as he returned to her side.

"The shaman will want to make sure you are not hurt."

"I am fine. I want to leave."

"You must show him respect, and do as he says, Nataya."

She flashed him a look of disdain, as if to say, *"Don't patronize me."* He understood now. Although she spoke simply, her thoughts and emotions were much more sophisticated than he'd realized.

Walker poured water into a cup and offered her a drink, which she refused. "I'm going to find the shaman. I promise I'll return."

He went to the door with Nataya yelling in the background, using her peculiar mix of English and Shoshone.

"Let me go—I have to leave here!"

He stepped outside and shut the door to keep the noise from the corridor.

Seeing Doc down the hallway, he motioned him over. "She must have injured her left ankle while running through the forest, or maybe during her struggle with the deputies. Discovered it when she awoke and tried to get free."

Doc cocked an ear toward the room. "I hated to leave her in the restraints, but I didn't know what she might do when she came to."

"From her reaction just now, I'd say you did the right thing. To help you out, I told her you're the shaman here." At Doc's puzzled expression, he explained, "You know—the medicine man. A shaman commands great respect in my culture. I believe she will do as you request."

"Thanks. I wasn't sure what kind of approach to take with her. This helps."

"You'll need to convince her she must obey your rules if she wants free of the restraints," Walker whispered as they entered the room and Doc closed the door behind them.

Nataya stared at Doc as he approached her. "You are the *pohakanten*."

"Yes, but you may call me Doc." He smiled at her. She did not smile back. "Walker says you injured your ankle. I'm going to touch it in different places and I'll be as gentle as I can. I need you to tell me where it hurts the most, okay?"

Nataya nodded, subdued for the moment. Walker watched fear once again replace the anger in her eyes.

Doc probed the tissue, at times making her wince. "I'm going to undo these straps, Nataya, and help you to stand." Looking up at Walker, he explained, "I thought this ankle seemed puffy compared to the other one, but it's swollen a bit more since I examined her. I don't think it's broken, but I'd like to see how much weight she can bear. Why don't you get on the other side and help me support her."

Doc began to remove her straps. When free, she sat up, rubbing her wrists and studying the two men. Walker watched her size them up, as if gauging whether she could make a break for it. But the injured ankle kept her subdued for the moment.

Both men each put one of her arms over a shoulder and helped slide her off the gurney.

"Now very slowly stand down on your foot, but stop when you feel pain."

Doc watched her face for any sign of distress. She had barely put any weight on her leg before she took a quick intake of breath, and grimaced.

Doc removed her arm from his shoulder and had her hold onto the gurney, Walker still supporting her. "Now, keep your weight off this leg while I move your foot around a bit."

After careful study, Doc straightened. "I believe it's only a bad sprain. Should heal quickly with rest and therapy, but we'll take x-rays to make sure. Walker, let's get her over to the bed by the window."

The two men helped her over to the hospital bed, where she sat on the edge, her body tense.

Doc pulled a chair over and sat down facing her. "Nataya, it's my job to make sure you have fully healed before you leave here, and it's going to take some time for your ankle to heal. I need you to do everything I ask. It's very important you do as I say, if you don't want to be tied down again. Do you understand?"

Nataya nodded.

"I need you to stay in this room and not run away. We'll make you as comfortable as possible. You'll have this bed to sleep in, and someone will bring you food and drink soon. For now, I want you to rest. Here, let me help you…you can sit up like this, but I'm going to put this pillow under your knee and another one to elevate your foot a bit. A nurse—my helper—will bring in some ice to put on your ankle. It's important to do as she says also, so you can get better."

"When can I leave?"

"When I tell you," Doc said sternly, but then softened it a bit. "Soon, I hope."

She looked away from the men and stared at the window. Walker noticed, walked over and fully opened the blinds, so she could see outdoors.

He was once again reminded of the wounded Flicker, caged to be kept safe so her wing could heal, but longing to be free.

They left her looking out the window from her bed, and made their way outside. Leaving the door open, they spoke softly in the hall. Doc ran his hand through his unruly, rust-colored hair and sighed.

"I really appreciate your help with this, Walker."

"What's going to happen to her now?"

Doc removed his glasses and cleaned them with the corner of his jacket. "Well, because I don't think we know her true identity, I can list her as a Jane Doe. That will allow me to admit her and give her care under the Mental Health Act. It'll give us some time to sort things out, without the authorities butting in."

"Good. I'll stay with her for tonight, in case she wakes up frightened."

Doc put his glasses on and gazed back into the room at Nataya, and Walker saw a deep sadness in his eyes. When Doc spoke again, he sounded distant.

"I can't be sure until I can do a psych exam, but right now I can only presume something horrible happened to Nataya, or whatever her real name is. If she indeed has blocked her memory of the past, I can guess she did it to mentally survive the ordeal. But that's all it is right now—a guess." He turned back to Walker. "If that's true, who knows if we'll be able to help her gain back her memory?"

"And do we have the right to try?"

"If we are to help her, I think we must."

Walker heard voices down the hallway and turned to see a deputy, his arms outstretched, blocking some people from approaching. Once the group had dispersed, the deputy joined Doc and Walker.

"What's going on?" Doc asked.

"Sorry for the disturbance, Doc. Oh—and before I forget—here are your truck keys, Mr. Walker. It's parked in space 33." The deputy tossed the key ring to Walker and turned to face Doc again. "Before we could even leave the building, the front desk nurses started complaining they were being hassled by reporters. I swear they appear like flies at a picnic. They must just drive around with one ear to the scanners. Morgan called the sheriff and he requested one of us stay here."

"Good idea. I should've known it would just be a matter of time before they appeared. Are you going to stay outside her room?"

"That's what the sheriff wants."

"Fine with me," Doc said.

Walker also breathed a sigh of relief. Not only would the deputy help protect Nataya from the curious, it would help guarantee her staying in the room. He knew that look in her eyes. She would run the moment an opportunity presented itself, injured ankle or not.

CHAPTER SIX

Elk Meadow, Colorado

he only light in the room glowed softly from the machines clustered around the bed. Their whirs and beeps were silent now. The noise had been a comfort, she realized. In the eerie silence she stood beside the bed, looking down upon the old man. His eyes were closed, but not in slumber. There remained a wonderful look of peacefulness on his face, so why did the sight of him hurt her so? Why the deep sense of loss? Sobbing, she reached out to touch him...

Nataya sat up in bed with a start. She tried to cling to the image as it faded like wisps of smoke in a breeze. It had seemed so real, more a memory than a dream. She closed her eyes and concentrated. The fading vision of the strange machines surrounding the old man's bed frightened her now, but during the dream she hadn't been afraid. She could still see the old man's face in her mind. Her hand involuntarily reached for the lone earring she wore and touched it. Why did she sense that she knew his face? But no matter how she tried, nothing more came to her. The vague recollections of the dream washed over her, leaving an undercurrent of loneliness and isolation.

It must be a message from the spirits.

She looked around the dimly lit room. Walker slept in a nearby chair, although how he could be comfortable enough to sleep, she couldn't imagine. Even though the Shaman had told her she must stay here until she healed, she had tried to sneak past Walker during the night, to explore and find a way out of this place. But a man sat outside the entry to her room. He made it clear she could not leave.

The dawn sky drew her out of bed and she limped to the window. Leaning against the glass, she gazed at the distant mountain peaks. She traced their silhouette with her finger on the glass as the sky glowed orange behind the snow-covered peaks.

Just yesterday morning she had been warming herself by the fire and drinking hot pine needle tea, content in her world. Now she stood here, trapped, in a lodge where windows allowed sunshine to enter, but no fresh air. And the constant noise—she feared it would drive her mad. How did this happen?

The spirits had told her someone would come, and she had believed Walker to be the one. She glanced over to where he still slumped in the chair. But maybe it had been a warning, that he would appear, and not to trust him. She must be wary.

She turned to again study the mountain range from her window, but couldn't see the peak that would guide her to her cave home. She needed to get outside, to see the entire horizon and find her direction.

Yesterday, as she'd watched out the window to the people below, she noticed the ones dressed like her were never allowed to walk far away from the building. To escape, she would need different covering.

Since Walker insisted he was her friend, maybe she could convince him to help her find a way out of this place.

Sunshine began to stream in the window and she heard Walker stir. She turned, the light behind her, infusing her in a halo. He looked up at her, shielding his eyes with his hand. She stepped out of the light and he could focus on her features. He smiled and stood, stretching the stiffness from his body.

"Did you sleep much, Nataya?"

"No."

"It's hard to sleep in a strange place. You will do better tonight."

Using the bed for support, she limped over to stand before him, demanding his full attention.

"I cannot stay here. I must leave."

"Your ankle needs to heal."

"You don't understand…last night…*napuisaitt.* I had a dream."

Walker nodded for her to continue.

She took a step closer, lowered her voice to a whisper. "You lied to me. This is not a place of healing. This is where people come to die. My dream told me. I *must* leave here, now."

His eyes held sympathy for her. She saw it. He took a step closer to her and placed his hands on her shoulders, staring into her eyes. "It's true some people die here, but only because they are very ill, or so badly hurt they cannot be helped, and it is their time. This *is* a place of healing. You will be safe here."

She pulled away and hobbled back to the window, her sanctuary.

After a moment, Walker spoke. "It's still early in the morning. We could go outside before they bring you food."

She turned to face him. "They will let me?"

"If I am with you, and *if* you let me push you in the wheelchair. Here, put on your robe and slippers and we'll go."

Walker helped her put the robe on over her gown, and handed her the slippers, but Nataya shook her head.

"You have to wear them. It's a rule here," Walker explained.

"But they are uncomfortable and they come right off."

"You have to wear them if you want to go outside. Besides, you will be in the wheelchair."

She snatched them from his hand, and put them on with no further argument. Walker helped her into the chair and wheeled her into the hallway.

The deputy jumped up from his seat. "Where do you think you're going? She can't leave this room."

Nataya looked up at Walker, who eyed the deputy. "You would deny her fresh air?"

"Well, no. It's just that the sheriff said I can't let her out of my sight."

"Then you are going to get some fresh air, too. We're heading outside."

The deputy shrugged and fell in behind them.

Walker pushed the wheelchair out the front entrance and immediately found himself confronted by a small group of reporters, all clamoring for answers to their questions.

"Tell us how you found the *Wild Woman*. What clues led you to her?"

"Can she tell us about her ordeal in the wilderness? What about an interview?"

The deputy intervened, and to Walker's relief, managed to dispatch the reporters to a comfortable distance away.

Walker shook his head, looked at the deputy. "There's only one little newspaper in this town. Where did all those people come from?"

"Looks like a couple of the surrounding towns have taken an interest, too."

Walker wheeled Nataya through the hospital grounds, away from the people, until only the birds' singing broke the silence. He watched her spend most of her time looking out at the mountains. The deputy followed at a distance, his presence keeping the curious at bay.

Walker inhaled the fresh air. He had to admit the suggestion to go outdoors had been as much for him as for her. Being stuck indoors in a hospital wore hard on him too, so he understood her desperation to leave this place. The difference being, he *could* leave whenever he wished.

He took full blame for her being dragged in here, and it irritated him he didn't know what to do next. Doc believed it their responsibility to help her recover her memories. Walker had mixed feelings about the role he might play in *that* scenario.

She continued to gaze at the trees and mountains beyond. A cloud rolled over the bright sun, blocking the warmth for a moment and Walker saw her shiver. He thought back to her primitive shelter. In his heart he wished to return her to her home, but wondered if she had begun preparing for the coming winter.

When they returned to the room, a nurse appeared. "So, you've had some fresh air already this morning. That's good. I'm going to help you with a shower and washing your hair. I think it will make you feel better."

Nataya looked to Walker, who nodded. He figured she'd do whatever it would take, to help her get out of this place sooner. He guessed correctly.

Walker turned to leave. "The nurse will take good care of you until I get back. I won't be long."

The slipper incident had given him an idea—that and seeing Nataya shiver in the cool air. Remembering the reporters at the entrance of the hospital, he found his way to the back of the building, and slipped away unnoticed. He headed downtown, a few blocks away, to a sporting goods store he often frequented.

A short time later, armed with his bag of purchases, he crossed the street and headed back toward the hospital. His step slowed as he passed the open door of a coffee shop, the aroma heavy in the air. He stopped. He didn't want to get back to the hospital too soon anyway. Nataya might not be ready.

He entered the little shop and waited in line to order. Looking around the room, he watched the businessmen and women beginning the day with their morning rituals, and friends sharing a moment of laughter together. Unbidden, a vision of Haiwi floated up to him…her raven black hair falling forward as she leaned over him…kissing him good morning. Then the pang of loneliness… hurt…then anger.

No, this is my life now—it is the only way.

He turned away from the people. His gaze fell upon a stack of newspapers. He scanned the headlines with minimal interest, until one of the front-page articles caught his attention. He read the headline again to make sure he hadn't misread it. He tossed money on the counter for the paper and left without ordering.

Walker saw Doc look up from his chart as he strode toward him. But the doctor still jumped when Walker slammed a newspaper down on the counter next to him.

"Look."

Doc picked up *The Elk Meadow Bugle,* staring at Walker with wide eyes, then scanned the headlines. Walker could see it didn't take him long to see what had caught his ire.

Wild Woman Captured in Gray's Forest

Doc shook his head. "Geez, sure didn't take the vultures long, did it? I thought the sheriff put out the word to hush this up for a while."

"Maybe, but the local paper decided not to listen. There are reporters hanging around out front, some from the surrounding towns."

"Damn. I'll talk to the staff and make sure everyone keeps a look out for anyone trying to sneak around Nataya's room."

"Sounds good. I will check on her right now."

The deputy stationed outside Nataya's room nodded in recognition as Walker neared. He returned the nod and stepped into the room, then stopped, dazed by her appearance. Now scrubbed head to toe, her tan skin gleamed, and her long hair shone in ripples down the back of her hospital gown.

It took him a moment to focus in on the fact that she glared at a pair of crutches propped up beside her, barely acknowledging his presence. When she spoke, it was to herself, not to him.

"They tell me I have to use these *huupi* to walk, and they cage me here like an animal."

He stepped into her line of vision. But when she turned to stare at him, he could see that her attention lay elsewhere.

"What have I done to be held here like this?"

"You did nothing wrong. The shaman only wants to heal your ankle before you leave." He held out the bag to her, hoping to distract her. "I have something for you."

She ignored both him and the package to resume her mumbling, limping over to the window, leaving the crutches behind.

Walker watched her for a moment, then put the package on her bed. "This is for you. When you are ready."

He left the room. No matter how upset she appeared to be, he'd bet her curiosity wouldn't allow her to ignore the package for long.

He smiled to himself, sure she would be happy with his purchase for her. It'd been a long time since he'd given a gift to a woman. His smile faded.

Don't get too close. Cannot walk that path again.

CHAPTER SEVEN

Elk Meadow, Colorado

Nataya turned from the window, seeing an empty room. *He left.*

She hadn't expected that. He was always around. A heaviness she didn't understand sank into her chest. Why the sadness? He had betrayed her and she didn't trust him.

Maybe having him here is better than being alone in this place.

She hobbled over to stand before the mirror, looking again at this stranger staring back. She had seen her reflection in water before, but she did not know the woman she saw now. And yet...somehow it was familiar, too. Little snippets of scenes flashed through her mind.

What is happening to me?

Nataya glanced over at the large bag on the bed. Walker had said it was for her. She stared at it a bit longer, then made her way over and peeked in. She picked up the material lying on top and brought it to her face, feeling the softness. The colors reminded her of autumn leaves, gold and bronze, against the blue sky. Holding it out at arms-length, she realized she held a...*long-sleeved shirt.*

How do I know this name?

Leaning against the bed for support, she impulsively slipped off the hospital gown and put on the shirt, buttoning it without effort. Why did that feel so natural?

Like I've done it a million times before.

She found her heart beating faster as she pulled out the next item, long pants. She put them on too. She *knew* these clothes, and their names. But how? Why were they so familiar? Now she pulled out a jacket from the bag and smiled. A warm coat. Her breath caught.

Earlier, when Walker had taken her outside, she had faked being chilled in the hospital clothes, hoping he would notice and offer to get her different covering. It had worked out better than she could have imagined.

Then she spotted something remaining at the bottom of the bag. A large box. She pulled it out and opened it, discovering a pair of beaded moccasin boots.

"Oh...*tsowon nambe*...so beautiful."

Nataya admired the workmanship, but couldn't wait to try them. She sat on the edge of the bed and pulled them on, being extra careful of her injured ankle. They fit perfectly. She stood and slowly limped around the room in the new footwear.

How did Walker know she would love these? She stopped in the middle of the room. Yes, how did he know?

She had to admit he had taken great care in choosing the garments. Her gratitude began to soften her reserve. Guilt seeped in. After this show of kindness, it made her sad to think about how she had tricked him.

No. She wouldn't allow those kinds of thoughts to creep in. The gift could be a ploy to make her trust him, and nothing more. She would cling to the anger and concentrate on the fact that now she could plan her escape.

CHAPTER EIGHT

Denver, Colorado

J ack Bailey pushed his chair back from the desk, sick to death
of staring at his computer monitor. If he had to write one more
story about alien abductions he'd slit his wrists.

Frames lined the wall in front of him, all containing headlines
for stories he had written for the *Front Range Chronicles*. Headlines
his boss loved. *Big Foot Spotted in Local Campgrounds, Two Headed
Calf Survives First Year* and *Freak Skiing Accident Claims Life of Famous
Actor.*

He leaned forward on his elbows and stared out the window
at the snow-topped mountains. Seasoned reporters told him to be
patient, that he was young and needed experience. But what he
needed right now was a real story—something exciting he could
dig around in—and do some sleuthing. Then maybe a reputable
newspaper or magazine would take notice of him.

He heard the slap of paper on his desk and turned to see his
editor, Dan Stevens, standing there, grim faced as always. Jack

looked over at *The Elk Meadow Bugle,* could see something circled in red on the front cover.

"What's up, Dan?"

"Elk Meadows, way out on the west side of the Rockies. One of our stringers sent this in. Some crazy, wacked-out woman just turned up in a forest, living out there like some wild creature."

"She isn't claiming to have been dropped off by a UFO, is she?"

"Funny. Do you see me laughing? Seems the local law is trying to keep this one quiet, but a couple of small-time papers are already all over it. This is our kind of story. I know you can put a fresh spin on it. I need you to make some phone calls and see what you can find out."

Jack perked up.

Now this is more like it.

"Sure, Dan. But you know…those small-town people can be pretty tight-lipped with strangers. I might not get far with just a call on the phone. I may need to go in kinda low-profile to get the locals to talk to me."

"In other words, you want an excuse for a road trip." Dan glared at him a moment, then gave in. "Alright, I guess it wouldn't hurt to have you go nose around. It *is* a tiny podunk town, not Denver."

"Super. Good thing I like to drink beer and play pool," Jack said and laughed. He could already picture himself tracking down this wild woman and getting the full story before anyone else. And not just the sensationalized scoop he knew Dan wanted—but a real piece of journalistic writing. Something to be proud of.

Dan grunted and tossed a map in his direction. "Here, you're gonna need this."

When would his boss ever get with the times and realize there was this gadget called a GPS? Jack opened the map to check out his destination.

Shit, it really is out in the middle of nowhere.

He had to think fast. "Hey Dan. You know, it's just a matter of time before the other national papers sniff out this story. Sure would be a shame to have one our big competitors beat us to this one."

Dan gave a sigh of resignation. "Alright. Catch a flight out of D.I.A. and fly into Gunnison. That'll save you a day of driving through the mountains. But from there you hit the road, and this place ain't on any tourist routes. Try not to get lost."

Jack shrugged. He never got lost. But he had to admit, this one might be more of a challenge to find. Good, that's just what he wanted.

CHAPTER NINE

Elk Meadow, Colorado

Late in the night, Nataya slipped out of bed and tested her weight on her ankle. In just the few days she'd been here, it already hurt less. She walked silently to the door and peered out into the hall. As usual, the man they called *Deputy* sat in a chair next to her door. She had questioned Walker about him, and about the strange tool he wore on his belt. Walker explained that it was a weapon, called a gun, and what it could do. But he said that the Deputy was there to protect her, not harm her. Still, it made her wary. And it hindered her plans on how to get out of the room and away from the medicine lodge.

It had become her routine to check on the Deputy each night when she awoke, disturbed by the dreams. Each one felt like a little piece of a puzzle she should know and understand, yet the meaning always eluded her.

Sometimes the old man from her first dream appeared to her, and she felt as if the young girl with him was her. But none of it made sense. During the dreams, she felt happy and content, but when she awoke, a longing filled her that she couldn't explain. She wished she understood the messages the spirits sent her, but for now she needed to have patience and keep planning.

She opened her locker and pulled out the shopping bag Walker had brought in with the clothes. Laying it on the bed, she slid out the items collected the last few days. Food included apples, bananas and oranges saved from her meals, plus a few bottles of water. Although she knew how to find food in her real world, she didn't want to spend time foraging during her escape.

She picked up one of the little soaps they gave her, inhaling the flowery smell. It reminded her of the wild roses blooming in the forest. Her hand moved to place it in the bag, but hesitated.

What if they send the barking dogs after me again?

They would smell the soap and find her. She decided against taking it. But this small bottle of liquid, which made her hair so shiny, gave out no smell. It had been given to her, and she didn't want to leave it behind.

On her first day here, before her cleansing, they had cut off her necklace and anklet, but gave them to her to keep. She had wrapped the pieces in some delicate paper from the shoebox, to repair when she got home.

Everything except the soap went back into the bag, and she placed it reverently in a wood box, which Walker called a locker, then walked over to the window.

Looking at the full moon and stars sprinkled across the sky, she pretended to be back in the woods, at her cave home. But the reality of her situation wouldn't leave. She couldn't forget the big, frightening manmade beings—Walker had called them x-ray machines. Nothing here felt like a place of healing.

I must escape.

Moonlight poured over the hills in the distance, drawing her attention. Thankfully, during her times outside with Walker, she had been able to study the surrounding landscape long enough to find the mountain range that would guide her back home. She knew which direction to go.

She turned from the window, removed her robe and climbed into the bed. Although most of the pain in her ankle had left, she exaggerated her limp whenever someone watched. The workers, and even Walker, seemed to believe her act. They wouldn't expect her to try and escape.

But she had clothes and supplies. The only thing left—find a way past the man at the door.

CHAPTER TEN

Elk Meadow, Colorado

Still dressed in the clothes Fox Walker had given her, Nataya stood at the window in her hospital room. She could feel the heat of the sun through the glass and remembered the warmth of it on her back earlier this morning, when Walker had taken her outside. It had made a nice contrast to the cool, crisp breeze on her face. No doubt autumn lay ahead, and then winter would take over. She must escape soon, so she could prepare for the cold months ahead.

Walker took her outside often. And he had discovered various ways to avoid the noisy people always waiting outside the building— shouting words. Grateful as she was for this, she wondered if he did it for her, or for himself. She could tell from his actions that being inside the medicine lodge bothered him, perhaps as much as it did her.

This morning, as he had pushed her wheelchair, she had especially enjoyed the quiet, with only bird song and the wind rustling the leaves in the background, instead of the constant rattling and clattering inside the medicine lodge. She inhaled as much of the fall aroma as her lungs could hold, and felt the energy of it flow through her, providing the strength to face yet another day in this place. But that had been earlier…

She looked around the room, glancing at the doorway. Yesterday an aged, bent man, referred to as a *security guard* had taken the place of Deputy. She noticed that this man did not wear the gun tool on his belt, and he had napped in his chair after lunch. So she thought to sneak past him this afternoon. But a different man had shown up this morning. He was a *tsugupe* as well, and walked with a limp, so maybe her plan would still work.

Hearing a conversation in the hallway, she strolled toward the doorway. It wasn't Walker's voice. Curious, she peered around the door and saw a man dressed similar to the Shaman, but younger, talking to the guard. She returned to the window. There were always people coming and going here. It irritated her, but Walker had explained they were simply doing their job.

She heard the man enter the room, and half-turned to study the youthful face behind the large glasses. He silently closed the door and, barely taking notice of her, walked over to the foot of her bed to look at her chart. When he glanced up, for the briefest of moments she thought she saw surprise in his eyes. But he spoke in a bored monotone.

"Miss…Nataya, I have been sent from the medical records department. To my understanding, you arrived at the hospital with scars on your torso."

When she stared at him without answering, he prompted her. "Scars?" he said, pointing toward his own stomach area.

He waited for her to acknowledge his statement with a nod, and then continued. "It's my job to take pictures as documentation. The photos will be kept with your permanent medical records. It's all just standard procedure."

The man's flat tone didn't fit with the sense of urgency Nataya caught amid the rush of words. And what did all those strange words mean? She would have to rely on her instincts to know how to react. Alarm stirred inside her.

The man watched her face intently. When he spoke again, His *words* sounded calm and soothing—but Nataya could see the tension in his body.

"Don't worry. There's nothing to be scared about. You won't feel anything. Do you remember when they did an x-ray of your ankle?"

There—a word she had learned. She nodded, remembering being frightened of the giant x-ray machine. Walker had promised it wouldn't touch her or hurt her, and it hadn't.

"Good, because this is just a small version of that machine." He pulled a small metal box-like object from his pocket and held it up for her to see. "This will take pictures, like the x-ray machine did."

He gently guided her toward the hospital bed, but she felt the tautness of his grasp.

"Here, let's have you sit on the bed like this, and now lean back against the pillows. Just relax, so you are comfortable. That's it."

Nataya followed his instructions. She had been made to lie down on a big, hard bed for the x-ray machine, so it must be okay.

"That's good, Nataya. Now I need you to undo these bottom shirt buttons, so I can pull back the material and show the scars clearly."

"I didn't have to do this for the x-ray machine."

"Well...that's because it was really big, wasn't it? This is very little, isn't it? It can't take a picture through the fabric like the big machine can. This one has to *see* the scars to take a picture."

It sounded like he spoke the truth. But it bothered her that he kept glancing nervously over his shoulder as she worked. Starting at the bottom of her shirt, she un-did the buttons, until she got to the ones that covered her bosom. Here she hesitated. This didn't feel right. When she looked up at the man, she noticed that he stared at her hands, biting his lower lip.

He frowned and leaned in closer. "These scars are partially hidden by your pants. I will need you to pull them out of the way."

She unsnapped the top of her pants, and he helped her roll the material back and away, to expose the entire scarred area. Then he picked up the little x-ray machine.

"That's good, Nataya." Holding the machine up to his face, he leaned over her. "Now hold real still. Don't move."

Sudden flashes of light startled and blinded her for a moment. She jerked upright in the bed, covering her eyes.

"I'm so sorry, Nataya. I should have warned you about the flashes. There's nothing to be afraid of. See, it's just because this room is too dark for the x-ray to work. It needs the extra light." He eased her back into position. "I only need a few more pictures. Please, just relax a moment longer."

Nataya stiffly obeyed. No matter what the man's words said, something was not right. She wished one of the medicine lodge people would come in. They were always in here. Why not now? They could tell her what to do.

After looking over his shoulder toward the door, the man once again leaned over her. The flashes started as before. This time there were many more and so fast she had to squeeze her eyes shut. And then they stopped.

She waited a moment, then peeked with one eye. No man. She turned and caught a glimpse of him rushing out the door. She eased herself up.

She sat on the edge of the bed, taking deep breaths to calm her rapid heartbeat while she buttoned her shirt again. The medicine lodge helper, Alice, entered with a lunch tray. She set it down and asked, "Are you okay, honey?"

"I don't know. A man dressed like the Shaman said he had to take x-rays of my scars. He scared me with the flashes of light."

"What did he look like?"

"He had black hair...and wore glasses over his eyes, like the Shaman called Doc wears...except these were bigger and thick... black edges."

"What else? Did he look old or young? Did he tell you his name?"

"No name. His skin looked smooth, younger than the Doc Shaman. He stood a little taller than me."

Alice frowned and picked up the phone. "Wanda, watch for a young male intern to come through. You may not recognize him— dark hair and glasses. Do me a favor and don't let him past the desk." She listened a moment, then spoke again, urgently. "I don't know how...just stop him and keep him talking while I send the security guard down there. I think we have an intruder."

Alice stepped out into the hall, and Nataya could hear her demanding that the guard go find the man. Then she came back into the room.

"Okay, dear. I'm sorry if the man scared you. Don't worry. He won't be back. Now, let's see how you're doing with your ankle. Stand up for me and put as much weight on that leg as you can."

Still rattled, Nataya performed her usual routine of exaggerating the amount of pain she felt when putting weight on her ankle. The nurse prodded the area a bit. Nataya winced.

"I just don't understand it..." Alice mumbled. "Nataya, just relax here for a moment."

She picked up the phone again and dialed, but this time got no answer. "I'm going to get Doc. Don't worry. Nothing's wrong. I just want him to take a look at your ankle. Keep it elevated and I'll be right back." She left the room.

Nataya sat there, stunned for the moment.

I'm alone. And no guard!

A quiver ran over her body. She slid off the bed and hurried to the locker, threw on her jacket, and grabbed the bag. She peered around the doorframe and down the hallway. Saw no one. The pounding in her chest made it difficult to breathe.

Stay calm—go now.

Forcing her feet to move, she walked away from her room, following the corridor. She didn't take time to acknowledge the slight pain in her ankle. The anxiety of being caught kept her focused on her escape.

Each time Walker had taken her outside, she had memorized the different ways he went to the back of the building, to avoid being seen by the people out front. When the corridor opened up into a larger area, Nataya walked close behind a group of *dioboo*, hoping she appeared to be with them until she could slip away unnoticed out a back door.

Once outside, she leaned back against the brick wall of the building and took a couple of deep breaths to calm down. Ahead of her lay a large open area Walker called a parking lot, full of things he called cars and trucks. She had watched them moving around every day and although everything about them felt familiar, no dreams or memories came to her. She did know that the empty ones never moved, and so she began to weave her way through them, crouching down whenever she saw others, until she reached the far end.

She knelt behind the last car in the lot and looked out across the fields that bordered the back of the medicine lodge, studying the distant mountain range in front of her until she found the one jagged peak she wanted.

She stood up from her hiding place and after a glance behind her, set off across the field, keeping her destination in view. She would have most of the daylight hours to travel before being forced to stop for the night. She smiled.

I'm going home.

⊯ ⊱

Jack Bailey drove down the back road from the hospital and followed it until well out of town. He pulled onto the shoulder and stopped the car. Laughing, he pounded on the steering wheel.

"Dammit—I love this shit!"

The *chameleon* had struck again. He took great pride in the fact that he had mastered the art of blending into his surroundings, whatever they may be. He used his good looks and charm on the women when he wanted, or became one of the guys when it suited his purpose. Other times he made sure no one noticed him at all.

In a town this small it had taken him no time to figure out where the deputies preferred to hang out after their work shifts, and even less time to get people talking about the most exciting thing to happen in these parts for a long time. And once he discovered the deputy guarding the wild woman's room had been replaced with a rent-a cop, he had known he was in.

Jack pulled out the digital camera and checked the shots. Excellent photos, even if he did stop short of getting the explicit pictures he knew Dan would pay big bucks for.

Jack opened the glove compartment, pulled out his flask and relaxed back into his seat.

Time to celebrate.

The shot of Blanton's Bourbon went down smooth and warmed him from the inside out.

Oh, Dan would get the sensationalized story he expected. It was what Jack excelled at. But this time he saw a better opportunity. This could be the big break he craved. The chance to prove to everyone that he could be more—a respected journalist.

CHAPTER ELEVEN

Elk Meadow, Colorado

Hospital cafeterias all smell the same.
Fox Walker attempted to eat the food on his tray. He lifted another forkful, but stopped midway to his mouth, noticing the security guard assigned to Nataya's room. The man moved slowly, limping with every step, but now he stood still and appeared to be searching the room.

Now what?

Walker stood and wove his way through the tables and chairs. "Is there a problem?"

"Mebbe. Seems some jerk posed as part of the hospital staff to get into the girl's room. The nurse thinks he took some photos of her. She asked me to find—"

Walker didn't wait to hear the rest. He took off in a sprint across the room and, dodging people, ran down the hallway. He turned the corner and saw Doc step out of Nataya's room, followed by a nurse.

Doc turned toward Walker, his face livid. "Damn reporters. I should have guessed one of them would figure out a way to get to her. I'm sorry, Walker. She's gone—all of her clothes too."

Walker stood motionless at the edge of the parking lot, gazing out over the fields. He had to admit relief, knowing she had made her escape. Now they were both free of the hospital and could return to the natural world they loved. The guilt had weighed heavy on him because she had been captured and dragged away from her home. He *knew* the spirits had asked him to be her protector...and he had failed.

Now he would follow her to make sure she arrived back to her cave home safely. Besides, tracking her would give him the opportunity to learn more about her.

Nataya would be using the mountain range near her home as a beacon. He had watched her study the peaks every day while they were outside and knew which direction she now headed.

The sound of hurried footsteps on the paved surface caught Walker's attention, and when they drew closer, he turned to see who approached.

Morgan. Great. Just what I don't need right now.

He stood, arms crossed, waiting.

"Hey, Walker. I suppose you're planning on heading out after that woman?"

"Yep." He braced for battle.

"Good."

Walker struggled to keep his surprise from showing, but fortunately Morgan continued talking before he could react.

"The whole reason we searched the forest was to make sure a fugitive wasn't hiding out there—a killer. Whoever killed that guy last spring had to be extremely strong, and smart, not some looney person living alone out there, surviving on roots and berries. As far as *I'm* concerned the department has already wasted too much time on this crazy woman."

Recovered now, Walker nodded and remained silent, letting Morgan do all the talking.

"Besides, she's not broken any laws, except maybe trespassing, and the owners of Gray's Forest have not pressed charges. That search wasn't even my idea in the first place. I'm washing my hands of the whole affair. So—knock yourself out, Tonto."

Walker watched Morgan's back as he retreated across the parking lot, relieved to know the law wouldn't be intruding. That still left the reporters, though. Once they discovered Nataya's escape, who knew what kind of frenzy they would set off again. Things might change for Morgan. Walker knew he had better take advantage of this time.

He strode along the edge of the parking lot and adjoining field until he found the spot where the disturbed ground indicated Nataya had entered the high weeds. The land held only a few low, rolling hills, but at the moment they hid her from his view. The relative flatness of the fields would let her travel far today.

He sprinted back through the parking lot and found his truck where the deputy had said it would be. He didn't know how long he might be out there in the wilderness, and he wasn't about to leave his truck in the hospital parking lot during that time. Modern society might not be good for much, but his 1986 Chevrolet Silverado pick-up truck faithfully served, year after year. He started it up and drove out onto the paved street bordering the field.

A half mile later he spotted an access road, a dirt path for tractors to drive into the field. The farmer wouldn't be using it this time of year. He drove into the field until the path crested a slight hill then headed downward. At the bottom he pulled over into the weeds, got out and made sure the truck couldn't be seen from the main road. The slight rise blocked the view of it.

He pulled a heavy jacket, as well as his moccasin boots, from behind the seat. This time of year the weather could change overnight with plunging temperatures and snowfall. Better to be prepared. After switching to the moccasin boots, he stowed the leather boots behind the truck seat.

Using loose brush in the area, he camouflaged the shiny metal of the vehicle. He didn't need someone spotting it from afar and checking it out. Then he opened the hitch cover on the rear bumper and hid his key inside for safekeeping.

Shielding against the sun, he peered at the distant landscape. He knew she would most likely head toward the tree-lined river off in the distance. She should arrive before nightfall. There she would find shelter and water. Walker continued to scan the land between him and the river. There, that little stand of trees in the middle of the fields. There would be water nearby. A good place to spend the night.

Now, to pick up her trail and follow.

CHAPTER TWELVE

The Open Countryside, Colorado

Nataya pushed her way through the shoulder-high weeds and grasses. At first her excitement over escaping from the hospital had given her unbounded energy, but it had drained after hour upon hour of struggling through the overgrown field.

Exhaustion consumed every part of her body as she strained to look ahead over the weeds towards her destination.

How much farther?

She yelped as her foot slipped into a shallow hole, twisting her sore ankle. She fell to the ground. Anger welled up as she sat there, attempting to rub out the pain. A loss of focus for one brief second. That's all it had taken.

She dug her fingers into the shadowed earth under the plants and packed the cool mud onto her ankle, hoping to stop any swelling and relieve the pain. But, perhaps because of her previous injury, the ache now settled into a constant throbbing and wouldn't ease. She could see the puffiness already starting. Her simmering anger now boiled over to panic.

I don't have time for this.

⊯ ⊱

Walker stopped and shielded his eyes against the setting sun, looking ahead to the trees lining the river. He didn't dare follow Nataya any further tonight. She would be stopping soon, where she could shelter within the trees.

He had followed her tracks for hours when, late in the day, he found an area of disturbance in the soil indicating Nataya had stepped into a shallow hole and stumbled. She may or may not have fallen, but at the very least she had sat on the ground long enough to create an impression. And soil had been dug up from under the plants where it would be shaded and cool to the touch. Had she made a mudpack for an injury?

Up to this point, her tracks had indicated she used equal weight on both legs while walking. No surprise to him, considering more than once he had caught her forgetting to exaggerate her limp while in the hospital. But from this spot on he could tell she again favored her left ankle. Perhaps she had overestimated how much it had healed, or re-injured it?

He turned, his brows furrowed in concern, and headed toward a small grouping of trees, in the opposite direction.

CHAPTER THIRTEEN

Portland, Oregon

Dean McClure walked past the police car parked in front of the large, brick house and stopped before the steps leading up to an expansive porch. The house number matched the one given to him. He ran his hand through his graying hair and took a moment to absorb the feel of the place, the multitude of flowers along the sidewalk, the sounds of cars and motorcycles passing through, kids playing in a nearby park…a siren in the distance. The older building sat sandwiched between newer condos, and had at one time probably been a mansion of sorts—its upstairs and downstairs rooms now divided into apartments.

When Dean made the top step, he lifted the yellow crime scene tape stretched across the porch entrance, and ducked under it. A fifth murder committed by the Art Critic, and no closer to finding the killer. He needed a break, something to stem the flow of frustration he battled. Something to give him hope.

Maybe this is the one. One too many.

Dean fished in his pocket for the key the police had given him as he walked toward the front door. But before he could slip it into the keyhole, a uniformed man stepped out of the shadows on his right, just at the edge of the porch. Dean stared at the officer walking toward him. Aviator style sunglasses reflected light, hiding the man's eyes. But his mouth curved into a slow smile.

"Special Agent McClure. Hope I didn't startle you. The department asked me to make sure none of the neighborhood teenagers messed around here."

Dean held up the key. "I was told I could have some time alone inside."

"Of course, and don't worry. I won't bother you while you work." The officer faced Dean, offering his hand. "It's a real honor to meet you, sir."

Dean sized up the man before him...shorter...medium build. Dean guessed him to be in his late twenties. He shook the offered hand, and took note of the man's badge number and name. "I'm sorry Officer Grey, have we met before?"

The officer gave a dry cough. "Uh, no," he said, as he removed his sunglasses, revealing deep-set dark brown eyes. "I guess I should explain. I'm applying to the Academy. I want to be an FBI Profiler like you. That's why I just *had* to take this opportunity to meet you. Been following your career for years. Truly inspirational."

The man's enthusiasm tugged at Dean. An inspiration? He didn't know whether to laugh hysterically or cry. Only another profiler would truly understand the toll this line of work took on one's life and health. "Then you know I just recently retired."

"Heard rumors. That's a big loss for the Bureau."

"It was *their* idea, not mine."

"But then, here you are."

"Yes, I'm working as a consultant."

"That's good to know. Especially since the Art Critic appears to be in Portland now."

Dean's eyebrow rose. "What makes you believe the Art Critic is involved?"

"Simple. Big profile case like this in our community—word gets out among the men. And like I said, I've been studying your career. And I'm betting you wouldn't be here if it wasn't the work of the Art Critic."

"That's a good observation, officer, but as for this case, you know I can't talk about it."

"Sure, I understand. But there's plenty we *could* talk about—stuff that was in the papers. Speaking of which, I haven't seen anything in the news about him lately. Wasn't he credited with killing someone every three months?"

"Correct."

"So following this killer's pattern, there should have been a murder back in April."

Geez, another naïve wanna-be.

Dean couldn't miss the eagerness in the officer's voice as he hurried to continue.

"But I never saw anything in the media about the Art Critic committing a murder during that time frame. Was there a gap? Or did the FBI hush it up or something?"

"Look, Officer. As much as I appreciate your interest in the case, you understand that I can't discuss any theories or evidence with you."

Officer Grey looked momentarily disappointed, but he recovered and nodded. "I get it. Maybe you guys laid a trap for this guy, and so you kept info out of the media. Maybe you hope he'll return to the scene of the crime?"

Dean gave him a weary smile, but remained silent. He certainly wasn't going to admit that they *hadn't* thought of setting a trap like that. He shifted his weight, glanced at the door awaiting him.

"Look, I know you're busy. But thanks for talking with me, Agent—I mean Mr. McClure. You have no idea how much this means to me, really. This is a dream I've had for a long time, and meeting you like this just motivates me more. I hope one day I can live up to your reputation as a profiler."

The words rattled up memories from a lifetime ago. This man had no idea the arduous days that lay before him. "You think you know what this is all about? But I'm going to tell you the truth of it, young man. *If* you even make it through the Academy, and *if* you do overcome the odds and become a profiler, to be any good at this, you'll pay—with your health—body *and* soul. And the gods be with you if you try to lead a normal life alongside your career, because *it* will take over. Your career *will* be your life."

Dean paused to let the officer absorb his words. But the man only watched him, silent. Dean's exasperation pushed to the surface and boiled over. "Don't you get it? My wife left years ago, hating me for letting my job destroy our marriage. And now her resentment is threatening to turn my grown daughter against me. Do you know what it's like losing the only people who matter to you?"

Officer Grey slid the sunglasses in place, but didn't speak.

Dean shook his head. "I should be enjoying my retirement, but instead I'm consulting for the Bureau. You know why? Because I'm so dedicated—self-sacrificing? No. It's because *that's all I've got.*"

Officer Grey stared at Dean for a long moment before giving him a curt nod. "I'll leave you to your work now, sir." But as he walked across the porch, ducked under the crime scene tape and took the steps, he threw one last comment over his shoulder. "Good hunting, Mr. McClure."

Dean turned away, a twinge of regret in his gut. He hadn't meant to go on such a rant. A side effect of his frustration with this case...and his life. He gave a sigh, then turned and unlocked the door and walked into the foyer.

The cloying scent of flowers greeted him. An assortment of mismatched vases filled with hand-cut blossoms sat on a table, alongside a snapshot of the victim. Perhaps a remembrance from the other tenants?

At the top of the stairs more crime scene tape stretched across an open door. He made his way up the staircase. The crime hadn't been committed in the apartment, so no need to prepare mentally for that. He'd already been to the actual crime scene and the morgue. He knew how the victim had died. Now he wanted to see how she had lived. He wanted to get to know this woman named Lisa. He ducked under the tape and stepped inside.

The only light in the room flowed in from the windows and open door, and Dean left it that way. He stood in one place for a moment, soaking in the atmosphere.

What made you special to the Art Critic. Why you?

He wandered through the main room, letting his gaze settle on each item before moving on…a small basket filled with pinecones, a glass box filled with rocks and fossils, a picture book of horses. He noticed still-vibrant plants spilling over into any available space, giving the place an organic and outdoorsy feel. Even the clutter looked organized. The roomy apartment gave a tree top view of the local park. A peaceful atmosphere, for a city place.

Art supplies, an easel and canvases of various shapes and sizes took up an entire corner of the room and beyond.

The easel.

This most recent murder scene in the woods crashed into his thoughts. Evidence indicated the victim had been tied to a tree and tortured, before finding relief in death. Every victim had suffered the same fate. Bound upright in some way, like a canvas on an easel, while the Art Critic created his masterpiece. Dean felt the burn of anger beginning.

Not now.

Every profiler finds himself drawn to a particular case and this one had captured Dean. Everyone in the Bureau knew it. They also knew he would not be able to let it go, even after retiring—far too personal now. The unidentified subject, or UNSUB as the guys at the Behavioral Analysis Unit referred to him, had been nicknamed the "Art Critic" by the media, because all of his young female victims thus far were artists.

Dean flipped on the lights and turned his attention to the paintings and sketches scattered about on the walls...ocean cliffs, mountains, and woodland scenes. He liked Lisa's artwork. He could identify with it, understand the earthy feel of it. Not like some of the stuff called a*rt* that he had seen in museums. Every one of the young victims had similar work... realistic paintings of nature. Not one of them did abstract or modern art. Each piece was a rendition of light and shadow, playing over and through views of the natural world.

A new victim every three months, like clockwork, at the new moon. And then suddenly—nothing—for six months. Dean had dared to hope the man had died, been killed, or captured for some other crime. Because he knew this murderer would never stop of his own accord. But this crime left no doubt the killer was alive and back at work.

Dean studied a painting depicting a deep, shadowed forest. How ironic Lisa had died in such a place. It hurt to know she would never create another piece of art.

You know better than to go there. Keep your emotions at bay.

An impossible task, yet one he strived to meet. Experience told him his very survival demanded it.

Focus on the room. Get to know her.

There. That easy chair.

Worn upholstery on the armrests, along with the sunken cushions declared this a favorite spot. The well-used piece of furniture sat in a corner, a reading light next to it, as well as a stack of art magazines and books. He turned on the lamp and sat down in the chair, forcing himself to relax back into it as she would have done. He could feel the contours of her body impressed into the cushions. They resisted conforming to his body, as if reluctant to give up her memory.

He looked again toward Lisa's artwork. It certainly appeared that this style attracted the Art Critic to these artists.

How could such beautiful art attract a killer?

Dean remained in the chair, studying the room around him until he spotted a photo of Lisa and her parents on a nearby table. The image of his daughter Kim flooded in. The pain of their separation tore at his heart, but he took refuge in the vague hope someday he would find a way to regain her love. The parents of *these* murdered young women had to suffer this agony every day, knowing their daughters were lost to them forever.

Focus. You can't help them this way.

"Of all the artists in this town, what made him pick you? Was it only the artwork?" Dean asked the empty room.

Nothing looked out of place in the apartment. In fact, none of the victims' residences held any signs of a break-in or struggle. Dean believed the killer knew his victims and their routines intimately, probably stalked them, and then abducted them as they traveled to or from somewhere using a familiar route.

And the Art Critic had evolved into quite an organized murderer. His abductions were honed to perfection, making Dean wonder how many years of practice he'd had before the FBI took notice eighteen months ago.

The victims were driven to some other location before they were killed. Lisa Webster's body had been found in a wilderness location, but some of the others had been discovered in remote warehouses. Either way, the killer worked where he was free from intrusions, alone to do whatever he desired.

He wants to feel safe. This guy doesn't take chances. He plans ahead.

Small traces of chloroform had been found in each victim's tissues, but only enough to subdue for a short period. Even with that, the abductions must have been blitzes, giving the victim no opportunity to fight back or flee. There were no defensive wounds—only the antemortem carvings on the torso. Aside from the slight bruising around the hips, there were ligature marks only on the ankles and wrists.

He needs total control, but lacks confidence he can over-power them without the element of surprise. All the victims were petite women. Perhaps he's not a big, muscular man, then.

Dean stood up from the chair and continued to study the apartment as he walked through the rooms. The used furniture and simple dishes in the kitchen were typical for a working student. But the closet yielded an abundance of clothes, shoes and handbags—most of them bearing designer labels.

Same as the other victims.

He had no doubt he would learn that Lisa, just like the other women, came from an affluent family, yet one that valued the lesson that it took hard work to succeed. It fit into the puzzle in some way.

A number of the victims had worked as sales clerks, like Lisa. Others had been waitresses or bank tellers. All held jobs that put them in contact with the public, making it easy to gain access to them in an unsuspicious way.

She fits the profile.

These murders weren't random. Each victim had been *chosen*. He just had to figure out the *why*. Then maybe he could figure out the *who*.

And he didn't plan on resting until he figured it out, until he could bring this killer to justice.

Personal satisfaction.

He had to admit that his career *had* given him much in *that* aspect. His life had purpose, knowing he had outwitted killers, had a hand in tracking them down and stopping them...finding vindication for the victims' families. Why else had he stuck with it, even as he watched it destroy his marriage? Even now, after the Bureau *encouraged* him to retire because he wouldn't embrace the new methods and philosophies, even now he couldn't walk away.

It's who I am.

His words to Officer Grey came back to mind.

The man's ambitions deserve more consideration than he had given him. The least he could do to make amends was try to contact the guy tomorrow when he dropped off the key at the police station.

CHAPTER FOURTEEN

Portland, Oregon

Dean McClure parked his car and briskly made his way to the North Precinct building of the Portland Police Bureau. He approached the desk clerk, checked out her name tag and waited for the woman's attention.

"Good Morning, Karen. My name is Dean McClure. I'm working with the FBI on the Lisa Webster case. Just dropping off the apartment key. Can you make sure it gets returned to Sergeant Reese?"

"Would you like me to buzz him, sir?"

"Nah, I'm sure he has far better things to do." Dean slid the borrowed key through the opening in the bulletproof divider, turned to go, then hesitated.

"Yes, Mr. McClure. Is there something else I can do for you?"

"Maybe. Any chance I can touch base with Officer Grey before he begins his shift? Badge number 867. I'll only take a moment of his time."

The clerk's eyes no longer held a neutral, business-only look. In fact, they squinted hard at Dean. She nodded to a couple of nearby officers who came to stand next to him.

"And may I ask how you know Officer Grey?"

Dean looked at the uniforms.

What the hell?

"I met him only yesterday. He was stationed at the apartment building over on Walnut Street…where Lisa Webster lived, before she was murdered."

"Mr. McClure. I'm going to have to ask you to wait here a moment. Sergeant Reese will want to speak with you."

Dean tensed. "Can you tell me what this is about?"

"Best if our Sergeant does that, sir. Please…"

The desk clerk picked up the phone and spoke a few words. A moment later the sergeant walked in the room. He approached Dean and offered his hand.

"Good to see you again, McClure. I hope you were able to get what you needed from the apartment?"

"Yes, and thank you again for the cooperation. The Bureau appreciates it. So what's this about?"

Sergeant Reese nodded to the two officers, dismissing them. "Let's go to my office."

Dean followed the sergeant down the hallway to an office door, where he was ushered in and offered a chair. Sergeant Reese sat heavily in his own desk chair and leaned forward, hands clasped on the desktop. Dean couldn't read anything in the man's guarded expression and waited for him to speak first.

"You say you met Officer Grey yesterday at the apartment building?"

"Yeah. We spoke about the Academy and profiling. He caught me at a bad time. Afraid I aired some dirty laundry. Wasn't the right thing to do. Thought maybe I'd set things right today before I head out."

"Can you describe the officer you spoke with?"

Dean stared at the sergeant. "Pardon me, sir. But can we cut the bullshit and you tell me what the hell is going on?"

Sergeant Reese picked up a photo from his desktop and held it up for Dean to see. "Any chance this is the officer you spoke with yesterday?"

Dean studied the photo, leaning in for a closer look. His gut tightened as well as his jaw.

"No, it's not. The man I spoke with *does* fit this man's description, perfectly. Only he's not the same guy."

Damn.

Sergeant Reese sighed and gently laid the photo on his desk. "Officer Grey never reported for duty yesterday. When he didn't answer any calls, we sent a patrol over to his place. But he wasn't there—his car either. He's officially listed as missing."

Dean's hands gripped the chair's armrest. "So, I take it he was never stationed at the apartment yesterday?"

"Nope."

⊱ ⊰

Scenery blurred past as Dean concentrated on the highway ahead, barely noticing his surroundings in the twilight. The quick stop at the police precinct had turned into a daylong ordeal, leaving him exhausted and exasperated. But he'd still rather drive the one hundred seventy-four miles from Portland to Seattle, versus boarding a plane. He hated to fly.

But the hours of driving along Interstate 5 left him alone with his thoughts. Someone had not only gone to the trouble to impersonate a police officer, but all evidence pointed to the fact that he did it to talk to *him*...in person. Why?

Hours had passed and the real officer was still missing, although his locked and empty patrol car had been located. Empty, except for the large pool of blood in the trunk. Dean figured the body of a young cop waited out there somewhere.

The impostor fit the missing officer's description right down to the dark brown eyes and late twenties age, making it clear why that particular officer had been targeted. A police cap had covered most of the impostor's hair, but Dean remembered black sideburns. A handsome man, well groomed, confident. Nothing about his appearance or speech had set off any alarms in Dean's psyche at the time, which did nothing to improve his present mood. He and a sketch artist had worked together to re-create a drawing of the impostor.

Dean passed a slow-moving truck and pulled back into his lane. He would not soon forget the moment he stared at the finished sketch. A chill of realization had run through his body, that he might be looking at the face of the Art Critic. A distinct possibility. In fact, for now it was the only thing that made any sense to him. The impostor had used the "wanna be a profiler" angle to gain Dean's confidence and pump him for information about the investigation. Who else would do that?

The impostor had known he'd be there.

But how?

Dean replayed the conversation. *I've followed your career for years. Heard rumors you'd retired.* Maybe the guy had an inside contact.

But why take that kind of risk, just to talk to me?

The guy had balls—that's for sure. Something about that conversation had to be the key to all of this. He replayed it over, and over again, in his head while mile after mile of highway streamed by in his rearview mirror.

One thing stuck out.

The whole point of the discussion kept coming back to the fact that there had been no murder in April.

But why the hell would the killer be asking about a murder that hadn't happened?

Unless there's still a body out there. One we haven't found.

Dean smacked the steering wheel with his hand. Of course! What if the Art Critic *did* keep to his schedule? But no one knew it. He wanted the body found. He couldn't stand it that his *art work* had gone unnoticed, without recognition. That had to be it.

But where the hell do I even begin to look for a body?

Maybe the impostor hid a clue within the conversation. What was that parting line…oh, yeah, "Good hunting, Mr. McClure."

He's goading me!

The Art Critic had let him see his face.

I know what he looks like—and he doesn't even care.

Was the killer *that* confident Dean couldn't track him down? A torrent of all Dean's inadequacies and fears broke free and flooded in. He could see the headline.

Washed-up Former Exalted FBI Profiler Duped by Nemesis, The Art Critic.

CHAPTER FIFTEEN

The Open Countryside, Colorado

Nataya stumbled through thickets and brush, trembling with weariness. Dark shadows rippled around her as the wind swayed the trees overhead across the face of the moon. After re-injuring her ankle earlier in the day, only dogged determination had allowed her to reach her goal, a line of trees that would give her shelter for the night. But the effort had cost her.

She collapsed to the ground and lie on the cool earth, waiting to regain her strength. When her breathing leveled out, she sat up, pulled a water bottle from her bag and drained it. The fluid revived some of her stamina. The rest of the water and food would be saved for tomorrow.

Nataya peered through the darkness, searching the ground for materials to build a shelter. The nights were growing colder. She could not count on surviving the long hours of darkness without a way to keep warm.

A huge tree on an incline, lit by the moonlight, caught her attention. Unless her eyes were playing tricks on her, the base of the trunk appeared to be hollow.

She forced herself up and limped over to it, rejoicing as she got closer. The tree was larger than she first thought. One hand clung to the bark as she steadied her balance and knelt to examine the hollow trunk. No forest creatures had taken up residence, and it looked to have plenty of room for her to squeeze in.

The snugger, the warmer it will be.

She used her fingers to scrape and pull loose pine needles from the surrounding ground into the hollow, covering the soft dirt floor inside with a thick evergreen mat. This would keep her body away from the damp ground, and deter insects from bothering her. Next, she gathered up handfuls of dried leaves from under the trees and packed the remaining hollowed space with them, for insulation.

Now what to do with her plastic bag of food and water bottles. She didn't need to attract any hungry animals to her space for the night. A nearby fallen log would do the trick. She rolled the log back a little and dug out a small depression in the soft ground where it had rested. Wrapping the plastic bag tightly around and around its contents, she laid the food pouch in the depression and covered it, then rolled the log back into place.

That should keep it safe for the night.

Her mission completed, weariness once again took hold. She crawled into her makeshift shelter and curled up among the leaves. Waiting for blessed slumber to find her, cradled within the tree, a final worry pricked at her mind as her ankle throbbed.

What about tomorrow?

Fox Walker sat on the ground, leaning back against a tree trunk, and enjoyed the peacefulness of the night. Moonlight dripped over the landscape, pooling in the flat surfaces, creating deep shadows in the hollows. The crickets sang their evening melody, and a small spring gurgled nearby.

The debris hut he had constructed would offer warmth from the chilly night air, but for now the openness of the night sky beckoned him to remain here a while longer. He breathed in the damp air, relieved to once again be outdoors, basking in the sounds of nature, no longer stuck in the confines of the hospital. But what about Nataya? Hopefully her injury hadn't kept her from reaching the shelter of the trees before dark.

The decision not to follow her and offer assistance hadn't been an easy one. But ultimately this journey had to be *her* quest, and hers alone. Whether she succeeded or failed must rest entirely on her own shoulders. Grandfather had taught him this lesson many moons ago.

Besides, she still distrusted him and believed he betrayed her to the law officers who had captured her.

That would be *his* journey. To re-gain her trust.

CHAPTER SIXTEEN

Elk Meadow, Colorado

Jack Bailey hit 'send' on the email and leaned back in the hotel desk chair. He'd written the story Dan Stevens expected, nothing more. But he had no intention of leaving Elk Meadows just yet. Word in town was that the *wild woman* had escaped from the hospital yesterday, and the tracker who originally found her had taken off after her. From what he'd gathered from the deputies talking in the bar, the sheriff's department had written her off, once they realized she wasn't a fugitive hiding from the law.

But Jack believed a bigger story awaited him, maybe a feature article…hell, maybe even a book deal and talk show appearances. He couldn't stop looking at the photos of those scars on the woman's torso. What the hell had happened to her? And why couldn't she remember her past?

He flipped open his cell phone, brought up Dan's number and clicked on it.

"Hey Dan. Just heads up I've sent that story to you. You should have the email now."

"Great. We'll be able to slip it into this upcoming edition."

"Cool. And I attached some kick-ass photos."

"Good job, Kid. I'll be anxious to take a look."

"They're top notch. Sure to make this an exclusive for you."

"I got it, Jack—you expect a bonus. If it's up to par with your usual work, it won't be a problem."

Jack smiled. "Oh, and Dan. I've decided to use some of my vacation time, hang out here for a while."

"You're going to—what?"

"Hang out here. Kick back for a while. I haven't had any time off for a year. This small town atmosphere is just what I need." Jack held his breath at the silence on the other end of the conversation, waiting for Dan to speak again.

"I don't know what you're up to, but I better not be seeing an expanded version of this story somewhere else—with your byline on it."

A frown creased Jack's brow. He hadn't thought Dan that astute. And he'd always considered himself a great judge of character.

CHAPTER SEVENTEEN

Seattle, Washington

Dean McClure opened the door and shuffled into his dark office. From outside, the city lights slid between the narrow slats of the window blinds, showing silhouettes of the sparse furniture in the room. Dragging his heavy briefcase to the desktop, he let it fall with a thud and then stared at the clock. He barely remembered driving here with so many thoughts rumbling around in his brain.

He flipped on the light and tried to ignore the wall of photos that stared at him accusingly. His hand went to his temple, rubbing at the dull ache there, then combed through his hair as he tried to suppress the aggravation gnawing at the edge of his consciousness. Being duped by someone impersonating a cop—possibly the Art Critic—hadn't made his day either.

Maybe I really do need to retire. Maybe I'm losing my edge.

He'd had more than enough time to think about it on his drive back from Portland. Too much time, in fact.

He opened the briefcase and pulled out the package of photographs from the crime scene and the morgue. Dean slid the photos from the envelope onto his desk. He walked across the room to The Wall. Standing before it, he forced aside his private turmoil and faced the all-too-familiar photographs. One by one, he focused on each victim's picture, and whispered each woman's name...Pam...Linda...Cyndi...Kate.

Dean stepped back and viewed the entire collection. Although all the victims had been blondes, their appearances differed. They didn't even have the same type of facial structures. But what never changed was the killer's signature. The scene remained the same for each murder. The photos displayed it clearly, in dismal detail.

Turning back to the desk, Dean fanned out the photos from the crime scene, still fresh in his mind. He picked up the first photo of Lisa Webster and added it to the others, then compared the wounds to her torso with the older photos. These cuts were different, more distinct. Closer examination had showed the cuts to still be the same pattern. And it would make sense that if the killer carved the same pattern obsessively over and over, he would improve with time. But the lab believed the killer had also improved on the *tools of his trade*. Dean's training told him this pattern was important to the Art Critic for some reason—but why? So far, the FBI symbology experts had failed to come up with a link.

Yet the face and the rest of the body were never harmed. And even though the bodies were found in remote locations, they were all left in the open—meant to be discovered. They weren't just garbage, to be disposed of. Perhaps the killer held some degree of respect for each victim, for none had been sexually violated. Dean believed the killer *wanted* the bodies found. Or perhaps he left them for display. A part of his gallery of artwork. Too soon to tell, he had to keep his mind open to other possibilities at this time.

He picked up the rest of the photos of Lisa and, one by one, added them to the wall. A hiker had found her. The story around the Bureau being the young guy became so unnerved by his discovery he wouldn't leave the deceased woman's side, even at the morgue. Not until a relative arrived to claim the body.

Stepping back from the wall, Dean viewed the entire collage. He knew the killer's MO. *How* he did it. He knew in detail the killer's signature. But he didn't understand the *why* of the murders. And if he couldn't comprehend that, how the hell could he stop the son of a bitch before he killed again?

The phone rang, startling him with its unwanted intrusion. He let the noisy rings continue, pretending the racket didn't irritate him, until the answering machine kicked in.

"Hey, Dean, pick up. I know you're there. Where else would you be? I know about the murder in Portland. It's our guy, isn't it? He's back at it, isn't he? You have crime scene photos, and I bet you're back in Seattle adding them to your collection as I speak, am I right? Come *on* Dean…you *know* you want to talk to someone about this."

Dean shook his head and reached for the phone. Yes, he did need someone to talk to and this wasn't just anyone. Clay Evans had fast become an expert on the Art Critic. The reasons for Clay's involvement, as Dean well knew, were personal.

He had come to respect the younger man and his computer skills after Clay helped him solve an earlier crime, similar to this one.

Dean picked up. "Hi, Clay. I don't even want to *know* how you got this info so fast." He could admire the results Clay's expertise could produce, but he didn't have to agree to the methods used.

"Hell, what else does this computer hacker have to do with his day anyway?" Clay laughed, but it was a bitter sound, laced with sadness. "So, what have you got? You share, I share. You know the dance, man."

Dean smiled before getting down to business. With Clay living in San Diego, many of their conversations had to take place via the phone.

Clay spoke before Dean could form his thoughts. "So, our boy is active again. We have the same MO and signature as all the others, eh?"

"Yes, but something new came up on this one. He didn't use the same knife as before. These cuts were surgically clean and precise, probably made by a scalpel. He is blossoming into quite the artist himself."

"Is the cut pattern easier to see?"

"Yes."

"Okay. Listen, Dean. You've got to send me those photos pronto. I have a theory, and I need to see those markings."

"Sure. Are you going to share your theory with me?"

"I promise—later. Right now it's just a guess. I'll have a better idea if I'm on track once I've seen these latest markings."

"I'll email you the torso shots."

"Thanks, man. So, I'm going to guess the Art Critic didn't use the scalpel for the final death blow to the victim?"

"Correct, it was definitely a larger knife—but not the same blade size as before. Looks like he replaced the original blade with two new knives."

"So, with the time lapse and knives being different, could this be a copycat?"

"I considered the possibility. But it's him, Clay. I know it. And his signature included all the things that have never been released to the public. Like the rope being cut from the woman's wrists and the exact placement of her hands, clasped beneath her breasts. I believe the changes only reflect he has grown. He's getting better at what he does, perfecting his ritual." Dean waited in the silence that followed. He knew he should tell Clay about the police impostor, but found his ego still stinging. Decided to wait until he knew more.

"Okay, I can buy that. So, what about our victim?"

"That stayed consistent. Besides her job, Lisa Webster took art classes. The acquaintances we interviewed all said her work had good reviews. But she hadn't had any real success in her field yet."

"The same as all the others," Clay said.

"Yes."

"That and the fact they all ended up dead."

"You don't need to remind me, Clay."

"Sorry, man."

"I have one more piece of news for you."

"There's more?"

"Yeah, I saved the best for last, I guess."

"Well, give it over, man."

"We got a break on this one. A hiker—the guy who found the body—was wearing a headlamp in the dark, when he heard screaming and ran toward the noise. We believe he just missed seeing the killer. He called the authorities within seconds."

"That's it?"

"There's more. While waiting by the dead woman, his headlamp beam reflected off some moisture on her chest. By the time the CSI arrived, it had dried, but he decided it strange enough to mention. So the team scanned the body using the ALS and they found traces of a dried fluid, consistent with the chemical make-up of tears."

"*Tears?* So, the Art Critic may have actually wept over the victim's body?"

"I believe so."

"Crap. So he kills her, then weeps in remorse? I'll be damned. What a minute...DNA!"

"Yeah. Lots of DNA in tears."

CHAPTER EIGHTEEN

The Open Countryside, Colorado

Nature sure knows how to be dramatic, Walker mused as he walked through the meadow bordering the wilderness. This third morning of tracking Nataya gave promise to be a beautiful autumn day. Dazzling blue skies and golden aspens blazed against the dark forests of the mountains ahead.

Although he began tracking at first light each morning, he stopped every day well before dusk, to give her time to create some distance between them. He didn't want her catching sight of him.

They should've covered the distance through the farms and fields during the first full day, another day for the open meadows beyond, instead of three days. The re-injured ankle made her progress slower each day. But he admired her determination to continue her quest despite the pain she must be suffering.

Aside from her slow pace, he found sign she had been quite clever during her travels across the landscape, making use of natural and man-made shelters alike, building a fire when necessary.

She had made a few forays into home gardens, although at this time of year the only things left for her to find were some root vegetables, such as turnips and carrots. The empty eggshells he found at her campsites told him she had raided a hen's nest along the way. She had packed mud around the eggs and laid them in the hot coals to cook. When done, she then peeled away the mud and shells to the egg inside. And there were still a few dried berries clinging to the vines found along the fence rows. After soaking in water, they grew plump and easier to eat.

What puzzled him, though, was the way she passed by many of the more readily available plants containing edible roots and shoots. Her food choices often focused on the common text-book plants taught in basic survival classes, not the wild plants she would have learned about through experience in the wilderness.

He had followed her path and made use of many of the same good fortunes, for food was scarce this time of year in the open fields and meadows.

But now, as they both entered the wooded foothills, the variety of food available would increase, including fish from the streams and ponds.

He had to admit, this woman continued to confound him with her knowledge for survival. How had she come by her talents?

Yes, she intrigues me.

Fox Walker checked the position of the sun and the moisture content of Nataya's footprints. Even with her slow pace, she should reach the safety of her cave before nightfall. He decided to stop and make camp for the night, while there still remained a good distance between them.

While tracking he had, out of habit, begun to gather dry materials to use in building a fire. It wasn't a conscious thought, simply a normal routine. Milkweed pods, cattails and thistle made their way into his pockets. The down from the plants would make a light and airy tinder, essential for catching a spark. He also gathered tiny twigs and slivers of wood for kindling.

He picked out his camping spot and walked around the area, gathering larger pieces of wood and stacking them next to where he wanted the fire. Kneeling, he scraped out a fire pit, and pulled out the flint he always carried, along with his steel knife. The tinder bundle was put together and placed on a large piece of bark on the ground in front of him, the kindling close by. Using the steel knife to strike the flint at the correct angle sent sparks into the tinder. He picked up the bundle, gently blowing into it until flames erupted. Placing the tinder bundle in the fire pit, he fed tiny kindling to the flames.

As the fire grew, he added larger kindling, then the pieces of firewood. Within a few minutes he had a fire blazing. He wanted to have a good bed of hot coals before evening. Once the sun sank behind the mountains, the air temperature would plummet because of the higher altitude.

Walker tended the fire, his thoughts going to Nataya and her cave home. She had chosen the place with care and forethought. High enough to avoid any flood waters in the creek below. And the entrance faced the east, where it would catch the first warm, early morning rays of sunshine. The cliff that supported the cave also protected it from the cold west winds and driving rains or snows of winter. Wood for fire could easily be obtained.

And she has now proved twice that she can survive on her own.

Walker placed another piece of wood on the fire. He used the smaller knife from his ankle sheath and whittled at a long, narrow tree limb. Once the end was shaped into a sharp point, he hardened it in the flames. Smiling, he laid the spear aside and leaned back to enjoy the warmth of the fire.

Tomorrow, some early morning fishing.

A cool wind blew through the flames and sent a chill down Walker's neck. He needed no reminder that the bitter winter would soon be here. The air turned colder every night. He watched the sky regularly. Soon the snows would come. Even with the survival knowledge Nataya exhibited, he did not believe she could possibly be properly prepared for the winter. Did she know how to hunt large game and dry the meat for storage? Did she know how to use the hides and fur to make warm clothing?

Her life was at stake, and not worth the gamble.

That is why the spirits sent me to find her. To protect her.

Soon he would have to convince her to leave the forest.

I'll need time to accomplish that.

He cursed under his breath. With cold weather approaching, time was the one thing he had in short supply.

CHAPTER NINETEEN

Gray's Forest, Colorado

Nataya plodded through the forest, barely conscious of her surroundings. Constant pain from her ankle dulled her senses. The idea of being almost home ran through her mind like a chant, overriding the agony of each step. The pounding of her heart served as the drumbeat propelling her forward, putting one foot in front of the other.

She stumbled down the side of a rocky creek bed, the water level low, and cried out. Stopping to let the pain ease, she looked up and stared ahead. Slowly the trees and cliffs came into focus and she recognized the area.

So close now!

A reserve of energy welled up from deep within and she focused all her strength on continuing.

Just a little farther...

Dirt and pebbles slid from under her moccasins as Nataya made her way up the side of the cliff to her cave. Previously an easy climb, her struggles this time brought home the extent of her injury and how much it sapped her energy. Reaching the level platform where her cave entrance stood, she lowered herself to one of the logs placed next to the fire pit.

She glanced around as she caught her breath and regained some strength.

There—my knife, right where I left it.

She picked up the knife and ran her fingers along the carved handle. Her chest tightened and tears of gratitude threatened. She had escaped that dreadful world of noise, machines, and people.

Thank you mukua for my safe return.

Gaining back some stamina, she arranged firewood in the pit, then pushed herself up, waiting to regain her balance. She tenderly put weight on the injured ankle, only enough to limp over to the mouth of the cave. Fallen leaf debris had collected at the entrance and she noisily moved through it as she ducked her head to enter the cave. She didn't want to surprise any wildlife that might have decided her cave made a good shelter. Better they hear her coming. The ceiling opened up as she stepped into the main chamber, allowing her to stand upright. She let her eyes adjust to the low evening light making its way in from outside.

Relieved to find the cave free of intruders, she continued searching in the dim light until she found her fire stones. She held them to her chest, thankful to have them again, remembering how difficult her trek had been without them.

The first night she had had no strength to make a fire. But by the second night, she had eaten all the food she carried and emptied the last water bottle. She needed a fire to heat water for safe drinking, and the warmth as relief from the cold at night. But without her knife and fire-making stones, she had to improvise. Using what she could find, she struggled to produce a tiny hot ember from her makeshift hand drill. She nurtured it into a small blaze, adding twigs to build it into a fire. She could remember even now the thrill of creating that fire, and the immense pleasure she felt that night, sitting by its warmth.

She opened her hand and looked down at her firestones, the shiny gold-colored one and the grey jagged one.

Gifts from the earth.

They had never failed her when she needed fire. As she stared at the stones, names slid into her mind.

Flint. Pyrite—fool's gold.

Stunned, she sank down onto the cave floor, and closed her eyes, concentrating.

Where did that come from? Did the spirits decide to give me names for the stones?

New words had started coming to her after the first night in the medicine lodge, and her dream of the old man. Things she had never seen before suddenly seemed familiar, and she knew their names, understood their function, like the clothes Walker gave her. Then there were the little flashes of scenes in her mind. Places she had never seen before, people she didn't know.

Do the spirits warn me of future events?

She stood and gingerly walked back out to the fire pit, sitting down next to the wood she had arranged. By striking the two stones together, she threw a spark into some tinder, and soon had a fire.

How she had missed the smell of a live campfire while trapped in the medicine lodge. The warmth of it soon soothed her tired and sore muscles. For the first time since her escape, she could relax.

Looking up at the moon through the treetops, she remembered watching it through the medicine lodge window, and the hopeless, trapped feeling.

I'm free again.

But then, from deep within, a sense of melancholy floated to the surface. Why?

I have no one to share this moment with me.

The answer startled her. She examined the thought. And had to acknowledge a part of her had grown used to Walker's company.

Maybe this explained the unearthly sense which had filled her every night as she traveled. The sense Walker watched over her, nearby. She had looked for him, but never saw him. Never heard anyone following.

Maybe I secretly hoped he would follow me!

This new emotion confused her.

I don't like this feeling.

She wished to go back to the days before meeting Fox Walker. Life had been simpler then.

CHAPTER TWENTY

Gray's Forest, Colorado

The first rays of sun slid into the cave entrance as Nataya pulled her body from the sleeping alcove in the cave. She had been warm and comfortable for the night. But hunger gnawed at her stomach. She tentatively stood, testing how much weight she could bear on her ankle. Pain shot up her leg.

I was sure it would be better this morning.

Instead of the mild tenderness she expected, a steady ache now settled in. Disappointment settled over her.

She limped through the cave, stopping often to let the pain subside a bit. She made her way outside and knelt by the fire pit. Blowing gently on the few remaining hot coals brought the fire back to life. She added tinder and larger pieces of wood until the flames blazed steadily. A cup of hot pine needle tea would help.

But as she made the tea new worries flowed through her mind. Now that she had returned to her cave, how could she keep people from finding her? And Walker knew of her cave.

I can't let anyone take me away from here...ever again.

One idea came to mind. She could set up signal traps around the area. Instead of setting a trap meant to capture an animal, she could set up hidden lines that, when tripped, created a lot of noise, warning her something or someone came close to the cave. This would give her time to escape.

She looked down at her swollen and bruised ankle.

I can't even make the traps yet, let alone run away from danger.

Walker finished his meal of fresh cooked fish and spent the morning scouting out the cliffs farther upstream from Nataya, until he found a small cave that would give him adequate shelter. He didn't need anything long-term, but he might as well be comfortable.

Digging a fire pit and collecting a supply of firewood became top priority. Once he had a fire blazing, he set to work creating a sleeping area within the cave. He scooped out an area in the soft dirt floor of the cave. Tonight he would heat stones in the fire. When ready for sleep, he would place them in the depression, and cover it all with dirt. The ground under him would stay warm all night.

After his immediate tasks were completed, Walker used the time to fabricate a few items that would make his stay more comfortable. Using some larger pieces of wood and his knife, he shaped the outside of a bowl and cup. He then hollowed them out by placing hot coals in the depressions at the top, scraping out the charred wood, and repeating the process until he created the depth he desired. Now he could fill the cup with water and boil it for drinking by placing hot stones in. Tomorrow he would make a few cooking tools and fashion a birch bark basket to transport water to his camp.

It would be dusk soon, so he made his way downstream to check on Nataya. Tracks near her cave home had indicated she still struggled to walk. Her left ankle must be giving her quite a bit of pain. He wanted to make sure she could get to water and had plenty of firewood to keep warm.

Walker moved through the brush at the edge of the creek in his typical unhurried fashion, each step measured and placed so as to not make any noise that might alert Nataya to his presence. He found a spot where he could see the cave and settled in to watch.

She sat by the fire. He noticed she had braided her hair again, but indeed still wore the clothes he had brought her.

Good, she will be warm as the temperatures continue to drop.

He could just make out the stack of wood near the cave, enough for a few days, at least. He waited, hoping to see how well she could move around on the ankle.

When Nataya stood, she hesitated a moment, then made her way toward the cave entrance. The overstated limp showed Walker she suffered in great pain. But she could still move around well enough to take care of herself, and she had the warm clothing and a fire.

He didn't want to make an appearance yet. It would serve his purpose better to let her settle back into her own routine before he let her know of his presence. But he would watch closely to see if her ankle began to heal or got worse.

Nataya entered the cave, giving Walker a moment to leave the area unnoticed. He would return tomorrow, and the next day, waiting for the right moment to approach her.

He glanced up to the cloudy sky. He had no idea how he would know when that moment would arrive, or how. His gut tensed. It better be soon.

He heard Grandfather's voice. *Patience. Watch and listen.*

CHAPTER TWENTY-ONE

Elk Meadow, Colorado

Jack Bailey hunkered over his beer and listened to the conversations going on around him in the Buffalo Bill Saloon. He didn't want the deputies to notice him as they gathered after duty, joking and giving each other a hard time.

His brush with their boss, Deputy Chief Morgan, hadn't gone well. The man had made it clear he wanted no more publicity regarding the wild woman. He wanted the entire situation to disappear, and the sooner the better.

No help there.

Jack had no choice but to ask one of the deputies for help. He hoped that sitting here, listening in on their conversations might help him discover which one to approach with his request.

That's when a guy in a cowboy hat sat down on the empty stool next to him and ordered a beer. The bartender nodded in acknowledgement. They knew each other.

Jack did a quick glance, noticed a guy in his late twenties, scruffy beard, flannel shirt. The man didn't acknowledge Jack existed, so he went back to his drink. But soon the cowboy spoke, still staring straight ahead, as if talking to no one in particular.

"You that reporter asking about the wild woman?"

"Yes, I am."

"I can help you."

"How so?"

"I figure the woman is headed back to where she was living in the wilderness when they found her."

"I think you're right...Mister..."

"You don't need my name."

Jack struggled to keep a straight face. This felt like he'd been plopped down in the middle of one of those spaghetti westerns, and a bad one, at that. "You're right, I don't. Please continue."

"My family's ranch butts up to the forest, right where they captured that woman. I can take you to where I saw all the vehicles. You'll have to hike into the forest to find where she's living, but I figure it must be close to where they chased her out of there."

"I like your offer. What are you asking for in return?"

The man took a drink of his beer. "I figure you're gonna sell your story for some pretty big money. Seeings you need to find the girl, in order to write your story, I'm thinking I'd need a couple hundred dollars for that information."

Jack's heart raced. *A couple of hundred, is that all?* He kept a sober face. "That seems like a fair trade to me. When can you take me there?"

"I'd suggest you take tomorrow to get you some supplies for being out in the wilderness. Then the next morning, at daybreak, I'll meet you over behind the hardware store. You'll give me the money and you can follow me out of town and to the forest edge."

"You've got a deal."

CHAPTER TWENTY-TWO

Gray's Forest, Colorado

J ack watched the truck ahead of him pull off the dirt road
and into the grass, stopping next to the edge of the forest. He
pulled his rental car in directly beside the guy he had dubbed
Cowboy, and parked. True to his word, the mystery man had
met him behind the hardware store and once Jack paid him,
promised to lead him to Gray's Forest—to the spot where he
insisted all the deputies and rescue trucks had parked the day
they captured the wild woman. Jack got out and grabbed his
equipment from the trunk of the car. Cowboy stepped out of
his truck and sauntered over to where Jack pulled a backpack
from the vehicle.

"Think ya have enough equipment there?"

I know sarcasm when I hear it.

Jack decided to ignore the comment. He hoisted the cumbersome backpack up onto his shoulders and almost fell forward from
the weight. The cowboy chuckled.

Jack's face turned red, both from anger and the effort. "I don't know how long I'm going to be out here, that's all. Need to be prepared for everything, you know."

"Sure you do. I guess that *is* better than wandering off into the woods without any supplies, like most of the tourists do, I *will* give ya that."

But Jack had already dismissed Cowboy, and mentally checked off his list of supplies...tent, sleeping bag, water filter, propane burner for cooking, dried foods, cooking and eating utensils, pocket knife, matches, change of clothes, rain gear, first aid kit, note book, pens, and most important—his camera.

He made sure the rental was locked, looked to the cowboy. "We square?"

The cowboy nodded and turned back to his truck. Jack stepped into the trees.

The intense fragrance of damp earth and evergreens hit him first. That and the silence. But the longer he walked among the trees, the more he could tune in to the subdued sounds of buzzing insects, birds calling high in the trees and his hiking boots rustling the dried leaves covering the ground. His shoulders relaxed, his breathing evened out.

So this is what being outdoors is all about.

The land had been flat when he entered the forest, the trees getting thicker with more undergrowth. But now ahead of him it sloped steeply downward. He knew enough to recognize that water would run downhill, so he made his first decision. Find water.

He began to ease his way downhill by holding onto tree trunks and strong plants. The pack on his back might be heavy and difficult to maneuver in the trees, but it gave him a huge advantage over the wild woman and that tracker guy. He had everything he'd need to survive comfortably in the wild, while the woman had left the hospital with nothing. He figured she'd be eating roots and grubs by now, or some such nasty thing.

Jack did a fist pump in celebration when he came to the bottom of the ravine and found a creek, the waters deep and swift. He dipped his hand in, surprised at the icy coldness.

Oh, yeah—snowmelt from the mountains probably feeds the creek.

Now that he had a handy source for water, he could set up his base camp. He planned to go out each day searching for the woman, and return to his camp each night. The Cowboy had been sure she would be living in a location not far from here.

He couldn't help but get excited at the prospect of finding and watching her. He knew it would take time, but he could visualize himself gaining her trust, talking to her and getting her story, taking photos.

Right before leaving civilization for the woods, he'd picked up the latest edition of the *Front Range Chronicles* and found his story. First thing he'd noticed was that Dan hadn't been able to restrain himself from doctoring up the photos.

Dammit. They were good without being sensationalized.

Oh, the scars were still there, but they had embellished them, to make them more dramatic.

What a cheap shot.

The whole thing made him even more determined to write this story the way it should be done. He'd prove he could do better than all that crap. He could visualize the printed story in his mind—complete with his byline—and then came the book. He'd be famous.

All this work will pay off.

CHAPTER TWENTY-THREE

Gray's Forest, Colorado

Nataya sat by her campfire, brooding over her injured ankle. Yesterday, after many hours, she had managed to create a couple of signal traps close by. They were simple designs, hurriedly made, but the effort had cost her, with more swelling and pain today. Still, knowing they were out there gave her some comfort. She placed them so if anyone approached the cave, they would set one off. The noise would give her a warning. She rubbed her ankle. But how could she escape?

I can at least hide.

She looked up into a cloudless blue sky and bright sun. But, all around her the signs of winter had begun. The animals and insects knew it. The trees knew it. She had much to do to prepare for winter. But the more she attempted, the more pain and frustration she experienced. At this rate, how could she possibly be ready before the snows arrived? How could she hunt and prepare food to sustain her through the winter? Her stomach tightened in a spasm of fear.

Panic will not help. I must clear my mind.

She took a deep breath to calm her thoughts and stood up, unsteady for a moment, then regained her balance. One chore at a time. Today firewood must be gathered, and water hauled up to be boiled.

She began to ease her way down the incline from her cave, each step with her sore ankle bringing shooting pain. Frustration boiled as the minutes fell by at her slow progress. Halfway down the incline, her ankle gave way. She lost her balance, arms flailing, and managed to keep from pitching forward. But instead she fell backward, her body slamming into the slope.

Dirt and rocks cascaded down with her as she bumped and slid, her arms instinctually reaching for something to stop her descent, finding only air.

She landed at the bottom of the incline, gasping for breath as the dust settled around her. A moment of stunned confusion and bewilderment ran through her brain until she could pull out and recognize one sensation. The back of her head hurt. She reached up and touched it, but found no blood, only a large knot forming. One by one she gently moved her arms and legs. Everything worked. Relieved, she eased her body into a sitting position and finished letting her head clear.

Time to try and stand up.

But the attempt brought pain in her ankle so intense it took her breath, and she had to sit back down.

Stay calm. Try a different way.

Leaning on her elbows for support, she rolled to her side and used her strong leg to push herself up. But the minute she put the slightest weight on her injured ankle, the pain caused her to fall to the ground again.

She took deep breaths to stay calm.

Think.

But taking stock of her situation didn't help matters. It only made it clearer she was in serious trouble. Even if she might be able to crawl back to the safety of the cave, she couldn't walk. She couldn't do any of the tasks she needed to do, gather firewood, get water, prepare for winter. She couldn't even go find help. Maybe the pain would subside if she waited. Maybe it wouldn't.

She pounded her fists on the ground. Anger at her helplessness washed over her like the rains of a thunderstorm. She lay back on the ground, squeezing her eyes shut to keep from crying in frustration, but that only forced the tears to roll down her cheeks.

Please mukua. Help me.

The wind rustled the dry leaves about her as she choked back the sobs that threatened. A shadow fell over her and she looked up with a start.

Fox Walker!

He knelt beside her. She tried to roll away from him, but Walker grabbed her shoulders and pushed her back to the ground.

"*Stop.* You're going to make your injury worse."

She twisted in his grasp. "You followed me!"

"Yes, I followed you."

"You plan to use *isapaippeh natesu'un* again. To take me from my home." Her eyes flickered with anger.

"No coyote medicine."

She stopped struggling and stared. "Words. All words. I don't believe you."

"When you left the medicine lodge, I had no reason to stay there. I followed, only to make sure you made it home safe."

She turned her head away. But he continued to speak.

"And you did it, Nataya. You made it back to your cave home without anyone's help, even with your injury."

"Yes, I did. So why are you still here—watching?" She heard what sounded like a sigh of exasperation. Turned to look at him.

"I want to prove to you I did not betray you. That you can trust me."

She watched his eyes. They looked truthful, but perhaps he had powers she did not understand. He removed his hands from her.

"Please, let me at least look at your ankle. I know healing herbs. I can help you."

She thought of her fall. She had asked the *mukua* for help, only moments before Walker appeared.

Did the Spirits send Walker to help me?

Maybe he told the truth. Maybe not. Either way, she didn't have much choice. She gave him a short nod and let him assist her into a sitting position. He gently removed her moccasin boot, then rolled up the pant leg and examined her ankle, causing her to bite her lip in pain.

"Good. Nothing is broken."

He handed her the moccasin and rolled the pant leg down. "We need to get you by the warm fire."

Before she could respond he gathered her up and cradled her in his arms.

"Hold on."

Taken by surprise, she did as instructed, and encircled his neck with her arms as he carried her up the incline.

Walker set her down close to the warm fire, her back propped up against a log. "Let's see what I can do for your ankle."

"Why are you helping me?"

Walker didn't respond, and left her sitting in silence as he worked, pulling soft dirt up into a mound. He tenderly lifted her leg onto it, to elevate her ankle. He pulled a handkerchief from his pocket and made his way down to the creek to wet the cloth in the icy water. After he wrung out the excess water, he returned and wrapped the cold compress lightly around her ankle.

"You need to keep your leg elevated as much as you, for at least the next couple of days, to get this swelling down. I am going to go look for some Burdock leaves to make a poultice, which will help, and get us something to eat. Stay still and rest."

She watched him walk down the slope and out of sight, a jumble of emotions flowing over her. He had followed her. Had he also watched, waiting to appear when she needed help—hoping she would trust him?

Then she remembered her signal traps. How had he gotten past them without tripping at least one of them? Her gut tightened. She again wondered if he possessed special powers.

Maybe he plans to heal me and then trick me. Take me away from my home again.

Her hands curled into hard fists, her jaw muscles tightened. She couldn't let that happen. Not again.

But bit-by-bit, the reality of her situation flowed back in. She didn't have a choice right now. She needed his help to survive.

She let a sigh escape, then pulled a small log from the stack of wood Walker had placed beside her, laid it on the fire and waited. She had to take advantage of his help for now. But that didn't mean she trusted him.

⊨≼╫ ╫≽⊨

The noon sun shone warmly on Walker's shoulders when he climbed up the incline to the cave, both hands full. He carried a spear and cleaned fish in one hand, a straight, long tree limb in the other, and a bunch of leaves sticking out of his back pocket.

After laying the items aside, he removed the cloth from Nataya's ankle and examined it. "The swelling has gone down a bit. Bet you're tired of sitting?"

"Yes."

He smiled, then leaned over and gave her the limb he'd brought back with him. "You can use this when you need to get up and move around." He helped her to her feet and made sure the flat area fit under her armpit, so she could put most of her weight on the handmade crutch. "But only for a short time. You need to keep the ankle elevated as much as possible."

"I need to relieve myself."

"Go then, and when you return I'll put the cold cloth back on your ankle. You can rest some more while I cook the fish."

Turning back to the fire pit, Walker studied the spit she had rigged up. It reminded him of a drawing he'd seen in a survival book. For all of Nataya's competence in the forest, she still showed a lack of experience that puzzled him. He impaled the fish onto the green stick she kept for cooking. He held the fish over the flames for a few seconds to sear in the juices, then set the stick into the wooden holders Nataya had placed at each side of the pit. He scraped some of the hot coals from the main fire into the area under the spit, to slow cook the fish. When she returned, he helped her get settled again and reapplied the cold cloth to her ankle.

The fish sizzled and popped in the heat, making his mouth water. He wondered how long it had been since Nataya had a hot meal. She remained watchful and quiet as he worked. Only after long minutes did she finally speak.

"You *say* you followed me to make sure I stayed safe."

Walker nodded.

"But what of the others?"

"What do you mean?"

"They will come again, with the barking dogs."

"I spoke with their leader. They will not come here."

"How can I believe you?"

"I cannot make you believe me. I can only hope to gain your trust by telling you the truth."

Nataya grew quiet again, and Walker didn't intrude. While the fish cooked, he boiled the Burdock leaves in water, then made a paste with them. He applied the poultice to her ankle, and then wrapped the handkerchief around it. He glanced up to see Nataya watching him as he worked. He kept his demeanor calm, his hands gentle. She had begun to relax in his company.

Soon, the fish were ready to eat and no one talked while they picked every bone clean. Nataya made some pine needle tea and shared her cup with him. Walker lounged at the fire, enjoying the feeling of a full stomach.

"That sure beats the medicine lodge food," he said.

Nataya laughed, then just as quickly stopped, and looked away, as if to regain her composure.

Walker didn't miss the meaning behind her actions. Winning her trust would take time.

He took the moment of her inattentiveness to gaze about her camp, taking in all she had done to create a home here. He especially admired the way she had built the fire pit. Lined around the edge with rock, the large area held the fire for both heat and light. Hot coals were scraped into the smaller, narrower area, and used for cooking. Green branches could be placed over it, like a grill. Or a large, flat stone could sit on top, making a stovetop of sorts.

"You made a wise decision for your home, Nataya. And the fire pit is perfectly built."

She turned her attention back to him, staring a moment before answering. "Thank you. I need to make a rock wall here, behind the fire, to make more warmth go into the cave." She looked up at the sky. "I can feel winter coming."

"Yes, it will be here soon." Walker stood and stretched. "I need to head back to my camp before dark. Will you be all right for the night?"

"Yes."

"Good. Remember, don't walk on that ankle any more than necessary. I'll stop by tomorrow and see what you might need, so rest and keep it raised, like it is."

He sensed her watching him leave and walk out of sight. But it could be wishful thinking on his part.

Walker returned to his camp and set about starting a fire. As he worked, his thoughts drifted back to seeing Nataya fall. How difficult it had been to not rush to her side, until he saw that she couldn't stand or walk.

No surprise she didn't trust him. Even at the hospital he understood she only tolerated his presence because he took her outside, away from the people and noise. In a way he had helped her escape. A secret part of him had wanted it to happen.

And now he had caught her at a vulnerable moment and taken advantage of that fact. No doubt she would become more independent as she healed and her strength increased.

Finding the signal traps she had set let him know she meant to stay free and in the forest. She would make him work hard to gain her friendship.

And it would be imperative he succeed. Her life would depend upon it. He prayed to the spirits that the weather would give him the time he needed.

CHAPTER TWENTY-FOUR

Gray's Forest, Colorado

The sun burned through the morning mist and peeked into Jack Bailey's tent. He moaned and pulled the sleeping bag up over his head.

What a night.

He hadn't been able to sleep until a few hours ago—and that had been fitful. First it had been the mosquitoes. His idyllic notion of setting up his tent next to the creek had certainly been flawed. Little did he know dusk would bring in hordes of the irritating, buzzing, blood sucking insects, intent on making him their evening meal.

He had just settled in again after the attack when the noises started. At first he liked the calming cricket songs…nice…but soon after, the screeching began. Haunting, scary-ass screeching echoing through the trees had convinced him banshees did indeed exist and lived here in this forest. All the ghost stories he'd heard about this place from the locals started sounding pretty damn real.

The howling he did recognize, of course…just coyotes, singing at the moon…or could it be wolves? Did wolves attack people? Should he build up his fire to keep the animals away? But he found he couldn't make himself crawl out of the tent to add wood to the fire. Instead he huddled further into his sleeping bag, expecting any moment to have a wolf or bear claw his way in, clamp deadly teeth into his body, and drag him away in the night.

Dammit. Now the birds were singing so loud he couldn't get back to sleep, and he had to pee anyway. He sighed and crawled out of the tent. But as he stood up, he banged his head into a low hanging tree limb, lost his balance and fell—face first into the mud at the creek's edge.

Is this story worth this? Is anything worth this?

CHAPTER TWENTY-FIVE

Seattle, Washington

Dean McClure sat alone at his desk in near darkness, the patter of rain his only companion. Neon iridescence from the city lights splashed amid the pouring rain. The shimmering colors ran in rivulets down his office window.

But Dean saw no bright hues in his world at this moment. The Art Critic had been his companion for the last few hours.

He avoided the wall of photos. No need to see them to remember the details. He had spent much time there in his mind, imagining the sequence of events, watching the killer at his work, trying to understand the need that drove him to this. And the frightening part, knowing that at some point he *would* understand and feel it—that buried deep inside he carried the seed of understanding. He shook his head to dispel the darkness seeping over him, the sick feeling twisting his gut.

He looked up then to The Wall, gazing at the photos of each victim, whispering their names. On impulse, his hand reached for his cell phone. He brought up his daughter's number...stared at it for a long moment. What would Kim say? Or would she merely hang up on him?

Tonight is not a good time for rejection.

Turning up the light on his desk, he reached for his scribbled notes, his fingers tapping the desktop in a staccato of frustration. He'd lost count of how many times he had replayed the conversation with the impostor in his mind—trying to remember every nuance, any hidden meanings. He could see the man's face clearly.

Dean's fingers stopped tapping. The impostor chose an officer who matched his own description.

He stole the man's identity.

His heart rate quickened. He grabbed his cell phone and pulled up Clay Evan's number, his eyebrows arching in surprise when it rang through to the voicemail and he had to leave a message.

"Hey, Clay, got your message. I'm flying in tomorrow. Looking forward to seeing what you have to show me regarding those torso shots. And I've got a project for you. Meet me for lunch and a beer at McCulley's, twelve-thirty."

Seagulls circled overhead in the bright sunshine as Dean made his way along the boardwalk at Pacific Beach in San Diego. He found the street sign he wanted and strolled the two blocks to a dimly lit pub. Nodding to the bartender, he seated himself at the far corner table. He liked the quiet privacy of Clay Evans' preferred watering hole, a favored spot for the locals. No one came here "to be seen".

Dean looked forward to the times he and Clay could meet in person. Even though the phone calls were more practical, he found the times they talked one-on-one to be the most productive. They had discovered a unique bond during the past case they had worked and solved together. And once Dean had retired from the Bureau, Clay became an invaluable resource for much needed research materials. Dean had learned not to ask questions about Clay's methods. It was better he didn't know the details.

Clay rolled in then and neatly maneuvered his wheelchair to their table. "Hey Dean."

The bartender brought over the 'usual' Sam Adams for Clay, and looked at Dean expectantly.

Dean asked for a Guinness, then added, "Bring us a tray of those bar burgers and fries, will you? I'm sure Clay here is starved."

Clay grinned in acknowledgement.

Dean turned to Clay. "So, you say you've had a breakthrough on the markings?"

"Yeah." Clay pulled a folder from the side pocket on his wheelchair and laid it on the table. "You were right. These latest carvings were made in minute detail. So much cleaner than the crude cuts we've been seeing up until now. Made *me* happy. The Feebie experts weren't the only ones frustrated. Trying to compare those other cut lines to all sorts of symbols, and getting nowhere, was driving me crazy. But this time, instead of just cuts into the flesh, he carved out slices of skin, to create intricate and varying widths to the lines. The entire design reminded me of Japanese characters—*kanji*. A friend of mine is learning to write Japanese characters. He created an ink drawing to match the carved pattern, and had his professor look at it."

Clay looked up as the bartender sat the Guinness down in front of Dean, then pulled the ink drawing from the folder and placed it in front of Dean.

"The markings represent the character *Yugen*. I looked back at my copies of all the other photos. They're definitely meant to be the same symbol as this latest one. They're just not as recognizable."

"Yugen," Dean repeated. "So, we *were* right about the symbol theory. Damn good news. Now what the hell does it mean?"

"It's a rather ambiguous term. Seems like most Japanese characters are." Clay reached into the folder and pulled out another page, squared his shoulders and started reading in his best academic voice. "The symbol represents the subtle and profound—indicating a mystical state in which beauty is but a premise, rather than being stated directly." Clay laid the paper down and looked up at Dean. "I know...all pretty woo woo stuff. But get this, everything I read mentioned that the symbol is considered a major big deal when it comes to the appreciation of beauty and art in Japan."

The bartender set down a platter of bar burgers on the table, catching Clay's attention, while Dean absorbed the information in silence.

Clay took a bite of burger then spoke. "So, now that we know the carvings are definitely a symbol, maybe this means that being a blonde artist is enough to be chosen by the killer, and then he adds the symbol to complete the image he wants."

Dean picked up the ink drawing and studied it. "But what image is he trying to complete? Unless, this could be about a real woman in his life. Maybe the symbol is on the body of the woman...a tattoo...or a piece of jewelry she always wears. It must inexplicably be a part of the person for him to go to these lengths to duplicate it."

He laid the drawing down, quiet for the moment. "I'm not sure just being a blonde artist is the only key. I keep going back to the victims, all young, promising artists. All struck down before they found recognition. I have to believe this plays into the equation, and especially now, with this new clue."

Clay nodded for Dean to continue.

"Think about it, Clay. You and I have had our share of experience with organized killers. But this is the first one who makes his victims look like they are a part of an extremely ritualized sacrifice. He even makes the kill during a new moon."

"True."

"So, let's apply our new evidence to that theory. Let's say our guy fashions his victims to be like this woman. She would have been influential in his life in some way, and for some reason she failed to fulfill her ambition in the arts."

"Okay. But the woman failing to find success in the arts doesn't seem to be a plausible enough reason to cause him to kill, even this nut case."

Dean stared out the window, to the scene beyond...sea gulls weaving in and out through the air...the waves crashing to the beach.

Clay waited, quiet and watching, until Dean turned his attention back to their conversation and spoke.

"What if the victims are truly killed as sacrifices?

"What?"

"What's the first thing you think about when I mention sacrifices...why were they done in the past?"

"To appease the gods...to ask for good crops...to atone for past sins...take care of that surplus of virgins..."

"There," Dean said with a finger jab in the air.

"The virgins?"

"Funny, Clay. No—atone for past sins."

"Sure. But I don't understand how *that* ties into the killer choosing unknown artists for the sacrifices."

"Maybe this woman committed some type of sin, at least in the killer's eyes, and it had something to do with the arts."

"What? Like she mixed the wrong colors or something?" Clay said.

Dean gave him a grim smile. "Seriously, maybe the Art Critic found the subject matter offensive and he murdered her, to stop her before she could fulfill her artist ambitions. He would have believed that he righted a wrong by doing this. But for some reason he keeps repeating the process—to compensate for her sins."

"He creates the victims in her image and kills them as sacrifices, to appease the gods for her sins. Maybe you have something there. No wonder everyone hates an art critic."

Dean continued to gaze at nothing, missing the pun. He mumbled to himself, "It just doesn't feel quite right yet."

Clay left Dean to his thoughts, finished off the last burger before speaking again. "Didn't you say you have a special project for me?"

Dean came out of his reverie and sat up straighter. "Yeah. Right. I need you to set up a program for me."

"What kind of program?"

"I need something that will allow us to search for missing person reports following some specific criteria."

"Like what?"

"I want to be able to enter a location—which can be expanded from a city, to a county, or even statewide. Then add a date—which can also be spread out as a time frame—a window of days, weeks or months. I want a list of any men reported missing during those time frames and locations."

"You're thinking of searching the city and date for each of these murders, to see if there is a male reported missing during that time."

"You got it."

"But why?"

"That's another story. We'll need another couple of beers and I'll fill you in."

Clay took a long drink of beer as Dean finished giving him the blow-by-blow account of his meeting with Officer Grey—or at least the impostor—who could be their killer.

"So, Clay, I figure that if the Art Critic killed a police officer who matched his own looks, maybe it fits a pattern. One we didn't even know existed. Perhaps he kills a man for his identity and uses it for each of the murders. He chooses men who already roughly fit his description, which makes it easier to use the stolen ID's. He disposes of the bodies, hence the missing person reports. The men don't mean anything to him, like the women do. The men are just a means to an end."

"You could have something here, Dean."

"It's just a hunch. But we aren't getting any clues to his identity from the crime scenes, so I need to try *something*. Hopefully the Art Critic won't expect us to examine his trail from this angle."

"And he's left a morsel for us to find."

"Exactly."

CHAPTER TWENTY-SIX

Gray's Forest, Colorado

Fox Walker gathered up an armload of firewood and made his way to the edge of the incline to Nataya's cave home. Smoke from her campfire filtered through the tree branches. He drew in the scent with a deep breath, savoring the aroma.

She sat in her customary position next to the fire, her ankle elevated, as he had taught her to do. He knew she followed his directions dutifully, only because she wanted to heal as quickly as possible. She looked up as he stepped into view at the creek and began the climb up the incline, as he had done every day these last few days.

Each day, as he approached, he began to hope he would be greeted with a smile from her, a hint he made progress with gaining her trust. Today she watched him and did not look away as before. He felt sure she wanted to smile, but held it back. Maybe...

He laid the firewood on the pile by her cave without a word, then sat down by the fire across from her. A subtle ritual had emerged these last few days between them—he, engaging her in conversation—she, trying to avoid it. But he had discovered she couldn't resist talking about her cave home, plants and animals of the forest, so he capitalized on that, evoking her into lengthy discussions. He could feel a bond beginning, even as she fought against it.

"Today I watched the squirrel hard at work making his winter home. Layer upon layer he builds, always at a frantic pace. But, have you noticed how the squirrel makes fun during his work?"

She nodded.

Walker began to describe the squirrel's comical antics and positions, stopping to mimic some of them. Nataya looked up at him. There. Just a hint of a grin.

"Squirrel knows that his task becomes lighter when he has fun doing it. When you are better I will take you to see him, if you'd like."

She smiled then.

He grinned in return, happy with any progress he could make. A chilly breeze ruffled the flames of the fire, making his smile fade.

The snows might come early this year. From what he had observed these last few days, she had not had time to prepare for the coming winter. And the daylight hours grew shorter every day.

Can I win her confidence soon enough?

CHAPTER TWENTY-SEVEN

San Diego, California

Clay Evans pulled a cold bottle of soda from the fridge in his studio's kitchen and rolled over to his desk. This morning he had listened to Dean's advice, "to get out and experience life beyond your apartment" and took advantage of the sunny weather. Being confined to a wheelchair was still fairly new to Clay, and Dean seemed determined to not let him become a bitter hermit.

He had to admit the notion pulled at him constantly. How much easier it would be to feel sorry for himself, for the hand life had recently dealt him. Working with Dean to find this killer kept his mind busy...but only with the thought of revenge....

He took a drink of the soda, hoping the caffeine and sugar would keep him going for a few more hours. He was still jazzed his program worked. Using the locations of the murders as a starting point allowed him to compile a list of men who had been filed as Missing Persons in those areas during each three-month span between the Art Critic's murders. He had emailed the names off to Dean earlier in the day.

But now he worked on another puzzle the two men had not been able to unravel as yet. Why had there not been a murder in April, to fit the previous time frames? Every three months, on a new moon night. That had been the pattern. Why the gap in time? And what about the fact Officer Grey—or the Art Critic—was so curious about it.

Maybe Dean is right. Maybe there is another body out there and for some reason it hasn't been discovered yet.

He jumped a bit when his cell phone buzzed. Looked at the number. Dean.

"Hey, Dean."

"Hope you enjoyed some of that sun for me today."

"Yep. I did. Rain for you?"

"You got it. But, that's okay. Been on the phone most of the day trying to get some info from the Bureau. Found out they didn't get any hits on CODIS for the DNA sample collected at this last crime scene."

"Crap. That's a disappointment."

"Yeah, well at least we have it for future reference. I did have some luck with the MP list you supplied me, though. Found what I was hoping for."

"Yeah?"

"Once I eliminated the men who have since been accounted for, I found that during the time span and location of each murder, there is still a missing man. No bodies ever recovered. And get this. Each missing guy was in his late twenties, similar build and appearance. All were 'suits' and considered good-looking, single and 'loner' types."

"Same description as the impostor for the cop."

"Yep. I've just got to believe it's the Art Critic, and he's killing these guys to use their identities while he stalks his next woman victim."

Clay listened to the following moment of silence on Dean's end before he spoke. "And if the impostor *was* the Art Critic you know he looks too *normal* for anyone to pick-up that he's dangerous."

"Yeah. And he may be a loner like the missing guys, but I believe he feels comfortable in social settings."

"Even more dangerous," Clay added.

"Something else I noticed. We've found victims in California, Nevada, Oregon and Wyoming. If you look at that cluster on a map, Idaho and Colorado would fit into that region. I'd like you to run your program for the month of April and for those two states. See what you come up with."

"Sure thing, Dean."

"I'm thinking maybe we've missed something."

CHAPTER TWENTY-EIGHT

Seattle, Washington

Dean stared out the window of the coffee shop, not that he could see much of Seattle outside. The wind had decided to make the storm more interesting by driving the downpour of rain in sideways against the glass. The waves of water rolled over the window, distorting the scenery. It reminded him of the funny mirrors he saw at a carnival when he was a kid.

And like a kid, he found sitting in his office waiting to hear back from Clay unbearable. So he sat here with his coffee, the steam rising lazily, like thin threads of smoke from a chimney. At least there were no photos here, staring at him from the wall. He wrapped his hands around the thick ceramic mug as if the warmth of it could penetrate his entire body. When his cell phone rang, he grabbed it up.

"Clay. What did you find?"

"I found one guy who fits all the same criteria as the other missing guys on your list. A Mr. John Littleton, from Colorado. He did have a Missing Persons report filed, but unlike the other men on our list, they found his body."

"Really. Let me guess. He was murdered?"

"Yep. Discovered May of this year. His throat had been slit. He was wrapped in plastic and weighted, on the bottom of Eagle Lake. Might never have been found, except they periodically dredge the lake to rid it of algae."

"Shit. So, I'm sure you're thinking what I'm thinking. Maybe we missed something in Colorado. It's never made sense the Art Critic missed a ritual for the month of April."

"That's what I want to work on. I'll take a look around that time frame and location, see what I can dig up."

"Good job. I'll double check with the Bureau for any murders reported in April, in Colorado. Maybe something got reported, but no one picked up on the MO and signature...or passed it along to the FBI."

CHAPTER TWENTY-NINE

Gray's Forest, Colorado

Nataya walked the distance from the cave to the campfire and smiled. Rest and Walker's daily compresses of burdock leaves had relieved all the swelling and pain in her ankle. To make sure she stayed off her feet and kept the ankle elevated, every day he had brought up water and prepared food for her. Often while they sat by the fire, he taught her various bird calls, including his favorite, the horned owl.

She had to daily remind herself his kindness could still be a trick. But it became more difficult to do this with each day. Good thing she would soon no longer need his help.

Something off in the distance caused her to look up. She studied the surrounding trees, waiting for the noise from one of her signal traps. Yesterday, after Walker left her camp, she had set up a few more of her warning signals. Since the first day he appeared, she had hesitated to tell him of their existence. Yet he managed to approach her every day without setting any of them off. Now it had become a personal challenge. She spotted Walker stepping into the clearing by the creek, and looked down, gritting her teeth.

How does he know?

Adding another log to the fire, she waited for him to make his way up the incline. He appeared over the edge carrying a pair of quail.

"Thought you might like to have something to eat besides fish."

She couldn't stop her grin, her mouth already watering at the thought of the roasted birds.

"How is your ankle today?"

"Better. I can start taking care of myself."

"Good."

A part of her wished to say "Thank You" for his help, but she stopped the words. He might take advantage of any gratitude she showed, thinking he had gained her trust. Instead she changed the subject.

"I'll heat water."

She removed hot stones from the edge of the campfire, and added them to a depression filled with water that she had hollowed into a log. Soon the water steamed. After placing each bird in scalding water the two of them plucked the feathers, working silently side by side.

⟞⟝ ⟞⟝

Walker glanced sideways at Nataya. Although she preferred silence between them, each day he had managed to draw her into conversation by showing interest in her cave home and her belongings. Her face always lit up when she showed him her hand-crafted items.

When they finished plucking and gutting the birds, he ran them through with the cooking stick and held them in the flames to burn off any remaining pinfeathers, and then placed the stick on the spit for slow roasting. In the lull, he said, "While we're waiting for the birds to cook, would you show me your cave home?"

Nataya at first hesitated, but then nodded and retrieved her handmade torch. She had already known how to gather pitch globules seeping from the bark of evergreen trees and heat it until it became a liquid. But Walker had suggested she soak a cattail head in the highly flammable pitch. Picking up the cattail by the stalk, she now tipped it into the flames and watched it instantly ignite.

She turned, and motioned for Walker to follow her. He watched her walk without any hint of a limp. She spoke the truth. She could do her own chores now. But could she prepare in time for winter snows?

He followed Nataya into the cave, stooping to enter, but found once inside he could stand upright. He studied the interior while she crossed the entrance, bent over and lit a flame right in the rock wall. She had created a candle within a rock depression, using pitch and a heavy cordage plant material. It gave off enough light to see by, but didn't use up the precious oxygen. He noticed the ceiling sloped down from the entrance and back to a solid wall that absorbed heat and sunlight during the day, then released the warmth at night. The floor of the cave was dry and sandy.

"This is where I work when it is wet or cold," she said, indicating the larger entrance room. "You see how the heat from the fire outside warms the back wall?"

Walker nodded. "In the early morning, the sun probably warms it too?"

"Yes." Nataya had led him over to a rock ledge protruding from the rear cave wall. "Here are all of my cooking and eating tools."

Walker noticed she had used the same hot coal method he did for creating depressions into the wood for her bowls and cup. She also had many carved, wooden utensils.

"This is my birch bark water basket. These other ones were my first tries, but I can use them for carrying *dekape*. Here is my digging stick I use for roots and plants."

He studied the items, taking note of the fishing hooks and sewing needles made from fish bone, and examined each piece carefully while listening to her stories about how she had created each one. Her knowledge of wilderness survival went well beyond what the average person knew, yet her actual skill level was that of a beginner. As though she had only read about the techniques before now, and was learning from trial and error.

Her story intrigued him. She lived simply, but the more layers he unraveled, the more complex the woven fabric of her life became.

They passed through the main room and continued farther back into the cave. To the left, a small alcove in the rock wall made a perfect place to curl up and sleep, retaining body heat in the tiny space.

As the flame highlighted the walls of the cave, Walker could see drawings. Not ancient petroglyphs, but freshly drawn charcoal art.

"Did you make these, Nataya?"

"Yes."

"I like your drawings of the deer and the hawk. You have studied them closely. What is this one? The lone tree...with a circle of trees around it?"

Nataya frowned. "It is a dream I have sometimes. Maybe the spirits send it, but I don't know what it means."

"It reminds me of a place..." Walker said.

"You know of this place?"

Walker didn't miss the eagerness in her tone. "Perhaps. Maybe I could take you see it?"

She nodded.

Good. Maybe a clue to her past.

Nataya moved, and he spied commercially made strands of yarn, lying among various materials she probably used for weaving and sewing. "Where did you get *this*?"

"I will show you." Nataya walked over toward her sleeping area and picked up what had once been a knit sweater. The arms were missing where she had pulled threads free. With the armholes sewn closed it created a shawl for her shoulders. "I used threads from this, until I could gather plants to make what I needed."

"That's very clever." He also spied a worn pair of sandals by the sleeping area. "Are these yours? You were barefoot when I met you."

"Yes, I wore them sometimes. I liked to walk barefoot then. But with winter coming I knew I would need to keep my feet warm. Now, I have these beautiful *tsowoon nambe* to wear," she said, glancing down at her moccasins.

She looked back up at Walker, her upturned face softly illuminated by the torch's flickering light. For one brief moment he'd swear he saw a warmth in her eyes he had not seen before. His breath caught, and an intense surge of passion ran through him. *What the—*

He tore his gaze from her. He had already noticed how much more beautiful she looked every day, being here, free in nature. To distract his mind, he concentrated on the items lying around them.

He spotted the odd knife she had worn the day he met her. He picked it up, and studied it closely. Intricate carvings of dragons and swirls covered the handle. "Where did you get this?"

Nataya took the knife reverently in her hands. "The *biawihi* is a gift from the spirits. When I awoke it lay next to me."

Walker studied the knife she held. What if he and Doc were correct—that she had been abducted and tortured? He could be looking at the very knife used to cut her. Strange the sight of it

140

didn't frighten her, but then, she didn't remember anything of her past.

"I also found this after I awoke," Nataya said. She held up a piece of glass. "I used it to make *kuna* until I found the firestones. Then I could make *kuna* without the sun."

Walker tried not to show his excitement as he looked at this latest item. She held a lens from a pair of eyeglasses. Had she been wearing glasses when abducted? He hadn't thought of that. But it would do no good to ask her. "Did you happen to find another piece of glass like that one?"

She shook her head. "This is the only one. I found it near me, with the *biawihi* and the rope. They were all gifts from the spirits." She motioned overhead to caches of food hanging to dry. "I use the rope to store my foods from the animals."

Walker thought the rope might have been used to bind her. But if so, how did she escape? He glanced around at the other personal items. A cotton-patterned material had been torn into strips and used to tie items together. Maybe it had been her blouse, torn by the attacker.

He felt his heartbeat speed up. Perhaps he could pull together a description of her from these items. She could have been wearing a print blouse, khaki-colored long pants, sandals and a knit sweater when she was abducted. And possibly she wore glasses. Perhaps there was a Missing Persons report out there somewhere, matching that description. It could be a starting point.

He glanced up to see her watching him. "You have done well with your forest home," he told her.

"Thank you." She sniffed the air. "It is hard, the waiting."

He looked at her, questioning her meaning.

"Waiting for the *dekape* to be done."

He laughed. "Yes, the food will be ready soon."

They savored the tender meat of the roasted birds and licked their fingers, not wanting to miss a single bit of flavor. In the relaxed quiet of enjoying their food, Walker thought about the cold days and colder nights that would soon descend upon this land. Here in the foothills the lower altitude would mean the weather would be less frigid, but it would still turn bitter cold at night. And even though the valley floor resided on the wind-protected side of the mountain, it could still receive great depths of snow.

Nataya's cave home didn't go deep enough into the earth to stay at the steady temperature of fifty degrees, as larger caves did.

He knew his ancestors had weathered the winters here for centuries. But they had worked together as a community, not as a single person trying to survive. And even if he stayed here to assist her, they should have started preparing months ago. To guarantee her safety, he still believed he would need to convince her to leave this place before the winter storms set in.

Thinking of his ancestors brought back memories of all the places he had come to know here in *muka sogope*. He thought of Nataya's drawing. He finished his last bite of food and broke the silence. "The place in your drawing. I could take you to see it. Do you feel up to walking tomorrow?"

"Yes. *Mia'yu* would feel good after all these days of sitting."

"Good. In the morning we will go."

He looked forward to visiting the Sacred Circle. It had been far too many years since he'd been there.

But what meaning will it hold for Nataya?

CHAPTER THIRTY

Gray's Forest, Colorado

It was just as Walker remembered it. He had taken them along the outer edge of the forest, knowing they would come upon the seldom used, crumbling asphalt road as it dead-ended into the forest. Taking his bearing from here, he knew exactly how to reach his destination.

The daylight was deceptive, for at night there were no streetlights, or light from nearby farms to break up the darkness. And during the right time of the month there would be only the stars for light. Walker knew all this, for he had been here at night many times before and had experienced the total blackness.

He turned to speak to Nataya. She stood transfixed, staring up at the two imposing evergreens guarding either side of the asphalt road.

"What is it, Nataya?"

"Those trees. I know them." She looked down and pointed to the road. "But, this…makes me scared. I don't understand."

"You will feel better when we get into the forest, among the trees. Here, follow me."

He led the way through the tall grasses, brown and full of seed heads, then into the tangle of tree branches and brush. They pushed through the underbrush until they reached the larger trees, dominating the sunshine and leaving little but cool shade under them.

Nataya followed Walker in silence. This place held special meaning to him. His expression when he talked about it told her this. And she wanted to show respect, but as they went deeper into the woods, a sense of dread came over her she could not explain. Everything felt...wilder. The trees were much denser here than where she lived, and the vast canopy of branches blocked the sunlight. A thick mat of needles and leaves choked out all but a few shade-loving plants. They could walk easily through the trees, but a dark and somber mood fell over her. A desire to turn around and run away settled over her.

Do the spirits warn me of danger ahead? Does Walker plan to hurt me?

She shook her head to dispel the thought. Even though she still believed he might trick her and make her leave again, he had healed her and helped her. Why would he harm her? But the longer they walked, the more difficult she found it to follow. Just when she thought she could bear no more, they came upon dense undergrowth where the light began to reach the forest floor once again. She followed close behind Walker as he pushed his way through the shrubs and weeds, to abruptly come upon a large opening, right in the middle of the forest. Before them spread an open meadow filled with sunlight.

All around the edge of the open area stood a ring of towering trees. Their boughs intertwined, creating a cathedral-like ceiling to walk beneath, until one reached the open grasses in the center of the circle, where a lone tree stood.

Nataya stared over Walker's shoulders at the remarkable sight. It matched her dream and the loveliness of it brought tears to her eyes. And yet, when Walker stepped out into the clearing, she stood looking on, confused. Again she tried to follow, but her body would not obey. A dark veil of fear slid over her. It dulled the vibrant colors before her, dulled her senses. She opened her mouth to call out to Walker, but her voice failed. She sank to her knees there at the forest edge, unable to go any farther.

She closed her eyes to the view in front of her, but it did not leave, instead became stronger in her mind. The vision grew sharper, more intense, and with it came physical pain. She moaned. This meadow...the lone tree...flames. A face!

No! Don't look at the face!

An agony gripped her and would not stop. Flickers of images rolled and flashed through her mind, then only darkness for a while...

She looked down then and saw the blood, her own blood! Near her, a fire lit up the night. The warmth of it beckoned to her. Why did it take so much effort to move? Teeth chattering and body trembling, she used the last ounces of her strength to crawl closer to the fire...then all went black.

Walker stepped out from the dark forest, into the sunlit area. The beauty and serenity took his breath, as it always did each time he visited this sacred spot. Deep in concentration, he soaked in the energies surrounding him. Passing under the canopy of tree boughs, he strode to the center of the open area and stood motionless. He glanced back to see Nataya sitting at the edge of the forest.

Each person reacts in their own way to this sacred place.

But as he stood within the circle of trees, he sensed a disturbance of some sort. Scanning the area, first the tree trunks and then the ground, he noticed it.

Fire had scorched the earth near the lone tree. He walked over to examine it closer. The blackened circular shape suggested it had been a large campfire, months old now. The tree next to it looked damaged in some way. Thinking it may have been scorched in the blaze, he bent over to take a closer look. But instead of fire damage, it appeared something had been tied around the trunk, cutting into the bark in places. The scars in the bark were not fresh, but had also weathered through time.

Walker stared at the scorched ground and then the tree. Instincts warned him. A travesty had taken place upon this sacred ground. He knelt at the tree to closer examine the scarred bark. A rope could make these marks if it had been tugged and pulled down the tree. But there were marks only on one side of the trunk. Something must have been wedged between the rope and the tree on the opposite side.

Walker remembered the rope in Nataya's cave. The same rope she had found along with the knife and eyeglass lens. These marks would make sense if someone were tied to the tree, and had then worked the rope down the trunk by twisting and tugging at it.

A burst of revelation fell upon his mind so rapidly that dizziness overwhelmed him. He closed his eyes. In the darkness a vision came to him…of a woman tied to the lone tree. Flames lit the night.

Nataya!

He opened his eyes to bright sunlight, his pulse pounding. He squinted and held his hand over his brow to shade his eyes. Did she still sit by the edge of the forest?

He could just make out her figure. She sat on the ground, her face in her hands. Forcing himself to stay calm and not break into a run, he strode toward her. As he approached he heard her sobbing.

She didn't react when he sat down beside her, so he tentatively laid his hand on her shoulder. She did not pull away as he expected, but instead leaned into him, still crying.

He encircled her with his arms and held her until her sobs slowly turned to sniffles, and then occasional choked breaths. When she straightened and looked up at him, a deep sadness filled her eyes.

"What is it? Can you tell me?" he asked.

She nodded. "I didn't think this place was real."

"What do you mean? Do you remember being here before?"

"I've always believed it a dream and nothing more, until... I saw it here for real. I couldn't follow you. And as I sat here, I began to remember being here. It's all very hazy."

Walker struggled to keep his expression neutral, for her entire speech pattern had changed. She spoke in complete proper English, and no longer slipped in the occasional Shoshone words to fill the gaps. Something had happened to her. "Please, Nataya, try to remember everything you can. It is very important."

He felt her body shudder before she spoke.

"I still don't understand why I would've been out there, cut and bleeding. It was as if I had been through an... initiation of some kind. A test of my courage. And I survived."

Walker realized she had no idea how much her language had changed, her words and expression. He held his breath to see what she would do next.

"Everything beyond that is blurred," she said. "I remember walking through the forest. It may have been only a few days. It may have been many days. It's so jumbled, but eventually I found the cliffs. All through this time the spirits of the forest gave me guidance. They showed me how to treat my wounds, and find food. I began to gain strength. After a while, I didn't believe the place in my dreams could be real. Until now."

Walker knew Nataya might be confused about her fear of the area, but he now understood it all too well. His vision matched the evidence. She had been brought here and tortured by someone. Why she had been left alive, he couldn't guess. But most importantly, she had begun to remember her past.

"Are you okay to wait here a few more moments, Nataya?"

"Yes. I'm fine now."

"It's important I take another look around." He gestured toward the lone tree.

"Of course. I'll wait here."

Walker began a thorough search of the area, at times crawling through the tall grasses and weeds. Any footprints would have been washed away months ago in the rains. But he knew to look for more than just prints.

He searched in an ever-expanding circle around the tree until he at last found his reward in a large clump of grass. Eyeglass frames. They were bent and twisted, which explained how the lens had been forced out. One lens was still in the frames. Walker smiled. He could have the prescription of the lens checked against the one in Nataya's cave.

The rest of the scene came together for him then. The knife she found must have been close to her. Perhaps on the ground, and she had used her foot to pull it towards her while still tied to the tree. Then she could have worked the rope down, a little at a time, until she could twist around the trunk and reach the knife. She must have cut herself free. But where did her attacker go? And why would he leave behind the knife?

CHAPTER THIRTY-ONE

Gray's Forest, Colorado

Jack Bailey stumbled his way along the creek. This morning he'd swear he smelled smoke from a campfire as he hiked. He had tried going downstream the previous day and had found nothing, so today he headed upstream. The smoke had to be a good omen. But his legs were getting tired now. He stopped to rest and look around.

Up ahead were some cliffs and what looked to be a small cave entrance high up on an incline. He hadn't thought about the possibility of caves in this area. What a perfect spot for someone living in the wilderness. He hurried forward.

At this point, the lower water level of the creek allowed him to easily scramble across to the other side of the bank, where he could see the cave entrance up above him. He took another step forward, felt a slight resistance against his pant leg, then jumped back in shock as a rush of leaves and tree limbs flew up into the air. A thin sapling now stood tall next to him, leaves and limbs vibrating with the force of motion he had set into play. A booby trap!

Lucky for him it had malfunctioned. Maybe the wild woman had set it. He hadn't expected that.

Jack stood still, barely breathing, and watched for any movement within his sight, especially up by the cave. Nothing. The birds slowly returned to singing.

Excellent! Maybe she had left her camp for a while and he could go check it out without her knowledge. He brought up his camera and took some photos before heading up closer.

CHAPTER THIRTY-TWO

Gray's Forest, Colorado

Walker glanced sideways at Nataya as they made their way back to her cave. She spoke little on the return trek, and as they got closer to familiar territory she occasionally reverted back to her former speech pattern. But clearly a change had taken place. He wondered if her encounter with the past might trigger more memories.

Might she have another upsetting vision?

Once they returned, he would find an excuse to stay with her at the cave for a while, to make sure she was going to be okay.

When, at last, they stepped from the woods into view of the cave, he noticed one of her booby traps had been sprung. No reaction from Nataya. She had never admitted their existence to him, so maybe she didn't want to say anything. Or could it be her mind wandered elsewhere?

Of course, the trap could have been triggered by an animal, but it put him on alert. As they began their climb up the incline, Walker spotted another disturbance. Footprints.

Dammit!

The prints indicated someone had entered and left Nataya's camp while they were gone. He didn't want to alarm Nataya. She sat down and began to get a fire ready, so he walked over to get firewood and scrutinized the ground for more footprints. There were dozens of them. Approximately size 11 hiking boots, shallow impressions—most likely a medium sized man. Whoever made them hadn't even bothered to try and hide the fact he had been there. Walker's skin prickled at the thought. He glanced over to make sure Nataya stayed busy with the fire. No reason to take chances. He brushed away the prints with his moccasin and then did a quick glance into the cave, to make sure their intruder had left. He couldn't imagine Morgan changing his mind and returning.

Think about this. What can I do?

Well, one thing for sure, he didn't want Nataya staying here alone at night. He'd have to secretly take up a watch of the place once she thought he'd left the area. He didn't look forward to the long night ahead.

He turned to see her huddled near the fire.

"Are you cold?"

She nodded.

He wondered if she shivered from the temperature, or memories. "I have a way to make your cave warmer for the night." He placed some rocks near the fire and once they were hot, he motioned for her to follow him into the cave.

With Nataya watching curiously, he dug out a small pit in the loose dirt of the floor. Then he stacked the hot stones in the depression.

"These will give off heat into the cave and help keep you warm."

She held her hands over the stones. "They give off so much heat."

Walker grinned and turned to leave. But she grabbed hold of his arm and he stopped, turning to look at her. Her eyes were wide in the dark of the cave.

"Don't go. You could stay here tonight?"

Walker hesitated, but only because she had taken him by surprise. She didn't plead or beg, but her eyes belied an undercurrent of panic. "Sure," he said as nonchalantly as he could. But his mind raced madly inside. This worked out perfectly. Now he could watch over her tonight, and make sure the stranger didn't return. Relief flooded in. Then he realized the other meaning it held. Maybe she finally trusted him. But, realistically, it could be a temporary situation. She must be terribly confused right now.

Walker put one last batch of green, slow burning wood on the fire, and banked it up for the night. Then as they entered the cave, he pulled one of the thatched mats across the entrance. It would block the drafty night air, at least at ground level. He waited awkwardly by the entrance as Nataya headed toward the sleeping area.

She turned and motioned him over.

"Come. There's room for two here and it will help us stay warm tonight."

Relieved that she seemed to have no problem with him being so close to her, he just as quickly realized it might not be so simple for *him* to be physically close to *her*.

Nataya crawled into the small space first, making room for Walker to slide in next to her. He maneuvered his body in, wedging his back against the wall of the sleeping chamber and lying on his left side to fit.

He had to admit she was right. Adding the blanket made of grasses and moss over their winter clothing, their combined body heat would soon create enough warmth to ward off the coldest night air. Nataya snuggled in, her back to him, and soon fell into a deep sleep.

Walker pushed his body back against the wall as far as he could, but the tight quarters still meant the full length of Nataya's body lay firmly pressed against the front of his. Her head lay against his chest as she slept and she hadn't minded that his right arm lay across her waist. He tried not to dwell on the fact that her body lay against his, but it was no use. He couldn't deny the physical attraction.

A memory floated up to him, of another he had held so long ago. Black-eyed, bewitching Haiwi—lost to him now. Forever. An ache of loneliness began to grow in his chest.

He watched Nataya as she breathed softly in slumber, her hair falling in waves across his arm and her face. His hand involuntarily reached up to brush aside her hair, but he jerked it back.

Don't go there! It only brings pain.

Besides, he'd only just gained Nataya's trust. He couldn't ruin everything now. He tried to relax and fall into sleep, but knew it would be a long night.

CHAPTER THIRTY-THREE

Gray's Forest, Colorado

E vening had settled in as Jack followed the creek back to his camp, dusk turning to dark. The night sounds of the woods replaced the bird song. Every shadow held the possibility of an animal lurking in the trees. Heart pounding in his ears, he fought the urge to take off running.

When at last his tent came into view, he did sprint for it, and dove inside. He pulled out his penlight and dug his notebook out of his pocket. Stretching out atop his sleeping bag, he began to scribble notes as fast as he could, a satisfied grin spreading across his face.

He had started to believe the Cowboy from town had fed him a line of crap, but then he found the cave. He had climbed up the steep embankment to the level top of the cliff where he found a ringed fire pit with log seats on either side, and a stack of firewood nearby. From what he'd heard, no one else lived here in this forest, so it had to be the wild woman's camp. And how lucky to find it when she wasn't around. Things were looking up.

He had snapped a flurry of photos and was headed for the cave entrance when he heard sounds of people talking coming through the nearby trees. He scrambled down the incline and barely managed to hide before Walker and the woman appeared. He hadn't had a chance to hide his footprints. But from where he watched, hidden in the brush at the creek, it hadn't look like either of them even noticed anyone had been there.

So much for Walker being some famous tracker guy.

But hiding in the brush and waiting for a chance to make his get-away had proved to be torturously boring. And every ant in the forest had discovered where he sat. So, the moment the wild woman and Walker entered the cave, he took off.

Jack finished up his notes, writing in big letters—*Must see inside the cave!*

No doubt about it. He *had* to go back.

CHAPTER THIRTY-FOUR

San Diego, California

The thin curtains only defused the bright California sunshine flowing into the room. Clay Evans didn't mind the added warmth on this cooler than normal autumn day, he just couldn't tolerate the glare on his computer screen.

Papers lay scattered across his desktop. Newspaper clippings tacked up on the walls served as the only decoration in the room. A bookcase held nothing considered as pleasure reading, not with titles related to serial killers, criminal profiling, and forensics. Clay had once quipped to Dean McClure if anyone ever broke into his apartment, they would believe they had stumbled upon a murderer's lair.

But for the moment, his focus remained on the monitor. The satisfaction of discovering the John Littleton murder story in Colorado had been short-lived. If the Art Critic indeed killed John Littleton in Colorado, and stole the man's identity, it meant there had to be a corresponding dead woman somewhere. A woman who could no longer speak for herself. A victim who needed someone else to take up the cause. It fueled his obsession to track down this killer. That and the photo of Stacy, gazing at him, as she would do forever.

All else forgotten, he had spent all morning searching online. Knowing the Bureau, or Dean, would have spotted a big, splashy front-page headline, he roamed through obscure stories and back-page articles.

At first he searched for any murders taking place four to six months earlier, in the same location where the body of John Littleton had been discovered. Then he expanded the search into surrounding counties. But Littleton's murder proved to be the only unsolved murder during that time frame. No female victims.

Clay did a head smack and cursed. Of course! If no one found a body, no murder would have been reported. But what if a woman was still missing? He ran his program again, this time searching for missing women. One report caught his eye. A young woman had gone missing last spring in April.

The right time of year.

He read further and noted that the woman's occupation was listed as a writer and illustrator.

Artist.

He pulled out his recently purchased map of Colorado and marked the spot where she'd gone missing. Big Pine, the same place Littleton had lived. The clincher though, was the thousands of acres of wilderness surrounding the small town.

Three items that fit the Art Critic's signature.

He picked up the phone.

CHAPTER THIRTY-FIVE

Big Pine, Colorado

Detective Thomas barely acknowledged the buzz of his phone intercom. He gave full attention to the report on his desk. He had grown used to the constant noise assaulting him from the surrounding desks, squeezed together on the central floor of the sheriff's department in Big Pine, Colorado. Others joked about his neatly stacked and organized desktop, but he secretly knew his obsession with uncluttered space was simply because it was the one place where he felt he had some control over his world.

"Detective, I've got a call here for you. It's a man inquiring about one of the Missing Persons you're handling. Shall I put him through?"

"Sure." The detective reached for the phone, one eye still on his report. "Detective Thomas."

"Detective, my name is Dean McClure. I'm working as a consultant for the FBI. Just wanted to let you know I have you set up on a conference call with my associate Clay Evans. We need some more information regarding one of your Missing Persons."

Now the caller had his full attention. The detective pushed the paperwork aside. "I'll need to have some credentials, as proof of what you say. You understand?"

"Of course. Mr. Jim Reeves is my contact at the Bureau. You can call the listed number for the Bureau and ask for him. He'll verify I'm legit. I'll hold, if you don't mind. Jim is expecting your call."

Detective Thomas dialed out on another line, half expecting to find out it was a prank call. But not only did he get through, by the time he finished the conversation he was duly impressed with this Dean McClure's credentials. He picked up Dean's line again—this time fully alert. "How can I help you Mr. McClure?"

"Jenny Long. Reported missing last spring from Big Pine, your jurisdiction."

"Yes, I remember. What does this relate to?"

"The FBI has been hunting a serial killer for two years. This particular UNSUB has a distinct MO and signature, leading me to believe he may have murdered someone in your area, but the body hasn't been discovered yet. The report mentions Jenny as an artist."

"I guess you could say that. When I did my interview with the person who reported Jenny missing, she mentioned that the young woman wrote scientific papers and did illustrations for nature-type books."

"Did this job bring her in contact with the general public?"

"No, not really. She worked from home. But she did visit elementary schools, and gave talks about nature and the Ind—Native Americans of Colorado. Outside of school, she took groups of kids on field trips to the woods and parks. I remember the teachers told us she was popular with the students and parents. In fact, we couldn't get one lead on anyone who would want to harm her. And she didn't appear to be the kind of person who would just up and leave, and not let anyone know."

"Who reported her missing?"

"Mrs. Becker, a family friend. Jenny stayed in a small cottage on her property. She told me Jenny took a walk every evening. One day she left for her walk, and never came back. Mrs. Becker told us that when Jenny's folks were killed in an airplane accident, she and her grandfather became close. But he had just recently passed away. There was no one to contact. When we investigated, the cottage showed no sign of a break-in, or struggle. All Jenny's belongings were there, as far as we could tell. It's as if she walked out and just vanished."

Clay spoke up then. "I noticed there are thousands of acres of wilderness close by. I presume searches were done?"

"Yes, for months after she disappeared, especially the places where we knew she liked to take the kids on field trips. But a body was never found. You have to understand though, these forests are immense, we could've easily missed her, or not looked in the right location."

"Any Jane Does found in the last six months who couldn't be traced?" Dean asked.

"Not dead ones—if that's what you mean."

"You've found a live one?"

"Yeah, couple weeks ago. A tracker discovered a woman living in the forest, the next county over. I called about her because the physical description was close, even though the woman didn't go by the name, Jenny, and I had no reason to believe that my MP would be living in the forest alone. But by the time I found out about her and contacted the sheriff for an interview, they informed me she had escaped the hospital where they had been treating her for an injury.

"Escaped?"

"They said she ran off for the woods again. Same tracker guy followed her to make sure she stayed safe. The two of them haven't returned yet."

"Didn't the sheriff go after her?"

"No need. She hadn't done anything wrong. It's not like she's an escaped convict or something, or a fugitive of the law. Besides, he seemed pretty sure the tracker would eventually bring her back."

"Why would he believe that?"

"The winter."

"What do you mean?"

"Winter will be here soon. It'd be certain death to leave her out there."

CHAPTER THIRTY-SIX

Gray's Forest, Colorado

Walker lay awake in the early dawn hours, enjoying the quiet of the morning, the warmth of Nataya's body next to his. He breathed in the scent of evergreens, mingled with grasses and leaves. He could hear the water of the creek below as it bubbled over the rocks and pebbles. It played the background music for the first tentative chirps of waking birds. Soon the chorus of morning songs would begin.

Staying with Nataya in the cave these last few nights, he learned to sleep facing the wall in the small alcove, letting her curl up to his back. It proved a far less torturous position for him, and made it easier to deal with the nightly battle of his physical attraction to her. If he wanted to gain her trust, he couldn't act on that instinct just yet. Common sense said it would destroy the fragile bond that had begun to form between them, a relaxed, comfortable companionship of sorts. Beyond that, he tried to avoid examining his feelings any closer. And he had no idea what Nataya's take on the situation might be.

She stirred and mumbled in her sleep next to him. Dreams, not all pleasant, had plagued her since their trip to the Sacred Circle. He believed they were memories trying to surface. And if he was correct in his theory, they would be unpleasant ones. No wonder her mind pushed them back from consciousness. Although her speech pattern had changed that day, she still slipped in and out of her old way of talking, as if trying to decide which personality best fit. He had to wonder at times which woman would greet him in the morning.

She mumbled again in her sleep. He lay still, listening. She moaned and then cried out.

He turned and leaned over her, calling her name to rouse her from the dream. She blinked away the sleepiness as he studied her eyes. "Did you have a nightmare again?"

She nodded. "The fire. Huge flames against darkness, and I couldn't move—couldn't get away."

"Anything else?"

"No."

"No face staring at you?"

"Not this time."

He reached out to smooth her hair back away from her face, caught his action and stopped, letting his hand fall to his side. "I'll get the fire going, so we can have tea."

Walker led the way through the last wisps of early morning fog, already beginning to dissolve in the sunlight, as he and Nataya left the campsite and headed downstream. A pair of crows cawed their boisterous greeting to the new day.

Nataya looked upward, spotted the ebony feathers glistening in the sun. "Good morning, *haih*," she shouted.

Ahead of her, Walker smiled to himself as he led the way. For the moment she was the Nataya he knew. The woman he met that first day, full of innocence and natural curiosity. Being among the trees usually brought out her former mode of speech, English mingled with Shoshone.

It had taken time and patience to gain this level of trust with her. And who knew whether it was really trust or if she instinctively knew she should accept his help, for now?

I was led here to find her and protect her.

He knew this. The spirits had shown him. But he hadn't anticipated experiencing this level of emotional connection on his part. Hadn't he vowed never to let himself become involved like this again?

Be honest. You desire her too.

Damn—of course he did. He was human, after all.

But each day, since their trip to the Sacred Circle, he had watched her change as these nightmares and memories assaulted her. He had no idea who would ultimately emerge from the ordeal.

He shook his head in frustration, then stepped off the trail and stopped.

"This is a good place to put the snare," he said, testing the springiness of a young sapling. He squatted, not letting his knees touch the ground. Nataya crouched down beside him to watch him set the trap. He found the closeness of her body distracting. To keep his mind focused, he explained the process as he worked.

"We must work quickly. It's important not to leave our scent on the surrounding ground. We will put the trap here because this is a run many smaller animals use to reach the water. Since the area is covered in tall grasses, we can easily hide the snare. The animals follow the path as routine and will not sense any danger. The snare we are making is for medium-sized animals, such as squirrel or cottontail."

From his pocket, Walker took a wooden peg he had carved the night before. He pushed the sharpened end into the dirt next to the run. He stood then and pulled the sapling down to the peg. "Hold this right here, while I tie the cord to the sapling."

Nataya watched as he fashioned a noose from the cord. Earlier, he had shown her how to unwrap a section of her heavy rope to make a thin, but strong cordage to use for the snare.

With Nataya holding the sapling to the peg, which remained firmly in the earth, he positioned the loop of the snare on the path, and pulled up the grasses to conceal his work. Then he delicately placed the end of the sapling to rest against the peg. Any animal heading down the run would have its head in the noose before it realized it. The movement would force the sapling to slip from the peg and spring into the air, snaring the animal. Walker explained the importance of good craftsmanship. The animal should not be made to suffer because of a poorly made trap.

He kept his attention on the snare, but moved his hand to lightly rest on her shoulder and spoke. "This type of snare has a touchy trigger, good for the quickest animals. We'll have to stand up carefully—slowly, or even our movement might set it off."

He watched her mimic his movements and back away from the area.

"Rabbit or squirrel *would* taste good," Nataya said as they turned to head back to the cave.

"Yes."

"And we could use the fur to make warm linings for our moccasins."

Walker glanced over at her. Her comment proved she still believed she could stay here for the winter. But Walker's woodland experience gave him the knowledge they did not have time to properly prepare. He knew how to survive, if forced to stay here. But it wasn't a risk he wanted to take. Not when they had other options. But how would he convince Nataya she should leave with him?

I'd better have some damn good valid reasons to give her.

Walker still brooded on how to bring up the subject of leaving the forest as they climbed up the incline to the cave. He stopped at the fire pit, knelt to blow the coals back to life and spotted a boot imprint in the dirt. Before he could speak, he heard Nataya gasp. He leapt to his feet in time to see a young man walking out of the cave, a camera hanging from a strap around his neck, his full attention on something he held—Nataya's knife.

⇒+ +⇐

Nataya raised her hand, pointed toward the man and shouted "You!"

One moment Walker stood beside her, the next he had the man pinned against the outside wall of the cave, his knife drawn and at the man's throat. It reminded her of watching a rattlesnake erupt from its coiled form and strike its victim. The man stared at Walker, his eyes wide, his hand dropping Nataya's knife to the ground.

"Stop! Don't hurt me."

Walker's knife pressed deeper into the man's neck. To Nataya, the growl that came from Walker's throat sounded more animal than human.

⇒+ +⇐

Walker felt a hand squeeze his shoulder…then a voice calling him. A soothing, calm voice…Haiwai's voice.

No she's gone. Nataya's voice.

The white rage in his head began to fade. Grandfather's voice had come to him this same way, the night he found Haiwi murdered.

The night I almost beat a man to death.

He squeezed his eyes shut at the memory.

Why did Grandfather stop me? The man deserved to die.

Bit by bit, the pleading words from the man in his grip soaked into Walker's brain.

"My name's Jack. I'm a reporter. I'm not going to hurt anyone."

Walker let go of the man, but kept his knife ready.

"I only want to write a story about your woman friend here—that's all. No harm done, really."

Nataya spoke at Walker's side. "You came to my room at the medicine lodge and pretended to be a shaman. "

The man looked to Walker for a translation.

"You're the reporter who sneaked into her room at the hospital, and took photos of her."

The man merely nodded.

"What the hell are you doing here? Wasn't *that* enough for you? Now you have to invade her private life too?"

"Look. I'm not doing anything wrong here. I'm on public property, just the same as you."

Walker leaned in closer. "Well, actually that's not true. This is private land, and I could contact the law to haul your ass off, for trespassing."

"You do, and I'll make sure you and your friend here get the same treatment."

The man squared his shoulders, stood up straighter, as if to add bravado to his words. But Walker saw that the man's hands trembled.

Walker's jaw flexed. "Believe what you want, but I *will* make your life hell if you ever come near here again. You understand?"

The man nodded and edged his way around Walker, then scrambled down the incline, trying to maintain some dignity along the way.

Walker watched the man go out of sight, then dropped down next to the fire and put his head in his hands. He had only reacted that violently one time in his life—the night he had discovered

Haiwi on the floor of her bedroom, raped and beaten beyond recognition.

I'm too emotionally connected with Nataya. Not good.

He heard Grandfather's slow, patient voice.

Time to let go of the fear.

But he didn't understand what it meant.

Nataya sat down beside him. Without a word, she wrapped her arm around him and leaned her head on his shoulder.

They sat that way until the sun dropped behind the mountain peaks and dusk settled in.

Thunder rolled over and over through the mountains and the first drops of rain splattered in the dirt around them. Walker stirred. He stood and reached for Nataya's hand. She didn't resist.

"We need to talk," he said.

She gave him a questioning look, but followed as he lead her into the cave entrance, and sat down just inside the opening, looking out to the forest. She joined him in silence, the rain now becoming a steady patter on the leaves and ground outside.

"We need to talk about the coming winter. Before long the cold will kill the few plants that still survive, and the snow will cover everything. The streams will freeze over."

"Yes, but I have dried plants for the cold months. And we can chop holes in the ice to fish."

"That is true. But we don't have enough to survive the winter, Nataya. To be prepared properly we should have hunted large game months ago—smoking and drying much meat."

"We still have time to hunt, and we have our snare. We can make more traps."

Walker shook his head. "It's too late. Soon the snows will be here." He picked up a pebble and tossed it out of the cave. "And now we have this reporter guy hanging around, spying on us. I know the type. He won't go away on his own."

"We can find a new cave home. Hide from him."

"He would still look for us. Besides...I think I have a better idea."

She looked up at him, waiting.

"I have a place where we could shelter from the winter. It's a home made from logs." He watched confusion cross Nataya's face. "It's a simple structure, like your cave, except made from logs— trees. It would protect us from the weather." Brows furrowed, Nataya's jaw clenched. Walker continued before she could reject his offer. "The cabin sits beside a lake, surrounded by woods. You could be outside as often as you want. Please consider it."

Nataya didn't want to leave her forest home. It frightened her to think of going away to a strange place. But an anxiety about her meager preparations had filled her mind every day since her return. And instincts warned her Walker spoke the truth about how dangerous it would be to stay the winter without the proper supplies.

When she first awoke from the Dream Time, she had relied on the spirits to guide her. Had they really sent Walker to help her, as she had first believed? She remembered the way he had reacted toward the reporter.

He did *just attack a man to keep me safe.*

She looked at him for a long moment. "Perhaps the *mukua* wish for me to go with you, so I can be safe for the winter."

"I believe this to be true. I have been sure, since the first day I saw you, that I was sent to help you."

Nataya gazed out to the trees and sky beyond the cave. If only the spirits would speak to her.

Maybe they do. Maybe Walker being here is their answer.

He had helped her and treated her with kindness. And he had protected her from the intruder today. Her distrust of him had faded, but she still watched him for any sign of betrayal. "If I agree, do we have to leave right now?"

"We can stay a little longer, to prepare for a hike out of the forest. But we *must* leave the moment I say. We will have days of walking ahead of us to reach my truck. It is parked not far from the medicine lodge."

"*Natesu'ungahni?*" Her gut tightened.

"Don't worry, we're not returning to the medicine lodge. But we are too far from my cabin to walk the entire distance. We'll need my truck, so I can drive us to our destination."

"Oh."

"So you will come with me to the cabin?"

"Yes."

⊷╬ ╬⊶

Walker held in a sigh of relief, and instead only gave Nataya a nod of agreement.

As much as I dislike that reporter, his appearance helped my cause.

He watched the rain pelting down outside the cave. The first snows would soon move in. He must keep a close watch on the sky while they prepared to leave the protection of the forest. They had miles of meadows and pastures to cross, to get back to his truck. Getting caught in a snowstorm on the open plains could prove deadly.

CHAPTER THIRTY-SEVEN

Gray's Forest, Colorado

J ack Bailey crouched by his campfire, puffing on the tiny flames and adding twigs. His hands shook, and not from the cold. Jesus! What the hell had he run into back there at the woman's camp? What he wouldn't give for a cigarette right now. And he wasn't proud of how frightened he'd been.

How can I become a great journalist if I get scared like a little kid?

He sat down next to the fire, letting the warmth of it relax his muscles. He pulled his notebook from his pocket and began to scribble down what he'd seen in the wild woman's cave. Wilderness survival had taken on a whole new meaning for him. This woman didn't have any of the modern pieces of equipment he believed were vital to stay alive out here. Yet from what he saw, she had created everything she needed. Her story took on new meaning. Curiosity took over. He wanted to learn more about her.

He had managed to take some photos in the cave, but even with a flash he wasn't sure how the photos would turn out. So he started sketching what he could remember of the knife he saw, the strange shape for the blade, the intriguing designs on the handle. He couldn't wait to get back to his laptop and do some research.

Thinking about holding the knife brought back the vivid image of the tracker guy attacking him. He was sure he was dead-meat from the look in the guy's eyes. Thank god the wild woman had intervened.

Maybe she likes me. She did save me.

That gave him some hope. But, in the meantime he'd better do his observing from a distance. At least he could get some photos while staying hidden, until he could figure out a new angle.

I've just got to be smarter.

CHAPTER THIRTY-EIGHT

San Diego, California

F acing the sun hanging on the ocean's horizon, surfers sat waiting on their boards for the familiar ritual. All along the boardwalk people stopped to watch, as the bright orb sank below the surface.

Clay Evans, once an avid surfer himself, sat at his desk, cup of coffee at hand, oblivious to the scene outside his window. The sun cast a red glow across the walls of the apartment as it descended. He reached up to flip on his desk lamp as the evening shadows invaded his room.

Hours had slid by as he searched online for stories or articles based on missing person reports, abductions and kidnappings. After wading through enough *alien abduction* stories to gag, he'd about called it quits, when a headline caught his attention.

A tabloid had run a story about a *wild woman* being found in a wilderness area in Colorado. It reminded him of the Jane Doe story Detective Thomas had told him about. The detective believed she might be his missing person, Jenny Long. This sounded like the right location, and there were photos of the woman. Maybe he could send the story to the detective. It might help his case. Then Clay looked at the photos closer.

"No way," He said, as he examined one photo in particular.

He leaned back in his chair. "I'll be damned..."

CHAPTER THIRTY-NINE

Seattle, Washington

Dean McClure ran his hand through his hair in frustration, leaned his elbows on the desktop and rested his face in his hands. His trip to Santa Monica, California had been a bad dream, one he couldn't awake from. Another young woman had lost her life because he hadn't been able to stop this bastard. The scenes were all too familiar now—although this time the Art Critic had truly gotten creative. The victim had been discovered in a warehouse full of giant wooden easels, meant to display large works of art—not a human body.

I can't take this personally.

He massaged his forehead, rubbing at the pain. The phone rang. He welcomed the interruption, picked up the receiver.

"Hey Dean, found an interesting story. Granted, it's from one of those tabloid papers, so most of it is exaggerated." Clay filled Dean in on the story, then added, "Thought you might want to send the story on to Detective Thomas. Then I noticed the scars."

"Scars?"

"Yep. There's a photo of the woman's torso, riddled with scars. They photo-shopped the hell out of the picture—trying to dramatize it. But I can tell which lines were faked in. Dean, they're the same as the scars on our victims! It's our killer."

"You're sure?"

"*If* this photo is genuine. We'll have to validate it. But it could be our missing piece. Maybe the Art Critic *did* abduct a woman in April and mark her. But she's still alive. For some reason he didn't finish the ritual."

"But it's been months. He believes she's dead. That's why he confronted me."

"Yeah, unless he reads this same article I just found."

"Shit! You're right. And he'd immediately know if this is his work. But why did he leave her alive to identity him?"

"Maybe he didn't mean to."

"Right. We've got to find her first, and make sure the scars are for real. She could be our only living witness."

"Well, that might be a problem, Dean. Her being a witness, I mean."

"Why?"

"According to the story, when they found this woman she had no memory of her past. She doesn't remember any kind of an abduction."

"No!"

"Yeah, a bummer, isn't it? But we both know that won't stop the Art Critic."

"Damn! Guess we better get some plane tickets for Denver."

"Well, that's the other rub, Dean."

"Now what?"

"Near as I can tell, all this took place in a remote little spot on the *west* side of the Rockies. We'd waste too much time trying to drive there from the Denver airport. We'll need to fly from Denver into Gunnison, in the mountains, rent a vehicle and drive to this little town."

"In the mountains…where it snows this time of year." Dean groaned.

"Yeah. And we need to do it pronto. I checked the weather on-line for that region. A large storm is moving down from the north."

"Great."

"Hey, I figure if a tabloid newspaper reporter could find this place, we should be able to."

"We have no choice, Clay. We have to find this woman before the Art Critic does."

CHAPTER FORTY

Gunnison, Colorado

Dean opened his eyes and sat up in bed, trying to remember where the hell he was. He looked across the room to see Clay, already up and in his wheelchair. Then he recalled the plane trip. His flight yesterday, from Seattle to Denver, had been a rough one coming in over the mountains. But then, what did he expect? He hated flying. Clay had flown in from San Diego and met him in the Denver airport, looking fresh, which irked him even more.

Their flight to Gunnison had been delayed due to mechanical problems, making him more nervous than usual. Luckily, they were able to catch the last flight out. But the entire trip had been a nightmare, as the plane pitched and bucked through the sky all the way to Gunnison. And to make matters worse, Clay had slept like a baby through the whole thing. By the time they made it to this hotel Dean had been so tired he barely remembered dragging himself to the room.

And now there sat Clay, already up and dressed. He sat at a large picture window, the long drapes pulled back only enough to peek outside. He must have heard Dean moving around and turned his wheelchair to face him. "Morning. You're going to love this."

"What?"

Clay pulled back the curtains to reveal nothing but white outside. "Looks like it's been snowing all night."

"Shit!" Dean's heart sank. They'd planned to drive out today. What a crock.

"Yeah, I checked the weather report online and it doesn't look good. Guess that storm made it in earlier than they thought it would."

Dean moaned and ran his hands through his hair, but left the bed to splash cold water on his face. Fully awake now, he slipped on his jeans and pulled a sweater over his head. "I'll go downstairs and get us some coffee and food. Maybe I can talk to some of the locals and see what they think the roads will be like out there."

"Sounds like a plan. I need to check my e-mails anyway."

Dean returned with two coffees and some breakfast sandwiches. He joined Clay at the desk, sat down and took a sip of the hot brew. He leaned back in the chair. "Well, the good news is that it's only been snowing about five hours, believe it or not. But it's expected to go on for a couple of days."

"Geez."

"Yeah. When I explained our situation, the locals urged us to head out, *now*. They said the storm is slow moving and we are still at the beginning edge of the weather front. We might be able to drive out of it. That would give us a chance to outrun the storm and get to Elk Meadow before it hits there. If we stay here, even a couple more hours, we might not be able to leave—maybe for days."

"Good thing you rented a four-wheel drive vehicle."

"Yeah. We're going to need it. Can you be ready to leave soon?"

"I'm ready. Checked my e-mails while you were out. Heard back from Detective Thomas. He said to thank you for sending him that story, and letting him know how to contact us for the next few days. He says that even though the woman called Nataya looks different in the photos, he's pretty sure it's his missing person, Jenny Long. He called the sheriff and found out the woman and the tracker are still out in the forest. I figure that's good news for now."

"Yeah. If our killer saw the story he could be heading back that way...or may already be there. As long as she stays in the forest he shouldn't be able to find her. She'll be safe until we can get there. But we need to show up before the tracker brings her back to town. Let's get packed up and head out. Elk Meadow would've been a long day's drive to begin with. Now it's going to be slow going for a while, and I'm damn sure not looking forward to driving in the snow."

"Don't you get snow up there in Seattle, Dean?"

"Sure. But nothing like this. And I still don't like it."

"I have a thermos. We can get some more coffee for the road. I looked over the maps to get us to Elk Meadow. Don't see any highways to take. There are a couple of main roads, but most of them look to be mountain roads."

"Yeah, I know. Winding, steep...and narrow."

"Don't sound so excited." Clay's lightness made him smile a little.

⚒ ⚒

The bellboy assisted Clay into the car and helped Dean lift the wheelchair into the trunk. What little luggage they had brought sat in the back seat. Dean eased the vehicle through the snow, creeping out of the parking area following the tracks of a car ahead of them. The driving snow made visibility difficult, but they had little choice. Locals told him that if they drove steadily, they should be able to get out of the worst of the snow by mid-day, maybe.

The GPS in the rental could give them directions, but Dean insisted Clay fiddle with the radio and try to find a station where they could keep track of weather and road conditions. But every time he found one, they lost it a few minutes later because of the surrounding mountains. Still, it gave them a sense of security—a beacon to civilization. Clay opened a map and studied, to get an overall sense of what lay ahead.

Four miles out of town they passed a car in a ditch, a tow truck trying to assist. Soon they would be on the winding, narrow roads high in the mountains. Dean knew the sheer drop-offs that came with those roads. He didn't want to think about what lay ahead.

CHAPTER FORTY-ONE

Gray's Forest, Colorado

N ataya awoke from yet another disturbing nightmare. Always the flames around her, unable to escape. Sometimes a face stared at her through the flames, making her wake from the nightmare. She reached out for Walker, found him missing. Wondering why he hadn't awakened her, she crawled from the alcove to look for him. The fire blazed with fresh wood, but she didn't see him anywhere close by. She gazed out over the creek and nearby trees, then looked up and spotted him.

Walker stood at the top of the cliff that supported the cave, as he had done the past two days. The short climb to the top rewarded one with an unobstructed view of the surrounding horizon. When she questioned him about it, he said he watched the sky for snow.

She studied him for a moment, his back to her, motionless. Then she gave him her best imitation of an owl hooting. He turned, smiled at her, and made his way down to the camp. Sitting by the fire, he rubbed his hands near the warmth of the flames. She sat down next to him, saw the seriousness of his expression. "What do you see today?"

"I see signs of a great storm coming. We must leave now."

"Right now?"

"Yes, it will be here soon." He must have seen the disappointment in her eyes, for he went on to say, "We have just enough time to walk back to my truck. This is going to be a bad one. We don't want to be stranded in it."

"Do I have time to make us some hot tea before we leave?"

"Let me make the tea while you get your things together."

Nataya nodded and rose to gather her belongings. She had already made up her mind which items she would take with her. It had been a difficult choice, almost everything she owned had been made by her own hands. Some pieces had required hours of hard work, while others were trial and error attempts, until she mastered them. When she had sorted through all the items, she realized she would be leaving behind little pieces of herself. And knowing she could return in the spring didn't make it any easier right now.

But in the end she had gathered only the bare necessities. She and Walker must be able to travel quickly. She slid her knife into the loop on her belt, added the firestones to her pocket, then gathered the food she had prepared and returned to the fire. Walker handed her a wooden cup of the hot tea.

She took a sip. "Thank you. I've brought us some hazelnuts, dried berries, and pine nuts." She patted her bulging coat pockets.

"Good. I've also brought smoked fish and some of the dried rabbit jerky we made together. We won't have time to forage for food, but this should be plenty to sustain us for the walk back." He finished his tea and stood, slipping the wood cup in a coat pocket. "Bring your cup with you for water. We leave now, and travel until the dark stops us."

Nataya nodded and stood to leave, but hesitated, looking back at her cave. The only home she remembered. She sensed Walker joining her. He put his arm around her shoulders.

"We'll return, I promise. Come...we must hurry."

She turned to follow him, not trying to hide the tears in her eyes. Making her way down from the cave, she followed the creek, keeping pace with Walker.

Sadness at leaving her home mingled with fear. She now traveled to someplace she had never been before. And she had to trust another person's word it would be safe. The confidence she had known in her own familiar surroundings receded with each step she took farther from her home.

She knew she must be brave now, trusting the spirits would protect her, because she followed their wishes. She took a deep breath, taking in the woodsy smell of fallen leaves and damp earth. Looking up at the trees and their strength and endurance, gave her the courage she needed.

Nataya followed Walker all day, first through the forest, then making it free of the trees by late afternoon. The remainder of the day took them into the level plains and meadows. The long shadows of evening stopped their progress. Walker built a fire and they ate some of their food, before darkness could overtake them.

"We made great progress today, Nataya. Better than I anticipated. And your ankle is doing okay?"

She nodded.

"I'm confident now we will make it back to the truck by evening tomorrow."

She could tell by his relaxed mood he was pleased. He laughed easily, the stress gone from his features. He encouraged her to practice bird calls, and they discussed the trek tomorrow would bring.

A breeze ruffled Walker's hair, giving her an idea. She offered to weave his long hair into traditional braids, and could tell the suggestion pleased him. She settled next to him and began her work. In the quiet that followed, she ventured a question. "Will you tell me about your shelter made of trees?"

Walker smiled. "I think you'll like it. It's small and will keep us warm. But the landscape around the cabin is the best part. It sits beside a lake, and you'll be able to walk down to the water and watch the ducks and geese. Many birds migrate through the area and there are always lots of waterfowl to watch. And of course, all around the cabin are woods. You can be outside as often as you like."

"It sounds beautiful."

"To me it is. I'm anxious for you to see it. But now we'd better get some rest. We'll need to start out again as soon as it is light enough to see our way."

Walker added some greener wood to the fire, so it would burn slowly through the night. Then he laid a few logs within easy reach, to add in the early morning hours, when it would burn down to glowing coals. The two of them built a simple shelter using debris from the ground: tree limbs and branches, grasses and dry leaves.

But as she prepared to join him inside the warm shelter, she took one last glance at the forest behind them...so far away now. An emptiness settled around her heart. Hopefully the long day of walking and fresh air would help her sleep without the haunting dreams of flames and pain. And let her forget her fear for a few hours of rest.

CHAPTER FORTY-TWO

San Juan Mountain Range: Rocky Mountains, Colorado

"Whoa..." Clay said, as he peered out his side window to the void below.

Dean gripped the steering wheel tighter and clenched his teeth. "That's at least the hundredth time you've said that. You can stop anytime now." With the tires just inches from a sheer drop-off on Clay's side of the vehicle, he maneuvered around the curve.

Clay laughed out loud. "Man, I'm sure as hell glad I *can't* see to the bottom of this ravine."

Dean grimaced. "Doesn't anything frighten you, Clay?"

"Oh yeah—like what if we crashed, and I became paralyzed?"

Dean surprised himself with a laugh. Clay had a way of forcing him to lighten up, even when he didn't want to. Or maybe he was hysterical with fear.

They rounded a bend, to the other side of the mountain. The fury of the storm diminished, and the constant howl of the wind died down. As they drove downward out of the steep mountain pass, the visibility improved.

"I think we're out of the worst of it, Dean."

"Yeah, looks like it," Dean said, relaxing his grip on the steering wheel. He took a breath and exhaled, to force the tension from his body. Now that he didn't need to focus every fiber of his being on driving the treacherous road, the exhaustion eased from his body. He glanced at Clay studying the GPS, and comparing it to the topo map in his lap.

Clay pointed to the GPS. "Looks like the roads ahead are straighter. We have a pretty direct route into town from here."

"Yeah, but we lost a ton of time back there. We wouldn't make it into Elk Meadows until late. I'm going to drive like hell and get us as far away from this weather front as I can. We can stop in Ouray for some food, and grab a few hours of sleep, then hit Elk Meadow tomorrow, during the daytime."

Two hours later, Clay spotted an all night diner up ahead, and they pulled in for a break. Clay wheeled off toward the restroom and Dean pulled out his cell phone, relieved to see he had a good signal. He finished his conversation as Clay returned.

They settled at a table and Dean filled him in. "I thought I'd better try to contact Sheriff Kimball over at Elk Meadow. Let him know why we are coming into town. We could use his help on this."

"Good idea."

"He asked that I call Chief Deputy Morgan. Seems he's the guy who headed up the search and brought the woman back from the woods."

"Did you speak to him?"

"Yes, Morgan wants to talk to us when we get there. He suggested we meet him and his deputies at the City Courthouse."

"What about Detective Thomas?"

"I asked Morgan if he could call the detective and let him know we'd be in town."

"Cool."

The waitress poured their coffee and took their orders. Dean grew quiet, staring out the window.

"What're you thinking about?" Clay asked.

Dean turned. "I wish I had enough hard evidence to feel comfortable calling the FBI in at this point."

"You don't feel confident about those photos, do you?"

"*I* do. But, knowing they were tampered with forces me to wait until someone can confirm they belong to the woman in the article. The last thing I want to do is call in the cavalry with false evidence. But then, if the photos *are* real, we're faced with the dilemma the killer may already be in Elk Meadow. I've thought about it all morning. Knowing the woman is safe out in the forest helped me make my decision."

"Yeah, tabloids don't have the best reputation. I have to agree with you on that. Hey, didn't the woman spend some time in the hospital? A doctor would have examined her."

"I talked to Morgan about that, too. He's going to ask the doctor to meet with us when we get there. Either that, or he'll take us to him."

"That's good."

"Morgan said the woman calls herself Nataya, just like the tabloid says. And she did have scars on her torso. So, that much is fact. He said the doc got a real good look, and will probably be able to verify whether the photos are of her or not."

"Sounds promising."

"If we can get confirmation on the photos, I'll be the first to call the FBI Director over at the Behavior Analysis Unit."

The food arrived, and neither man wasted any time digging in.

"Tell you what, Clay, when we've eaten, we'll stop at the first motel we find along the road. Maybe we can grab a few hours of sleep before we head into Elk Meadow tomorrow, and still beat that storm."

"No problem, man. Just wake me when you're ready to roll."

CHAPTER FORTY-THREE

The Open Countryside, Colorado

Nataya awoke during the in-between time, when night gives way to the new morning. The sky would soon lighten in anticipation of the rising sun, and she knew Walker wanted to set out the moment they could see to travel.

She lay curled up against him in the tiny shelter, relishing the added warmth. In contrast, the icy cold air on her face made her reluctant to move.

I want to lie here just a little longer.

But the looming fear of being caught in a snowstorm prompted her to rouse Walker from his sleep.

"The temperature has dropped," he said before they crawled from the small shelter. Even as they pulled their bodies free into the darkness, they could tell a heavy frost covered all the plants and grasses. Walker scraped back the campfire ashes and found a few small hot coals from last night, added some tinder and coaxed it into flames.

"We have a little of the fish left for this morning," she said, handing him the food.

"Good. And we can finish the jerky as we travel today. We'll need to keep moving."

As they ate the morsels of food, a strong breeze came up, followed by colder gusts a few minutes later. Nataya shivered, huddling closer to the feeble flames. Moments later the wind gained momentum, threatening to whip the fire out of existence altogether. Nataya didn't miss the serious set to Walker's jaw when he stood and peered into the darkness. Shapes of the surrounding landscape had begun to appear in the growing light. He then crouched next to the fire.

"We must leave now." He covered the struggling flames with dirt, took Nataya's hand and helped her to her feet.

"Come...moving will help keep our bodies warm." They gathered their meager belongings and he led the way forward across the open ground, treading carefully in the minimal light.

Nataya tucked her head down and pushed forward, thankful the ever-increasing force of wind pushed at her back. But the absence of trees or hills for shelter meant there would be no respite from the buffeting their bodies would endure. Winter had finally decided to move in.

The meadowland ended, forcing them to enter a large field. Shoulder high grasses and weeds threatened to obscure her sight of Walker as he moved steadily through the field. She never let her eyes wander from his back, stepping carefully to avoid holes or ruts in the nearly frozen ground. The winds drove the energy from her body, and sent it out over the fields.

The sky before them began to lighten, its gray hue turning to a light pink. Up ahead Walker stopped and turned around, gazing past Nataya to the landscape behind them. She turned to follow his gaze and stood still, staring in awe.

Glowing red just above the mountain peaks, the sun blazed into the sky before the heavy cloud cover above extinguished it. Nataya's gaze continued upward, and upward, taking in the enormous wall of towering clouds, rolling in over the mountaintops. They reached high into the sky, filling her vision.

The constant blast of frigid air on her face made her eyes water as she watched the approaching storm, realizing this same wind drove the storm clouds directly toward them.

She and Walker turned as one, and without a word between them, forged onward.

CHAPTER FORTY-FOUR

San Juan Mountain Range: Rocky Mountains, Colorado

Clay would swear he had just closed his eyes when Dean woke him, saying they had to leave. But now he peered out the window as the scenery sped by, alert. Every mile they drew closer to their destination, he perceived a new level of anticipation building. They finally had a real chance at catching this son-of-a-bitch. He knew it.

The morning sun quickly warmed up the interior of their vehicle as they traveled, despite the cold outside. He lived in sunny California, but his sunglasses were no match for *this* brightness. *Intense.* That's how he would describe the sunshine out here. In fact, intense described everything about this place. The snow storms, the bluest skies he'd ever seen, dark brooding mountains, and rich green pines. Even the land itself came in extremes. Hundreds of miles of flat prairie lands erupted into snow-covered mountain peaks, jutting up into the clouds above.

Driving through the winding foothills, the landscape changing with every turn, he had to admit it. He could understand how someone might fall in love with this land.

Dean let Clay enjoy the scenery for a while. A native Californian, Clay hadn't traveled much, nor seemed interested in it. Dean wanted him to get a feel for it—especially now with Stacy gone. He broke the silence reluctantly. "I'm guessing we're just an hour away. Can you check the GPS?"

Clay studied the digital map for a moment. "Yeah, looks right. We'll be turning back north before we reach Elk Meadow though, closer to that storm."

"Okay. I'm going to pull over at the rest stop up ahead. We'll take a break and I'll give Morgan a call, ask him to set up that meeting with us."

An hour later, Dean pulled into a parking place on the square where the courthouse sat. Morgan had spoken the truth, it was easy to spot, there wasn't much else to the town.

They had lost the sunshine as they neared Elk Meadow, and when he stepped out of the vehicle to assist Clay, the force of the wind startled him. That and the initial shock of bitter cold, after enjoying the warmth of the vehicle. Clay grumbled as Dean helped him into the wheelchair.

"And just when I had decided I liked this place."

Chief Deputy Morgan met Dean and Clay inside the courthouse doors and led them down a hall to a meeting room. They stopped short of going in, though, as Morgan turned to face them. Dean studied the thin, wiry man with a somber expression, recognized the defensiveness in Morgan's stance. The man's tone was *all business.*

"Mr. McClure, I know Sheriff Kimball sent you my way, but before we go in there with my men I need to fully understand the scenario. In what capacity are you here? The Sheriff said you work with the FBI?"

Dean gave a curt nod. "Before retiring from the FBI, I began working on a case involving a serial killer. They've asked me to stay on the case as a consultant. Recently we had a breakthrough. Much of the credit goes to Clay here. He's been instrumental in keeping this case alive."

Clay spoke up. "Don't be fooled by this man's modesty. He's one of the top profilers...ever. I just tag along for the ride."

Morgan shifted his weight, his impatience showing. "So, are you here on official business, or is this just some hunch you're following?"

Dean made sure he had Morgan's gaze and held it. "We're here because we believe there is a strong possibility one of your citizens is in extreme danger. I'm sure you want to protect anyone in harm's way, am I right?"

Morgan matched Dean's hard stare for a long moment, then relaxed his attitude. "Of course. We appreciate your offer of help."

They entered a small room, devoid of any décor other than clusters of tables and chairs filling the space, and uniforms scattered about. Morgan introduced them to Doctor Baker, Detective Thomas and a few of the deputies. The rest of the uniforms talked quietly amongst themselves, checking out the newcomers.

Morgan led them to the front of the room and asked everyone else to take a seat.

"Thanks for your attention." Morgan nodded toward Dean. "Mr. Dean McClure here is a former FBI profiler, and is currently working as a consultant for the Bureau." He motioned toward Clay. "And this is his...assistant, Mr. Clay Evans. Sheriff Kimball has requested our assistance and cooperation in a matter he deems of high importance. They will fill you in on the details."

Dean repressed a smirk as Morgan moved to stand aside. So much for inciting his men to cooperate. He'd made it clear this was the sheriff's idea, not his. No problem. After all, he'd had years of experience handling similar scenarios.

"First, Clay and I would like to thank all of you for your time today. The information we are about to share with you has come through an ongoing investigation. This particular case, now two years old, involves a serial killer. He abducts young women, taking them to remote warehouses or wilderness areas, where he murders them in a ritualistic fashion. A ceremony of sorts, one only he fully understands. Part of this *ritual* entails carving a pattern into the flesh of the victim's torso with a knife. The cuts form a design we believe has a significant meaning to the killer. It is identifiable, once you've seen it." Dean paused, then added, "We've seen it six times."

Dean let the silence in the room hang for a moment, saw he had everyone's attention now. "We've come here to Elk Meadow because of an article we read in a newspaper. We believe the woman found in the forest near here—the *wild women* as you call her, or Nataya, as she calls herself—may have been an intended victim, but somehow managed to survive. You see, the killer cuts his victims *before* he kills them. And Morgan has confirmed Nataya has scars on her torso." Dean looked at Doctor Baker. "Would you be willing to look at the newspaper photos and confirm if this is the woman you examined?"

"Of course."

Clay rolled his chair over and handed the doctor a printout from the paper.

Dean gave him time to study the photos. "Is this the woman you call, Nataya?"

Doctor Baker looked up from the paper. "Yes. This is the woman Fox Walker found living in the wilderness."

Dean glanced at Clay, saw him give a little fist pump.

Doc continued. "The scars in the photo don't exactly match what I saw, though. Did someone alter the photo?"

Dean pulled photos from his jacket pocket and walked over to the doctor. "We believe so. Could you take a look at these? I warn you, they're not pretty. These are crime scene photos of the victims we've investigated so far."

Doc took the photos. He studied each one, his face grim. When he handed the photos back, he shook his head.

"So many."

Dean tucked the photos into his pocket and returned to the front of the room. "Do *those* markings look familiar, Doctor?"

"Yes, they do. Please understand, Nataya's markings are scars, completely healed. And these photos show fresh wounds. But they clearly match the pattern I saw on Nataya."

"Thanks. We appreciate your appraisal. This is very helpful." Dean looked out over the men and women gathered in the room. Every face turned to him. "This convinces me we now have hard evidence linking Nataya's scars to those of six other victims. I believe we can safely conclude she was abducted and tortured by this serial killer. How she survived, or escaped, we don't know."

Dean held up the newspaper. "But, if the killer sees this same article, he will immediately know it's her. She's the only living witness we know about. We believe he'll come back to finish what he left undone."

Clay added, "Detective Thomas has identified the photos of Nataya as his missing person, Jenny Long. He has confirmed she has no close living relatives. And the article we read mentions she doesn't have any memory of what happened to her. Can you give us confirmation of that fact, Doc?"

"It's true. At least during the time she was under my care, she called herself Nataya, and didn't remember anything except months of living in the wilderness. I believe the trauma she suffered caused her to block out the memories. She didn't *want* to remember what happened to her."

Dean looked down for a moment, frowning. "So she has no idea of the danger she is in."

"I would say that is correct."

Dean looked at Morgan. "Detective Thomas mentioned this woman has returned to the forest with the tracker who first discovered her. Is she still there?"

"As far as we know. Walker followed her into the forest. He said he would make sure she arrived safely. I presume he would convince her to return to town, before winter set in."

"Considering the storm due in here, is it a possibility that they may be returning at any time?"

"Could be. We can send someone out to his cabin and check. If he hasn't returned yet, we can leave him a note, warning him to come into town when he gets back."

"Isn't there any way to reach him by cell phone?"

Morgan shook his head. "He doesn't own one. He has a phone at the cabin, but no answering machine."

"Sounds like the note is our best back-up option, but keep trying to call the cabin as well. We need to warn him Nataya is in danger."

Dean grabbed a stack of papers from Clay and passed them out to the group. "Through this ongoing investigation, we've been able to compile a sketch and profile that might help you to spot this man. Make no mistake, the killer is highly intelligent. He is organized, putting much thought and planning into his abductions. He has eluded us for two years."

Dean waited until everyone had a paper. "We know he is a white male, of medium build, probably in his late twenties. As you can see from the drawing, he is what you would consider a handsome man, with polite mannerisms. We also believe he has an extensive education, with an active social background. This makes it easy for him to blend into any scene and not be noticed. He feels comfortable striking up conversations with strangers."

Dean paced across the front of the room, turning to look at his audience as he spoke. "What this man is *not*, is a social misfit. He doesn't live as a recluse, hiding from people. He won't be easy to spot. He even impersonated a police officer. He's not afraid to go outside his comfort zone. He moves across state lines often. We have a theory he steals identities of men who closely match his description. His hair color appears to be black, but most likely he alters his appearance as needed, such as contact lens for eye color."

Everyone in the room followed Dean's movements. He stopped in the middle of the room and looked into the eyes of each person there. "You know the people in this town. We need you to take special note of any strangers in your area. Ask around, see if anyone new has shown up matching the description. We believe this man would feel especially comfortable being out at night, since all of his abductions appear to have taken place during the early evening hours."

Dean answered a few questions and thanked everyone for showing up. Clay wheeled up beside him and Morgan.

"Okay, Clay. Now I feel comfortable contacting Wheat." Dean turned to Morgan. "Considering the evidence we have, I'll be alerting Harold Wheat, the Director of the Behavioral Analysis Unit for the FBI. He'll probably elect to send in some people via choppers ASAP. If so, they can form search teams or set up surveillance. I suggest you make use of their skills—"

"The FBI?" Morgan's face turned red. "We're a small town, and we know everyone here. We can handle this without the Bureau crawling all over the place."

"And we know this killer," Dean said. "He *will* be back to kill Nataya—may already be here. It won't matter the woman has no memory of him or the abduction. He'll be driven to finish the ritual *and* get rid of a witness. The FBI will keep a low profile in case the killer is here in the area." Dean softened his tone. "We will need your co-operation to save this woman and capture the killer.

I'm sure we all feel the same way about finding this guy. Let's make *that* the important issue right now."

Morgan gave a curt nod.

Dean extended his hand. "We do thank you for your support in this matter."

Morgan shook the offered hand. "It's not like we have any choice, is there?"

"You're not the first person to get a bit protective about your town. Please understand. We really *do* need your help here. In a small town situation, the locals can be the most important link in locating a stranger."

"Good." Morgan stuck his hands in his pockets. "Maybe this is kind of personal, but if you don't mind me asking, why are *you two* so involved in this particular case?"

Dean glanced at Clay, who nodded his head solemnly, spun his wheelchair around and rolled away.

Morgan gave Dean a dumbfounded look. "Did I say something wrong?"

"No, you didn't. It's just even to this day, Clay can't talk about what happened to him. He hasn't made peace with his situation yet." He saw the question in Morgan's expression and continued. "Clay's fiancée, Stacy, was a victim of a serial killer, not this one—a different man. Clay walked in on the murder, surprising the bastard. They struggled, and as the killer got loose and fled, he shot Clay, paralyzing him from the waist down."

"Damn! I had no idea…"

"As Clay would prefer it."

"But how did he end up with you?"

"Clay became relentless in tracking the killer down. The FBI dismissed him at first, but he approached me and we began working together. There's no doubt Clay has been instrumental in the capture of at least two other killers, but he's never been able to track down the son-of-a-bitch who murdered Stacy."

"Putting other killers away hasn't eased the pain for him, has it?"

"No. Like I said, Clay hasn't come to terms with this yet. He lives for revenge. It's all he has."

"That's a sad thing."

"Yes, it is. Each time we solve a case I hope it takes him a step closer to healing his pain."

"What about you?"

"Well, all I can say is, every now and then a particular case gets under your skin. It's hard to explain. I can't let go of this one. I know this killer. He will never stop. I can't rest until I finish this one. He *must* not win."

Morgan didn't doubt him. He had seen the pain in the younger man's eyes, and he saw Dean's determination in the set of his jaw.

"Then I'm glad I'm not the Art Critic."

CHAPTER FORTY-FIVE

Elk Meadow, Colorado

The deputy stepped up onto the porch of Fox Walker's cabin and knocked on the front door. He looked around the property as he waited. When no one answered, he walked to a window and peered in, then returned to the door. Glancing around once more, he slid an envelope between the screen and the wood door, down near the threshold. His task completed, he returned to his car.

In the dark shadows of the treeline bordering Walker's property, a man watched, waiting until the uniformed man's car had time to travel back down the long gravel driveway and the accompanying dust cloud dissipated.

Only then did he slip up close to the cabin and sprint the short distance to the closest wall. With his back against the log exterior, he worked his way around to the front. Crouching, he made his way across the long front porch to the entrance. The man tried the outside screen door and found it locked. He took out a knife and, using the tip of the blade in the holes of the screen, tediously worked the envelope over to where he could grasp a corner. He pulled it loose from the door, stuffed it into his pocket and hurried back to the trees for cover.

Once safely secluded from view, the man opened the envelope and took out a piece of paper. After reading it, he crumpled the paper into his fist, and turned to make his way back to his vehicle. The one hidden from view on the long ago forgotten grass-covered access lane.

CHAPTER FORTY-SIX

Gray's Forest, Colorado

The wind rattled the sides of the tent and found ways to sneak inside, sending chills over Jack's skin, even through his clothing. He peeked out through the tent flap and watched the high-reaching, brooding clouds cover the sun and hang over the mountaintops.

Nothing for it, he had to brave the weather and leave his shelter if he wanted to see how the wild woman fared.

Better than me—I'm sure.

He held a new appreciation for her knowledge and mindset. In the short time he'd been out here, completely separated from the modern world, his lack of survival skills had become a little too apparent. He struggled with the simplest tasks. But each day he accomplished something new, and gained more confidence.

Bundled up in his coat, he added his knit ski hat, and forced his body outside the tent. He leaned into the wind assaulting his body and tucked his head down, plowing forward.

Tears streamed from his eyes from the wind whenever he tried to look up, so he kept his head down and followed the creek, hoping this ordeal was going to be worth the effort.

Closer to the cave, the cliffs protected him somewhat from the windy onslaught. He breathed a sigh of relief at the reprieve and stopped to watch for any movement ahead. After watching the cave for days, he could tell, even at this distance, the cave and campfire appeared deserted. His heartbeat increased. He strode up the incline, watching and listening for any movement, then approached the campfire pit. Cold ashes. And no sign of either the Indian or the wild woman having been here for a while. He walked to the cave entrance and tentatively peered inside. No one. He stepped inside and let his eyes adjust. It looked deserted as well. But on closer inspection he could see rope bundles of Nataya's handmade tools and dried foods hanging from the cave's higher ledges. It appeared she planned to return. But maybe this colder weather had forced her and the Indian to leave and find shelter beyond the forest.

Maybe I should do the same.

A moment ago he had been ready to battle the elements for the opportunity to talk to the wild woman. But standing here alone in the vast wilderness, a winter storm brewing overhead made him rethink his strategy.

He turned and headed back to his camp.

Thankfully my vehicle is only a short hike up the side of the ravine. But now what?

CHAPTER FORTY-SEVEN

Elk Meadow, Colorado

Nataya forced one foot in front of the other, pushing her way through the high grasses behind Walker. She glanced over her shoulder to the scene behind them. The massive cloud bank hadn't advanced and still hung over the mountains, but Walker had encouraged her not to ease up, for the temperature continued to drop. The storm would still come, he explained, even though it moved slower than he had anticipated. The color of the sky told her the sun, hidden now behind clouds, would soon drop below the mountains. Why hadn't they stopped to set up camp for the night?

The grasses opened to reveal a dirt path running through the field. Walker stopped and turned to her.

"It's not far now. And it'll be easier walking on this path."

Nataya could only nod.

The land ahead fell and rose in gentle hills. At the bottom of one such hill, just before the land ahead began to rise, she saw metal shining through the weeds. Walker stepped off the path and began to brush off the loose debris, revealing what he called a truck. She had seen these things at the medicine lodge, in the place named parking lot. Sometimes she saw them moving, sometimes sitting still.

Nataya stood in place and stared. Her relief at reaching their goal was replaced with anxiety about what would happen next. A vision flashed across her mind...she sat inside one of these. How? A chill ran through her body, not entirely from the cold wind. Walker glanced at her.

"Here, I'll unlock the door and let you get out of the wind."

Nataya watched him walk to the back of the truck and return with a metal piece. He used it to open a door. The big truck intimidated her, yet part of her sensed familiarity. And getting inside offered shelter from the wind. Exhaustion prompted her to let Walker assist her. She climbed onto the seat, relishing the warmth of the air inside and relief from the never-ending winds. Walker finished removing brush from the vehicle, while she watched. He opened the door opposite of her and climbed in. He leaned over and began to pull a strap across her. She grabbed his arms to stop him.

"No!"

Walker stopped, surprise on his face. Then he nodded. "I understand your fear. But it's okay, Nataya. These are called safety belts, for riding in the truck. I'll be wearing one also."

He showed her how to fasten the belt, and true to his word, also put one on. She watched as he put the same little metal piece, that had opened the doors, into a little slot and turned it. A groaning noise startled her, the truck sputtered and shook, then roared loudly. Nataya put her hands to her ears.

"You will be fine," Walker reached over to touch her shoulder. She gradually brought her hands down, allowing her ears to get used to the noise. Besides, Walker appeared to think everything was okay. The truck began to move slowly over the bumpy ground.

Then it left the field and Walker explained that they were going to ride on a paved road to get to his cabin.

She sat up straight, looking from window to window, but the scenery flew by at such a blur it made her dizzy. She studied Walker. He stared straight ahead out the biggest window in front of them. She did as well, and the dizziness went away. When she relaxed back into the seat, the motion of the moving truck reminded her of her vision earlier.

I have done this before.

The road stretched ahead of them forever. She worked to keep her focus on the road, but after being in the cold wind all day, the warmth of the truck and its gentle rocking motion made her sleepy. She nodded off, her head sliding over to rest on Walker's shoulder.

Sitting up as tall as she could in the seat, she could just peek over the dashboard. The sun shone through the windshield warming the inside, but when she touched the window next to her with her finger, it was cold. She leaned over and breathed on the glass, watching it steam up in a circle. She drew little squiggles in the fogged up area.

The man driving the truck glanced over at her and smiled. His gentle eyes had little creases beside them. She grinned back and promised herself to remember this moment. It was a special game she played—her own little secret. Whenever she was extra happy like this, she tried to remember every-thing about it, the smell...the sounds...the way the sun shone. That way, she could remember it whenever she wanted to, and be happy again. Just like now.

The man motioned to the bag of fresh-picked apples sitting beside her on the seat. She selected one and rubbed it on the front of her jacket, like she'd seen him do, and handed it to him. Then she took one for herself. When she bit into it, the sweet juices ran down her chin, causing her to giggle.

The noise and motion of the truck changed slightly. Nataya stirred and sat up, the dream fading away. Walker slowed the truck and turned off the paved road onto a gravel drive.

"Is this the driveway you told me about?" she asked.

"Yes. We'll soon be there."

She strained to see down the road. Walker had described how his cabin would be at the end. They drove over the crunching stones until they passed through a stand of stately evergreens.

Even in the late evening light she could make out the details of the land as they came through the trees. It looked exactly as Walker had described, only more beautiful than she had imagined. A lush valley spread out in front of them, including a lake. Beyond the hills surrounding the valley loomed the mountains, shrouded in clouds.

A small cabin sat on a slight rise and overlooked the stunning scene.

"It's beautiful," she said, leaning forward to better see.

Walker smiled and parked the truck next to the cabin. Still sitting in the warmth of the cab he pointed out the different buildings on the property, making special note of the large structure where he held his classes. "Take a good look. Soon it will all be covered in snow. Are you ready to go in?"

"Yes."

Her heart fluttered, but she tried to remain calm. She wanted to observe everything around her as she followed Walker across the large porch. He hesitated before opening the door.

"When we go inside it will feel colder than your cave at first, but I'll build a fire and soon it will be warm."

She followed him through the door, then stopped to scan the interior of the structure. She had visualized it being small like her cave, but the top stretched tall above her, the space around her, large. Walker was right, the air did feel cold, but the enclosure was still cozy, compared with being outside.

"What do you think, Nataya?'

"I believe you, that I will be safe from the winter weather in here. And I like being surrounded by the tree logs."

Walker smiled. "Good. Let me get a fire started. It'll warm up quickly."

She watched as he started a fire in something he called a wood burning stove.

"This will heat the room just like your campfire, but warmer. And we can heat water right here on top, instead of heating rocks by the fire and putting them in our wooden cups."

With the fire blazing, he walked her around, showing her the section of the room he called the kitchen, where he prepared food and ate, and then the furniture where he relaxed.

"I built this as one room to make it easier to heat in the winter, just like your cave."

"You were very smart. It's not what I imagined. I didn't know it would be so...comfortable."

"There's more." Walker grabbed her hand and tugged her toward an opening in the wall. "Down this hallway is a bath, and two other rooms. An enclosed porch runs the length of the south wall."

Her head was spinning with questions, but all she could blurt out was, "It's all so much." Walker must have sensed how overwhelmed she was, and to her relief they returned to the main room.

The warmth of the stove had already taken away some of the chill. She breathed in the aroma of the burning wood. It did remind her of her cave, and not in a sad way.

I can do this.

Walker pointed toward the furniture. "Go ahead and make yourself comfortable—sit wherever you want. I'll heat water for tea, to help warm us up." He turned and busied himself in the kitchen.

She chose the chair closest to the warm stove and curled up in it. The cold, difficult walk from the cave behind her, she could finally relax. She studied Walker as he worked. No matter how she struggled to keep distrust for him in her heart, his good deeds and kindness over these many days had made it an impossible task. Coming to this place proved to her the spirits indeed sent him to find her…to help her survive the winter. But then an unexpected thought came into her mind.

I like being with him.

Walker had watched Nataya's body language and expression closely ever since they entered the cabin. It was imperative that she want to stay the winter. If she decided to escape back to her cave, he didn't believe she had much chance of surviving. During the trek here, he wanted to believe a bond had formed between the two of them. But he couldn't be sure. More than once she had proven she could strategize and use circumstances to her advantage. Might she be doing so now?

He put water in the enamel coffeepot and carried it to the top of the wood stove. He saw her eyeing it with curiosity. "I use this to make a drink called coffee," he said. "But tonight it will heat water for tea. I'll make coffee for you another time."

When the water came to a boil he fixed two large mugs and handed one to her. "This is different from your pine needle tea, but I think you'll like it. It's made from herbs and will help you relax." He watched her taste it.

"It's good."

They sat by the fire drinking the tea, until the chill had left their bodies and the cabin.

"I like the campfire in your cabin. It reminds me of my cave. But this is warmer."

"Now that we are warm, are you hungry?"

Nataya nodded vigorously.

Walker laughed. "I thought so. We haven't eaten anything, except some jerky, since this morning. I'll find something to fix." He walked into the kitchen, opened a can of beef stew, poured it into a pan and brought it to the stovetop to heat.

As they waited for the soup to warm, Nataya asked questions about all the items she saw around her. She wanted to know about the furniture, the rugs on the floor, and the hanging pictures. She especially showed interest in his bows and arrows mounted in a rack on the wall.

"I prefer to hunt as my ancestors did," he said, taking down one of the handmade arrows. He fingered the feathers on the wooden shaft. "The bow and arrow, and my knife are the only weapons I use."

"And the snares you taught me to make."

Walker looked up from the arrow and smiled. "Yes, and the snares."

"You don't use the gun?"

"What gun?"

"Like the one the man called Deputy wore on his belt. He sat at the door to my room in the medicine lodge."

"No, I don't like to use guns. They make it too easy to kill. Hunting the old way takes skill. I must know my animal brothers and their way of life before I can successfully hunt them. They in turn give up their lives that I might survive. I have respect for their spirit and what they give to me."

"Was the Deputy hunting?"

Walker rubbed his neck. "Guns are a part of this world now, and sometimes good people, like the deputy, use them to protect others. It's not simple."

The stew came to a boil and all talking ceased when Walker filled their bowls. Nataya managed to ask a few more questions, between bites of stew, about how he built the cabin. But the warmth of the stove and a full stomach soon caught up to her. Walker watched as her eyelids grew heavy. Sleep beckoned him as well.

He stood and came to her side. "I think we can both use some sleep. It's been a long day."

She smiled up at him, her face still radiant from the wind and cold. Her eyes held a tenderness he had not seen before. It caught him off guard. And his physical reaction to it also meant he had to rethink the sleeping arrangement.

Snuggling together in a cave for warmth had been one thing. Crawling into his bed with her beside him, another. The temptation would be more than he could handle. And instincts told him she was nowhere near ready for what he had to offer.

I can't destroy her trust in me now, after all this.

He offered his hand and helped her from the chair. She stretched her lean body and smiled, eyes half closed. Walker tensed. Didn't she have any idea how enticing she was? But then, she still mostly lived in her pretend world. What would happen if she regained her memories?

"Come, Nataya. Let me show you to the sleeping room, so you can get some rest."

Walker showed her the guest room and pulled back the blankets on the bed. "I'll put extra blankets on here to keep you warm for the night. The bed is soft and you will sleep well."

Nataya touched the soft blankets and smiled, until Walker turned to leave.

"Are we not sharing the sleeping space?"

"We don't need to, here in the cabin, like we did in the cave. It will be warm all night. We'll talk more about this tomorrow, okay?"

Perhaps she was too weary to argue, for she only nodded. Walker laid one of his flannel shirts on the bed, along with a pair of wool socks. "You can wear these to sleep in, if you want." He showed her a hook on the back of the door where a wool poncho hung. "If you need to get up in the night, you can put this on for extra warmth."

"Thank you. This is very kind." She didn't meet his eyes and he wondered at her quiet mood.

"Good night, Nataya. Have a pleasant sleep."

"Yes. You too."

He added enough wood to the stove to last the night, damped it down, and went to his bedroom. Exhaustion tugged at his body and yet he stopped at the doorway and stared into the room. Now he understood Nataya's quietness. Without her presence, the room looked lonely and empty. She must have experienced this sensation as well.

He looked back toward her room. But the woman who called herself Nataya, didn't even know her real name, or her past. She had not shown him any evidence she felt a physical attraction to him. In fact, he had no idea how any of this would fit into her current world.

You can't take advantage of her when she doesn't yet know her own mind.

He stood in the doorway a long moment, then forced himself to crawl under the covers, alone.

CHAPTER FORTY-EIGHT

Elk Meadow, Colorado

F ox Walker sat upright in bed with a start.
What the hell!
Something had awakened him from a deep sleep—a scream?
He held his breath, listening, every muscle in his body taut. The
full moon had slid from behind the clouds and momentarily lit up
his room like daylight. He saw nothing out of place. Then he heard
crying.
Nataya!
He rushed down the hall and into her room. She sat upright in
bed, hands covering her face. He sat down on the edge of the bed
and put his hands on her shoulders.
"What is it, Nataya?"
"The dream."
"The fire one?"
"Yes."
"Tell me what you remember."
"I don't want to think about it."

"Telling me about it will help you lose the fear."

She took a breath to stop the sobs. "It's the same as the other times. It starts out all blackness, and then I see the flames, bright orange flames of fire. I try to get away, but I can't move. All I can see is the fire, until a face appears in front of me, blocking out everything else." She shuddered. "But this time, his eyes—were like the black openings of caves—and when the fire reflected in them, they scared me! I couldn't breathe. Then I woke up."

She trembled. Walker slid his arm around her, pulling her close, and talked to her. He talked of the hikes they would take into the woods, and told her about the injured flicker he had rescued, how he mended her wing. He talked until her breathing slowed, and he felt her relax once again. Still holding her in his arms, he looked down into her eyes.

"Do you think you can sleep now?"

"Yes, I think so."

He meant to give her a quick hug, but found himself pulling her tightly against him, not wanting to let go. She didn't resist.

His entire being cried out to lie down beside her. He wanted to feel her body next to his, make love to her. So many years had passed since he had allowed himself to experience those emotions.

Memories of Haiwi came to him then, and the anguish of losing her brought him back to reality. He didn't want to ever experience that kind of pain again. So why did he tempt himself with this?

Besides, I've already fought this battle once tonight. Seducing her would be wrong—and I know it.

If he gave into his wants now, he might lose something else more precious, Nataya's trust and her friendship.

Reluctantly he loosened his embrace and helped her lie back onto the bed. He gently tucked her in, and returned to his own room.

Nataya may have succeeded in appearing brave in front of Walker, but alone in the dark, tears spilled down her cheeks. "What is happening to me?" she whispered in the dark. The dreams came more often now, but gave no clues as to their meaning. More frightening were the broken bits of visions flashing in and out of her mind when she didn't expect them. People she didn't know, and places she'd never been. Many of them were recurring scenes, over and over, but never making any sense to her.

And to complicate everything, she struggled to understand these new sensations her body experienced whenever Walker came near her. Ever since she began to trust him and believed the spirits had indeed sent him to her, waves of emotions periodically washed over her, overwhelming her at times.

When he had held her only moments ago, a longing arose in her she didn't understand, except that she didn't want it to end. She wanted him to stay with her, and she believed he wanted to keep holding her. But then his body went rigid, and he let go, leaving her alone once more. She didn't know if she cried now because of the frightening dream, or because he had left.

CHAPTER FORTY-NINE

Elk Meadow, Colorado

J ack Bailey switched on the old Bearcat police scanner he'd picked up for a song, and smiled at the instant burst of noise and activity. It had taken some additional wiring and Yankee ingenuity to hook up the scanner to his rental vehicle, but he had succeeded. Being out there in the wilderness had given him a new level of determination, and confidence.

Once he had discovered the cave abandoned, and the weather forecast began taking a turn for the worse, he figured the tracker and the wild woman must have returned to town. He hadn't seen them yet, but they were still a topic of discussion in the bars. More than a few times he'd heard someone mention the tabloid story he wrote. Maybe the law wasn't looking for them, but at least the scanner would allow him to pick up bits of information and keep in touch with activity in the small town.

The scanner had been only the first part of his plan. In fact, his next destination would be the hospital on the outskirts of town. He knew Doctor Baker had treated the wild woman, and he knew what days the doctor was on call. He would present himself as a professional journalist, and refuse to leave until he got a promise of an interview.

The reality of his dream job as a top journalist had been brought home with some painful conclusions. This would take some damn hard work.

But I want it—warts and all.

CHAPTER FIFTY

Elk Meadow, Colorado

"*N*o *school today, little one. It's been cancelled due to snow.*"
Eyes still closed, she smiled and snuggled deeper under the covers. Outside, the wind howled, rattling the shutters on her windows. But she remained safe in her soft cocoon of blankets. The smell of bacon cooking began to find its way into her room and she knew it would eventually coax her from the cozy bed, but not yet...not yet...

Wrapped in warmth, Nataya shook off the fogginess of the dream, another one that made no sense to her, yet felt as real as the moment right now. She lay still in the early morning light, listening to the wind pummel the outside of the snug cabin, searching and clawing for a way to get inside, just as it had in her dream.

But Walker had been right. She'd stayed warm all night under the layers of bed covers. She looked around the room, wondering at this new sleeping arrangement. She understood Walker spoke the truth, that inside the cabin they no longer needed each other's body heat for survival. But it made her sad to be alone in here, to awaken without him next to her.

Loneliness. She didn't remember ever being lonely, until she met Walker.

What does it mean?

Did his companionship mean so much to her now? Maybe she should tell him she did not like sleeping alone.

Another noise, something other than the wind, caught her attention. She didn't recognize what it might be. Curious, she crawled from the covers and peered out her door into the hall. Nothing. Then she heard it again. It came from the main room. Still wearing the long flannel shirt and wool socks Walker had given her, she pulled on her long pants and quietly walked down the short hallway.

Walker stood in the kitchen, opening and closing the little doors that lined the wall. He looked into each one, and every once in a while made marks on something he held in his hand. She watched him until he sensed her presence and turned.

"I hope I didn't wake you."

"No. The wind did."

"Yes, the winds have grown stronger, but the snows have not yet arrived. The spirits of nature do as they please. Come on over and I'll pour you some coffee. I promised I'd make you some."

She joined him at the table and he handed her a steaming mug.

"See if you like it."

She took a small sip. "It tastes…familiar. I like it."

"Good." Walker smiled at her. "Did you stay warm last night, Nataya?"

She looked down and couldn't meet his eyes "Yes. You spoke the truth. The blankets kept me warm." Should she tell him of her sadness?

"I'm sorry the nightmare woke you last night. Were you able to get back to sleep afterwards?"

Many answers jumbled about in her mind and she struggled with what would be the right thing to say. Silence hung between them, until in frustration she blurted, "If you had not left, you would know." She glanced up to see Walker staring at her with wide eyes, but his mouth slowly formed a smile.

"That's what I like about you, Nataya. You speak the truth. You are right, of course. It's just that—"

"Then I will tell you *all* the truth. I do not like being apart from you for sleep time. I don't like being alone and waking up alone. I miss you."

Walker looked away, and her stomach lurched. Maybe he didn't feel the same way. Maybe she had been wrong to speak the truth. But when he turned and looked at her again, the intensity of his gaze made her suck in her breath.

"I missed being with you, too."

Her pulse quickened. She felt her face grow warm.

He laid his hand over hers and she wondered at the sudden dizziness in her head.

"Thank you for letting me know how you feel, Nataya. It means more to me than you may believe. And now I must be as honest with you. I want to be with you too. We must talk, though—"

A loud ringing made her jump. When it rang again she heard Walker curse. The noise came from the phone, like in the medicine lodge. He walked over and picked it up to stop the racket.

Walker couldn't believe the bad timing. But a phone call usually meant the sheriff's department needed his assistance. Who else would ever call?

"Walker here."

"Fox Walker?"

"Yeah. Who's this?"

"Deputy Ellis. I'm calling for Chief Deputy Morgan. He asked that I check in every day, to see if you and Nataya had returned to the cabin yet."

"Yeah, you can tell him we're here."

"Okay. Hold on."

Walker heard muffled yelling through the phone. Then the caller came back on.

"He says he needs you to come in to Elk Meadow ASAP."

"The hell he does. He realizes a storm is heading our way?"

"Yes, yes. He knows. He says it's imperative you get here as quickly as possible."

"I'd like to know why, before I head out into this weather."

"I'm sorry Mr. Walker, but he's on another line now. But he was adamant about you coming in here, though. Can I tell him you're on your way?"

"Yeah, but this better be good."

Walker hung up.

What the hell was that all about?

The wind could've caused damage and trapped people on the mountainside, he guessed. He turned to Nataya. "I've been called in by the sheriff's department to help them with…something. We'll take the truck, but you'll need to dress warm. I'm not sure how long we'll be in town."

Nataya stared at him, her eyes wide. "There will be many people there? Like at the medicine lodge?'

"Maybe, but I won't let them bother you, I promise."

She began to back away from the kitchen counter. "Please do not make me go there."

Walker saw the panic in her eyes. He glanced out the window. A few scattered flurries were flying around out there now. Damn. He didn't want to leave her here alone. But someone's life might be on the line.

"Please, Nataya. I don't want to go without you, but I need to leave right now. And I want to get back before the snow gets serious."

"I'm sorry. I…can't."

Walker understood her fear, but at the same time understood the sheriff needed his help. He was torn between the two.

Nataya touched his arm, looked up into his eyes. "It's okay to go. I will wait here."

Walker sighed. "On one condition. You stay here in the cabin. Don't open the door for anyone, except me. Promise?"

"I promise."

He hurriedly added wood to the stove, filled the enamel coffee pot with water and showed her how to make more coffee. After adding the sheathed knife to his belt he walked over to the coat rack by the door and slipped on a heavy overcoat.

Nataya stood watching him, the warmth in her eyes made him want to change his mind. But he had no idea what danger someone might be facing, especially with this storm moving into the area. He reached out and gently touched her cheek, then turned to go. She followed him to the door, where he showed her how to lock it after he left.

"Make yourself comfortable. And don't let anyone in the cabin."

She nodded.

He opened the door and stepped outside into the cold.

Nataya stood at the window, watching Walker drive off. When she turned and stared into the now-empty cabin, the solitude wrapped around her like a heavy blanket. Before knowing Walker, she had never experienced this sense of isolation. Perhaps she spent too much time in his company, and so missed his presence when he wasn't there. She would have to think about this aspect of being here. She would need alone time.

To make the time pass, she walked through the cabin, examining all the items sitting about, pottery and baskets. The bows and arrows hanging on the wall still intrigued her the most. She studied the handmade arrows, with their painted designs. Maybe she would ask Walker to teach her how to make them.

The hallway beckoned and she decided to explore the smaller sleeping rooms, going to Walker's room first. She ran her hand over the wood frame of the bed and the soft wool blanket that lay on top. Next to the bed stood a wooden chest of drawers—that's what Walker had called it—just like the one in the room where she had slept. But this one had lots of items sitting on top. One of those items caught her eye. She carefully picked it up to get a better look. The moment she did, snippets of images flashed through her mind, causing her to gasp. A word came to her.

Photograph.

There it was again, words she did not know until she heard them in her mind. But now she remembered. She had seen photographs before. But she did not know how. What were the spirits trying to show her?

She looked at the photograph. A woman's face stared back at her. A beautiful woman with ebony hair and dark eyes. Her skin color matched that of Walker's. What did she mean to him? Where was she?

The room began to spin and she had to sit down on the bed. The waking dreams were coming more often now. She tried to block them, as she had in the past. But now they ignored her pleas and came at her unbidden. Scene upon scene began to bombard her, people she didn't know and places she didn't remember visiting, and with the scenes came words—new words she didn't know.

And yet when she heard them in her mind they became familiar. She knew them somehow. But each word brought with it pain.

Home. Childhood. Family. Happiness. Safety. Love. Fear. Pain. Death.

The words wouldn't stop. They were taking over her thoughts. She covered her ears with her hands, but still the words kept pouring into her mind. Panic gripped her chest in a spasm. She screamed and the voices stopped. She ran from the room, rushed to the kitchen window to stare out to the lake and woods before her—open and free as far as she could see. If only she could hear sounds of nature…birds…the wind in the trees. She had to get outside before the words came back.

She hurried to the sleeping room, where she replaced the over-sized shirt with her own flannel shirt, and pulled her moccasin boots over the heavy wool socks Walker had given her to wear. She returned to the main room, grabbed her coat from the hook by the front door and pulled it on, then stopped. What about her promise to Walker that she wouldn't leave the cabin? But she had to get outdoors, even if for a short reprieve. Besides, she could be back in the cabin long before he returned.

He won't even know.

She stepped out onto the porch and caught her breath. The temperature had plummeted. Being sheltered in the cabin had given her a false sense of the weather outside.

She hesitated, not because of the cold, but because a sense of urgency to return to the safety of the cabin came over her. She usually trusted her intuition, but this made no sense. The cold air made her feel so alive. Nature surrounded her, not empty rooms filled with scenes and words she didn't understand.

She ignored her instincts, stepped off the porch and walked across the open lawn in front of the cabin. She passed by the large building, where Walker said he held classes, and headed down toward the lake.

CHAPTER FIFTY-ONE

Elk Meadow, Colorado

Dean walked through the lobby of the Winchester Hotel and found Clay sitting in his wheelchair near one of the large picture windows. He joined him, and stood gazing out at the flurries of snow.

"You know, Dean, I do love the California weather, but I admit it's kinda cool watching this snow, now that we're not trying to drive through it."

"Yeah, agree with that. Looks like the storm is finally making its way here. I'm glad it got stalled over the mountains for a while though. It gave the FBI chopper a small window of opportunity. They just made it in."

"That's good news."

"Yeah, they're grounded now until the storm passes, but at least they were able to bring in our ground support team."

"Cool. The more eyes watching for our guy, the better."

"Yeah. This storm complicates things, though. The Art Critic may just hole up somewhere and wait it out."

Clay looked up at Dean. "Or he'll take advantage of the weather to move before we can track him down."

CHAPTER FIFTY-TWO

Elk Meadow, Colorado

The windshield wipers swiped at the snow steadily flying into Walker's view. His hope to get into town and back before the storm settled in had already been dashed. But he remained optimistic he'd be able to take care of business, whatever the hell it turned out to be, and get back before the snows were too deep.

More than a couple of times he had caught himself speeding faster and faster, the anxiety of getting back to the cabin taking control. And not just because of the approaching storm. He hadn't wanted to leave Nataya there alone. Instincts told him not to. But he understood her fear of coming here.

Thinking of Nataya brought to his mind her statement about missing him last night. He didn't try to stop the smile that spread across his face.

His truck bounced hard over a pothole in the road, jarring him into awareness. He needed to slow down. But even as his foot lifted off the accelerator, the backend of the truck began to fishtail. It all happened in slow motion, the tires losing traction, the truck now skidding sideways down the road. He knew not to touch the brakes. With his foot off the gas and gripping the steering wheel, he held his breath, waiting to see where the momentum would take him. The weight of the backend sent the vehicle into a slow spin as it slid down the highway. But at least this slowed the speed and he could lightly pump the brakes. He wound up facing in the correct direction, as the tires on the passenger side slid off the pavement. The heavy truck pushed the wheels deep into the loose gravel, slowing it more. The truck skidded to a stop, half on the road, half off, leaning at an angle on the uneven surface. He sat for a moment, just staring out the windshield. Fifteen feet ahead, the road crossed over a now dry riverbed. The drop could have been deadly if the truck had slid much farther.

First, he thanked the Great Spirit for sparing him from harm. Then he began to wonder at his own actions.

I don't do things like this!

His focus had not been as it should be. His thoughts kept wandering back to Nataya.

He heard Grandfather's voice.

Get control of your mind.

The roads would only get worse now. He had to stay alert.

After the near disaster, the rest of Walker's drive into town went without much incident, but only because he stayed to a torturously slow pace. Which only gave him more time to regret leaving Nataya behind. He should have insisted she join him. At least they would've been here together if he ended up getting trapped in town by the snow.

Rounding the last curve before arriving at the small community, he stared at a large black helicopter sitting in the field next to the road.

What in the world?

A couple of sheriff's cars sat off to the side, some uniforms gathered nearby. Slowing down, he peered through the driving snow as he drove by and could swear he saw the letters *FBI* on the chopper. He couldn't imagine why *they* would be here. And how had the chopper even managed to fly in through this wind and snow? Did this have something to do with Morgan asking him to come into town?

Okay, they had his interest now. He drove into downtown and parked in front of the Sheriff Department building. Winds buffeted the truck and rocked it. He knew from experience to get a good grip on the door handle before easing open the door, to make sure the wind didn't jerk it out of his hands. He slid out of the seat, and slammed the door behind him.

"Walker. Hey, Walker!"

He turned and spotted a uniform waving him down. The man hurried across the snowy road, and as he got closer, Walker recognized Deputy Harris. The deputy caught up with him, and breathing hard, shouted through the wind.

"Have you talked to Morgan yet?"

"No. About what?"

"Wait here a second." Harris pulled out his cell phone and punched in a number. "Mister McClure. I have Fox Walker here. Morgan's still out with the chopper. I figured you might want to talk with him. Sure, I'll bring him right over." He turned back to Walker. "I need you to follow me over to the Winchester Hotel."

"What the hell is going on, Harris."

"No time to explain. Trust me on this. Follow me."

Harris ran off toward his car and Walker shook his head. What was this all about? He pulled his coat collar up against the wind and clenched his jaw. Somebody better be coming up with answers soon.

CHAPTER FIFTY-THREE

Elk Meadow, Colorado

The light flurry of snowflakes Nataya had watched from the cabin window took on a more serious mood, growing heavier by the minute as she stood by the lake taking pleasure in the quiet peacefulness. The ground, lakeshore, shrubs and trees steadily turned into a magical wonderland as the snowstorm covered everything in its path with a pristine white coating. She flipped up the hood on her coat and let the snow settle on her as well. And still she stayed, even as the winds picked up and sent chills down her neck.

Minute by minute wildlife retreated into the shelter of the nearby trees, and she alone stood by the waters of the lake, snow gathered around her boots, covering her shoulders. She tilted her head back to stare up into the heavy clouds above. White specks flew downward into her face, catching on her eyelashes. The storm had settled in now, bringing with it a numbing cold. Perhaps she should follow the lead of the birds, and return to the shelter of the cabin. She reluctantly turned, surprised at the strength of the wind now as she faced into it. She lowered her head and pushed forward, heading back up the slight rise toward the cabin and away from the lake.

Movement in her peripheral vision made her look up. She stopped and squinted into the snow and wind. A man walked across the open grounds, hunched over, eyes on the ground. She tensed to run. But his steps were unsteady, his body showing signs of exhaustion. His wavering path led him toward her. The dim light cast his face in shadow, and dark shades covered his eyes, but she could see he wore a backpack. A lost hiker?

As she watched, bewildered about what to do, he stumbled, then caught his balance. He stood still a moment, and she held her breath. Should she run back to the safety of the cabin?

But then the man tried to take another step, swayed, and collapsed onto the ground.

Her fear dissolved, replaced with concern as she hurried toward the fallen man, the wind buffeting her, snow flying into her face. She couldn't leave him out here to freeze to death.

CHAPTER FIFTY-FOUR

Elk Meadow, Colorado

Walker pulled his truck in next to Harris in front of the hotel, watched the deputy leap from his cruiser and appear at his door before he could even get the seat belt off. Harris opened Walker's door.

"Follow me." Harris took off toward the hotel entrance leaving Walker to hustle to keep up.

Good. About time people got in a hurry around here.

The snow wasn't slowing down and the plummeting temperature meant business. Hopefully he'd finally find out what the ruckus was about and get back to Nataya at the cabin.

Walker followed Harris into the lobby where two strangers waited, apparently for him, although he couldn't imagine why. The younger man had that California surfer look about him, except he sat in a wheelchair. The gray-haired man standing next to him looked all business. They both wore grim expressions and gave him the once over, taking special note of the knife he wore at his side.

Harris motioned to the two strangers. "Walker, this is Dean McClure and Clay Evans. They are here as consultants for the FBI. Gentlemen, this is Fox Walker."

Walker shook their offered hands and stared at the two men.

FBI consultants?

Had someone dropped him into the middle of a movie, and not told him his part?

The gray-haired man, the one named McClure, motioned to some chairs in the corner. "Let's have a seat, Mr. Walker."

Walker stayed planted where he was. "What's this all about?" When neither man spoke, he lost what patience he had left. "Look. I'm not in the mood for games. Why are you here, and what do you need with *me*?"

McClure motioned toward the chairs. "Please, time is of the essence."

"Exactly." Walker stared at the man.

McClure pulled a paper from the folder he held. "Is this the woman you call Nataya?"

Walker stared at the newspaper clipping and nodded. "Where did this photo come from?"

"It's from a newspaper story."

"A story...about Nataya? That damn reporter!"

McClure again motioned to the chairs. This time Walker strode over, took a seat and looked to each man. "Do the scars in the photo look like the ones Nataya has? Study them closely. This is important."

Walker stared at the photo, felt his heart rate increasing. "These do," he said, pointing to a spot on the photo. These other lines weren't there."

The younger man in the wheel chair, Evans, pulled some Polaroids from his pocket and reached out his hand to Walker. "I'm sorry to ask you to look at these, but it's important, I promise."

Walker stretched out his hand for the photos, as Evans continued. "These are from crime scenes and difficult to look at, but we need to know if the markings in these match Nataya's scars. Can you do that?"

Walker gave a short nod and looked down at the first photo. His throat tightened.

How could this be possible?

He studied each photo, his hands shaking by the time he finished. "Yes. They look like Nataya's scars. Okay, enough of this. Tell me what the hell is going on—*now.*"

McClure leaned forward, and the intensity in his expression did nothing to calm Walker's nerves.

"Doctor Baker agrees with this as well. We have hard evidence indicating that Nataya's real name is Jenny Long. We believe she was abducted in the spring of this year from Big Pine, and has been missing ever since."

"In spring. That's when Nataya says she awoke in the forest."

"With no memory of her past, right?" Evans asked.

"Yeah, but how did you—"

"So, when you saw the scars, you thought perhaps she had been attacked?"

"I was sure of it. Doc thought maybe her lack of memory was a result of an attack."

McClure nodded. "That's a high possibility. We believe the person who kidnapped her is a known serial killer. We've been trying to track him down for two years. He marks all his female victims with that same pattern. Right before he kills them."

Walker's heart thumped in his chest, his mouth moved, but nothing came out. McClure answered his unspoken question.

"We don't know how *she* managed to survive. As far as we know she's our only living witness."

Walker struggled to put together all the parts to this surreal movie he'd been dropped into. He forced his mind to calm and concentrate on the fact. "All the pieces fit, the time frame...the scars...her loss of memory."

Evans chimed in. "Yes, you see it, don't you?"

Walker looked up at the men. "I think you may be right. But how did you figure out—?"

"No time for that," McClure said. "More importantly, where is Nataya right now?"

"Back at my cabin."

"You didn't bring her to town with you?"

"When the department asked me to come into town, I thought they had a search and rescue. Nataya didn't want to come here, around people. She's safe in the cabin, though."

"Didn't you find the note?"

"What note?"

The men looked at each other, and Walker didn't like what he saw. He jumped to his feet. *"What note?"*

McClure spoke firmly, but Walker could see the empathy. "We've got to keep a cool head, if we are to help her."

"What do you mean—help her?"

Evans wheeled his chair closer to Walker. "We have good reason to believe the killer thought Nataya was dead. But it's possible he discovered she's still alive—just as we did."

"From that damn newspaper article."

McClure stood and faced Walker. "And if he did, we have no doubt he will return to finish what he started. He may already be here. We left a note in your door to warn you to bring Nataya to town for protection."

Walker's chest tightened until he could scarcely breathe. He grabbed the chair back, waiting for the room to stop spinning.

Evans rolled his wheelchair in front of Walker. "Look man, we've brought in the FBI. They'll set up surveillance and watch your place. We'll catch him."

Walker sidestepped the wheelchair.

McClure took a step toward him. "Wait—where are you going?"

Walker stopped and turned toward the men. "I have to get back to the cabin and make sure Nataya is safe. But thank you. I mean that." He motioned the deputy over and added, "Harris can give you directions to my cabin. Please, hurry and send someone. I have a bad feeling about this."

Walker managed to maintain a calm exit from the hotel, but couldn't control the need to break into a sprint back to his truck.

McClure stood beside Evans, pulling open his cell phone as they watched Walker exit the building.

The younger man spoke. "I didn't want to say anything in front of him about what it may mean that the note was missing. Maybe the Art Critic *is* here and took it. For all we know, the woman may already be dead."

McClure hurriedly punched numbers into the phone. "He knows."

CHAPTER FIFTY-FIVE

Elk Meadow, Colorado

By the time Nataya reached the fallen man, he had pushed himself up on one elbow. A knit ski hat was pulled down low to his dark glasses, his collar up. But she could see beard stubble, as if he'd been out in the woods for days. She knelt in the snow and reached out to help him sit up, noticing he shivered.

"Move slowly. Where are you from?"

His raspy voice forced out words between breaths. "Lost...I got lost hiking up there." He pointed feebly to the hills behind them. "I saw the buildings down here..."

"I need to get you out of this cold wind. Do you think you can stand now, if I help you?"

The man nodded and Nataya supported him as he got to his feet. She waited for him to regain his balance and then let him lean on her as they started forward. "It's just up over this rise. You can see the top of the building from here. Can you make it?"

"Yes."

Together they trudged up the slight rise from the lake in silence. The man struggled to catch his breath, as if not used to the altitude, but she attributed it to his signs of exhaustion and hypothermia. Once they made it to level ground, where he could walk easier, she guided him to the large outbuilding where Walker said he held classes in the warmer seasons. He had explained why he always kept it unlocked, in case someone came by in bad weather and needed shelter. Just like today. She liked that about him.

She halted in front of the large door. "Can you stand alone, while I open the door?"

"I...think so."

He removed his arm from her shoulders and she made sure he had his balance before she turned and walked over to the door. The wind had swirled the already accumulated snow into a small drift against the bottom, and the cold moisture had swollen the wood. She had to tug hard, but managed to swing it open. The aroma of raw cut wood greeted her.

Stepping inside, she looked up. She could see all the way up to the roof, where wood beams joined together like a huge rib cage. She glanced around the large open room. One side contained long flat wood boards, each row higher than the one in front. Opposite, on the far wall were bookshelves, like in Walker's cabin, and a large board with markings on it.

She sensed the man behind her.

"I really appreciate you helping me."

His voice sounded different. Her scalp tingled, instincts warned her of danger. She started to spin around, but a blow from behind slammed her up against the wall next to the door. Her breath knocked out from the blow, it took a second before the adrenaline kicked in. She struggled in panic to get free of the man's hold. She tried to kick out from the wall, twisting at the same time. But the man slipped his arm around her neck, pulling her backwards. Her balance, thrown off by the awkward position, let her arms flail wildly as she attempted to hit him. His hand pressed a cloth against her face. She tried to twist her face away from it, away from the smell.

I know this smell!

It was her last thought before everything went black.

CHAPTER FIFTY-SIX

Elk Meadow, Colorado

The driving snow assaulted Walker's truck from all sides, mimicking the chaos of his thoughts and turning the surroundings into a surreal landscape. How could normal life be going on around him, while his life played like a nightmare, where the world moved in slow motion and no matter how hard he struggled to go forward he couldn't make any progress?

He had to get back to Nataya. Had to know she was safe. His mind kept returning to the missing note. What had happened to it? Maybe the wind had simply blown it away. But McClure's statement—that the killer may already be here—wouldn't stop playing in his mind. What if the killer had already been to the cabin? What if *he* found the note first? He could've been watching, could've seen Walker leave this morning. Damn! He *knew* he shouldn't have left her there alone.

"Stop it!" he yelled and slammed on the brakes, causing the truck to skid sideways to a halt.

He sat quietly in the still cab, listening to the wind howling outside, and to his own heavy breathing.

What's happening to me?

He didn't lose control of his emotions like this. Which gave him an inkling of how much Nataya had come to mean to him. But that wouldn't help her. Right now he needed to concentrate on driving this truck through the storm and returning to the cabin. It would do her no good if he ended up in a ditch, or worse.

He set off again, slowly adding speed, gauging how hard he could push and still maintain control of the vehicle. The slow pace gave him too much time to think about what might be occurring, right then. He forced the thoughts down, and focused on driving. But that didn't stop the rapid thumping in his chest.

Walker slowed for the entrance to his driveway up ahead, leaned forward in the seat and squinted through the snow hitting his windshield, checking for tire tracks. Nothing. He savored the moment of relief and hope. Of course it didn't mean someone hadn't been here earlier and the tracks were already covered by fresh snow. Gravel sprayed out in all directions as the truck pummeled its way through the snow and down the driveway.

He stopped the truck next to the cabin and took a moment to scan the grounds and outbuildings for any signs of an intruder, then jumped down from the cab. Sliding his knife from its sheath at his side, he took two large strides and cleared the steps, then sprinted across the porch to the front door.

He tried the knob and found the door unlocked. Dammit. He'd made sure Nataya locked it when he left. He closed his eyes and said a silent prayer to the Great Spirit before slipping inside. Silence met him. No sign of a struggle.

Good.

He called out for Nataya and hurried through the cabin, checking each room. No sign of her, but the coat rack was empty. Maybe she had simply gone outside to walk. Maybe he was jumping to conclusions. But the gut feeling of dread would not leave him.

He went back outside. Snow already covered much of the ground. And there were no fresh prints leading from the cabin.

That doesn't mean anything. Maybe she left the cabin before the snow started accumulating.

He scanned the property through the wind and driving snow. He could see the outbuilding where he taught classes. She knew he kept it unlocked. Maybe she had gone inside. He hurried for the door.

As he neared, he could see that the door had indeed been opened, for snow had been shoved aside in the process. And there were footprints under a thin layer of new fallen snow. He didn't stop to examine them, but hurriedly opened the door and stepped in. Empty.

Disappointment filled his heart. He had to force his mind to concentrate. He stepped back outside, and knelt, carefully brushing the newer snow away to study the footprints.

"Shit," he said, closing his eyes.

A man's footprint.

A heavy weight pressed in on his chest and a bubble of panic threatened to rise to the surface. He shook his head to clear his thoughts. He heard Grandfather's voice in his mind.

You must take the time to study the sign.

Walker knew from experience it would unravel the story like a loose string from a ball of twine. He continued his search, finding more prints coming across the yard from the opposite direction. He traced them backwards. There—Nataya's prints and the man's, side by side. Her prints were too deep for her weight. Perhaps she had let the man lean on her for support. Maybe he had been hurt?

He had to track the prints back to where Nataya and the man had met.

Shit. That'll take so much time.

But it had to be done. Only then would he have the entire picture to piece together. By widening his search he found where Nataya had started to walk back up from the lake. Then her prints veered off, digging into the soil, her strides lengthening. Something had made her run.

He followed her trail until he discovered where the man had fallen. Nataya had knelt beside him. A spark of hope began inside. Maybe she had only helped a stranded hiker. Maybe his imagination had run wild with his worst fears. But Grandfather's voice came to him clear and strong.

If that's true, where are they? Know who you track...follow the sign.

He had to follow the man's tracks backward as well. Maybe they would reveal a hint as to who he was. He blew out a breath of frustration and started to track the man's footprints. The covering of snow deepened as he searched, making him stop to brush it aside to find more tracks. The prints indicated a staggering walk, clumsy from exhaustion...until Walker neared a thick tree standing at the edge of his property. Sign indicated the man had stood there for some time, perhaps spying on Nataya? He followed the tracks backward from there. The man walked normally. No sign of exhaustion.

No doubt about it. The man faked his condition. Probably to lure in Nataya.

The tiny ray of hope that the man had indeed been injured fell away. Adrenaline pumped into Walker's veins. He took off at a run through the snow, back up to the outbuilding, and to the door. He studied the tracks again. Nataya and the man had made it to the door at the same time and stepped inside. But try as he may, he could only find the man's prints leaving the building, heading off to the right, toward the trees at the edge of his property.

He crouched and studied the prints closer. These were the same strong, purposeful prints he'd found up by the tree. But something else, they were deeper impressions in the snow.

The sign left no doubt in his mind. Now he knew exactly what had happened here.

Nataya had helped a man posing to be in distress. They had entered the building, where he attacked her. Then he had carried her off, hence the deeper impressions.

She would have never gone willingly. Which meant she had been unconscious—or dead.

Total despair crashed over him as he knelt in the snow. She had been stolen right out from under his watch, and his heart ached with the knowledge he had failed her, again.

Hundreds of times he had been called upon to track a lost or missing person, and even though he came to know the person he tracked, it had not been like this. He had been able to keep a clear mind and focus on his work.

Nataya has captured my heart.

There—he admitted it. But now the fear of failure carried an even heavier price.

The keening cry of a hawk broke into his troubled thoughts and made him look upward. How could a hawk possibly fly in this weather? No matter how he strained, he couldn't find a silhouette in the whiteness of falling snow. Nonetheless, he knew what he heard. He wondered what his spirit brother could be trying to tell him. *Beware...*or... *Be Aware.* He took a cleansing breath to clear his mind.

This isn't over yet.

Nataya had been kidnapped by the killer.

Now, what to do from here?

He could follow the footprints. He had a direction to go. Walker crossed the open space quickly, stopping every so often to brush aside the snow and check for tracks. At the tree line he came to an abrupt halt. Ahead of him lay an overgrown and rutted dirt road. He'd forgotten about this old access road. The pieces of clues fell together. The killer had driven down here, and then walked in from the trees. There had to be tire tracks somewhere on the path. He searched until he found them, hoping he could narrow down what type of vehicle the man drove.

Looking at the width of the tracks and the tire tread, he determined that it wasn't a truck. It had to be a car of some type—but with a wider wheelbase—possibly one with four-wheel drive.

Wow, I've narrowed it down to a few hundred different types of vehicles.

He kicked at the ground in frustration.

Grandfather would tell me to start at the beginning.

He replayed the conversation with McClure...that the man was a serial killer, which meant he had abducted other victims, and killed them. McClure believed this man would come back to finish what he left undone with Nataya. Well, he *had* returned. But where could he be taking her?

Examine the possibilities.

The authorities believed she had been abducted from Big Pine in spring...the same time as when Nataya remembered waking up in the forest. In fact, when they had visited the Sacred Circle, Nataya insisted she had awakened right there in the meadow, in pain and bleeding—*the cuts!*

He pictured the lone tree in the meadow, where he believed Nataya may have been bound. There had been a fire burning next to it. Her dreams of the flames, and the fact she couldn't move fit the clues he had found. Lately her dreams included a face. It all made sense now. The killer had taken her there, tied her to the tree, and tortured her. But somehow she had survived the ordeal.

"He'll take her back there. To finish it this time," he said aloud.

He pushed himself up off the ground, new energy surging through his body. He reviewed all the clues as he struggled through the snow, hurrying back to the cabin. He couldn't get any of it wrong. It would mean Nataya's life, of that he was sure.

He pulled open the cabin door and rushed in, grabbed the phone and called Chief Deputy Morgan's office. A deputy told him Morgan had left, along with some of the FBI agents. They were headed here, to his property, to set up surveillance.

"What about that man I met today—McClure. Is he around? Good, let me talk to him. And deputy, I'll need you to stay on the line as well. I'll need to give you some directions...Mr. McClure? He's got Nataya, but I know where he's taking her...doesn't matter how I know. Is the chopper grounded? Yeah, I figured that. There's a deputy on the line who will give you directions. Deputy, get everyone out to the old 'haunted lane'—the road that stops at the edge of Gray's Forest...yeah...that's the one. McClure, about one mile straight into the forest from that road, there's an open meadow, surrounded by trees. That's where the killer is taking Nataya."

Walker hung up the phone before they could question him more, in auto mode he checked his pocket for his flint, grabbed his ankle sheath and knife and strapped it on, then headed out the door to his truck. He couldn't wait for Morgan and the FBI. Hopefully the deputy or McClure could get them turned around.

Standing by his truck, he looked out over his property toward the access road. It struck him that even though he knew where the path exited out onto the main road, the possibility existed the killer could still be out there on the dirt road. With the snow falling at such a rapid rate, it may have only been minutes since they were here. The vehicle could be just ahead of him, or even stuck in the dirt and snow of the rugged, overgrown road. He would have to drive it. He had to be sure he didn't miss them. Damn! He hated the delay but had no other option.

His truck barreled across the open ground, then slowed to enter the access road. He pushed it as fast as he dared over the dirt path, the truck rolling and listing like a ship over waves. He stopped before rounding the curves, got out and walked it first, making sure he didn't surprise them on the dirt road.

The minutes ticked by like hours before he reached the end and sat at the intersection with the paved street. The snow now covered any tire tracks, but Walker knew they were there. And the tires would've picked up mud in the tread all along the dirt road.

He put his truck in park, walked out onto the paved road and found what he was looking for. As the vehicle left the access road, it flipped bits of snow and mud out from the tire treads. The car had turned right. Good. The killer had to go that way to reach Gray's Forest, where the Sacred Circle lay. So far, he had guessed correctly. He pushed back against the thoughts about how far ahead the killer might be, or what the consequences would be if he'd made the wrong call.

CHAPTER FIFTY-SEVEN

Elk Meadow, Colorado

Dean McClure hung up when he heard Walker's call go dead.
He stared across the room at the deputy, who stared back.
With Morgan and the FBI on the road, he didn't have time to worry about protocol.

"Deputy, can you find me someone to drive us to those directions? Good. Get in contact with Morgan. Fill him in on the conversation we just had with Walker. Let him know we'll leave from here, and meet him at Gray's Forest."

The deputy gave Dean a nod and went into action.

Dean glanced across the office, recognized the FBI pilot talking with Clay. He hurried over.

"Good to see you again, Mac. I wasn't sure you'd make it through this storm."

"I'd hoped to be more help, but this weather has us grounded."

"Yeah, a pair of eyes in the sky would've been good. But, at least you were able to get some men in here. With any luck the snow will let up enough to get you back in the air.

"I'll be ready."

Dean turned to Clay. "Follow me to that map on the wall over there, and I'll fill you in the conversation I just had with Walker."

By the time they crossed the room, Dean had Clay up to speed. They checked out their destination on the map. It would be quite a drive, especially in this weather. Dean recognized the stress in Clay's expression and figured he looked the same way. So close now. They both wanted this bastard out of circulation, and they didn't want anything to go wrong. The deputy waited for them at the door, ready to head out.

Clay looked up at Dean. "I *have* to be there. You know that, right? Even if I can only wait in the car."

"Wouldn't have it any other way, my friend."

⇒‡ ‡⇐

Morgan steered the car with one hand and called the officer in the car just ahead of him.

"Everett—just got a call from the department. Plans have changed. I need you to go ahead to Walker's place without me," he said as he slowed to make a U-turn on the slippery road, then accelerated in the opposite direction. "Check out the cabin and grounds and set up surveillance. I'm heading to Gray's Forest. McClure believes the killer is headed there with the woman. Walker is far to the south, and headquarters is to the north. I'm smack dab in the middle and have the best chance to get there before the killer makes his move."

"Roger that," Everett said.

Morgan smiled. For once Walker wouldn't be able to upstage him.

⇒‡ ‡⇐

Jack Bailey's pulse raced out of control. He couldn't believe what he had been hearing on the police scanner. It sounded like every officer in the county had been called in, along with the FBI, to hunt down a killer. And if he understood the directions he heard from the sheriff's headquarters, he actually had a good chance of reaching Gray's Forest before anyone else. He appeared to be right in the goddamn middle of it all.

He started his rental and pulled out onto the road, picking up speed as the weather would allow. He put together the puzzle in his mind. Too many pieces were missing for him to comprehend the full story. But he'd figured out the wild woman had been kidnapped. The sheriff's department believed the kidnapper was headed to a particular road leading into Gray's Forest—and he, journalist hero to be, could possibly be the closest person to the road right now.

A career opportunity, if he'd ever seen one.

Time to step it up.

CHAPTER FIFTY-EIGHT

Elk Meadow, Colorado

Walker pushed the gas pedal to the floor and his tires spun, flipping mud and snow as the truck pulled out from the dirt access road. The engine whined in protest as it strained to keep up with the acceleration between shifting gears. Snow pelted the windshield as he worked to subdue his racing thoughts for Nataya's safety and instead concentrated on the man who had taken her, and where they were headed. There would only be time for one plan of attack.

They were far ahead of him. Of that he was sure. He had to find an advantage here—something to make up for lost time. The snow made the pavement dangerous to drive. It would slow the killer down, but unfortunately it affected him as well. He pictured all the roads leading from here to the forest area, thought of the short cuts and side roads. But if the killer had a map or GPS, he could discover them too.

I've got one more option.

The railroad had been built through this area long before the highways were. He knew of one such line that ran along the edge of the foothills—no stoplights or intersections, no other cars. And as for his truck, driving alongside the tracks in the gravel would be far faster to negotiate in the snow than the slippery pavement. He took the next turn-off and headed toward the foothills and the railroad tracks.

Minutes later his truck groaned in protest as it slid down through the loose gravel at a steep angle alongside the tracks, leveling out at the bottom. The land ahead, running alongside the old train tracks, spread out flat before him, and he'd take full advantage of it. The ride would be rougher than the road, but he preferred snow-covered dirt to snow-covered pavement any day.

Every minute counts now.

CHAPTER FIFTY-NINE

Elk Meadow, Colorado

Nataya moaned with the pounding headache as she regained consciousness.

What a horrible dream.

She attempted to open her eyelids, but the moment light entered, the stabbing pain increased. With her eyes closed and her head throbbing, it took her a moment to recognize the noise of an engine running, and the fact she sat in a moving vehicle. None of it made any sense.

She tried to raise a hand to her aching head and discovered her wrists were bound. Involuntarily her eyes flew open, and she squinted against the pain. She tried to move her feet, but her ankles were also bound. A rush of adrenaline chased away any remaining fogginess.

She turned her head and focused on the driver. She couldn't see much of his face, but he had on the same hat and dark glasses as the lost hiker.

He attacked me!

It hadn't been a dream after all. She had landed in a real-life nightmare.

"Who are you?" Nataya demanded, surprised at the strength in her voice.

The man kept his eyes on the road, and said nothing.

"Where are you taking me?"

Again, nothing. Did he mean to frighten her with his silence? She felt more anger than fear. What right did he have to take her away? Besides, when Walker returned and saw she was missing, he would follow and find her.

Follow me to where?

The realization hit her like a physical blow to her gut. How could Walker possibly know where this man was going? They were speeding away in a vehicle. He had no tracks to follow.

Panic rose from the pit of her stomach.

Stay calm...must be able to think...

The mountains loomed closer as Nataya studied the passing landscape. At first they sped along the highway so fast she wanted to close her eyes in fear. But after a nearly disastrous slide on a sharp curve, the man had slowed the vehicle to a crawl. The snowfall intensified every minute, making the man grip the steering wheel until his knuckles were white. Maybe he had never driven in this kind of weather.

Turning from the main highway onto a side road, he pulled off the pavement and stopped. She held her breath.

What now?

But the man only leaned his head down and studied the piece of paper in his lap. She had seen him look at it many times as he drove, and wondered if maybe the paper told him which way to go. But where *were* they going?

She stared out her side window. Given the position of the mountains, maybe they were headed toward the forest. But she'd never seen it from this perspective before, and could only guess... and hope.

If only I can reach the forest.

In the woods she could run away from this man and find the way back to her cave home. Walker could find her there. But the road possibly led off to many other destinations. Her hope dangled like a fragile thread, and she struggled to keep it from breaking.

The man still studied the paper, so she took the opportunity to study *him*. She wanted to get a good look at his face, but the hat pulled down low, the turned up collar, and the dark glasses hid most of his features. Why had this man lied to her, made her think he needed help, then attacked her? She couldn't understand the reason for this.

She reviewed her memory of the incident, recalling how his voice, right before he attacked, had sounded different. It had made her skin prickly, made her... afraid. The spirits had warned her of danger. But now he wouldn't speak. Did he keep silent only to frighten her, or so she wouldn't recognize his voice? She'd never seen this man before today. So why would she know his voice?

Fragments of dreams floated into her consciousness...scenes, places, people's faces. Did he fit into one of them?

But he's real—not a dream.

She closed her eyes. Could it be true the dreams were more real than she believed? What about the vision she saw when Walker took her to the place in the forest called the Sacred Circle? *He* believed it was a real memory. That it did happen to her. She had to consider it—a past she couldn't remember. And maybe this man fit into it somehow. She shuddered and didn't want to remember.

That was it maybe. She didn't want to know her past. She had been content living in the forest, and now she had found happiness being with Walker. He was kind to her and she had grown to trust him.

Why did this man have to take me away?

A tear slid down her cheek and she turned her head so the man couldn't see. She would not let him know of her fear and confusion.

The car lurched forward, and they were on the move again. She quickly swiped the tear away with her sleeve and sat up straight, alert. She had to pay attention.

Walker cannot save me this time. I must save myself.

CHAPTER SIXTY

Elk Meadow, Colorado

Dean glanced at the deputy driving the cruiser. The crazy weather didn't even seem to faze the man.

"In the rush to get on the road, I'm afraid I didn't even ask your name, deputy."

"Harris. Deputy Harris."

"We appreciate you helping us out on this."

"You're welcome. But I have a personal interest, as well.'

Dean looked sideways at the man. "You know Walker?"

Harris nodded.

"Interesting fellow, that man."

"You could say that. If anyone can find that woman, it's Walker."

Dean looked over his shoulder at the back seat. Clay had only made one comment about the "shitty weather" when they loaded the wheelchair into the trunk and got him settled in the car. Since then, he had been quiet. Dean knew him well enough to understand the silence that underscored their tension. So much hinged on catching this guy, not only to hopefully save the life of the woman called Nataya, but also to spare future victims.

It had been too late for all the others. But this time...*this time,* they had a chance to make a difference.

He figured it also bothered Clay they had to put so much trust in Walker's assessment of the situation, that he sensed they had lost control. But Dean had done his own evaluation and agreed with Harris. Walker said he knew where Nataya had been taken when she had been abducted last spring. Dean believed the killer would return to that same place. He would have to, in order to complete the ritual.

He had to trust not only in Walker's instincts, but his own. He learned long ago the importance of removing *ego* from the equation, but it had taken him many more years to be able to *do* it. They had to work as a team now to make this happen.

Snow pummeled the windshield, turning their world into a blur of white, and the wind swirled it around on the road, creating drifts where the driver least expected it. Dean likened it to driving inside one of those snow globes that someone had shaken up. The unavoidable slow pace left him agonizing over the head start the killer had on them. There would be no high-speed chase to beat the bad guy to the final destination. The weather had taken that out of their control, as well.

"This is killing me," Clay said, breaking the silence.

"Yeah, I know what you mean."

Walker's truck bounced and bucked as he shifted gears and pushed it to the limits, maintaining a fragile balance between speeding and keeping control of the vehicle.

The mountains loomed ever larger in his windshield. A good sign. He had covered a great deal of distance in a short period of time. It wouldn't be much farther. This was the edge he needed.

His gut twisted in anticipation. What was happening to Nataya...right now?

Don't fall into that trap. You know better.

He focused instead on the landscape ahead of him. There could be no mistakes.

CHAPTER SIXTY-ONE

Country Roads in Colorado

Mile after mile Nataya sat helpless while her captor took her farther away from Walker's cabin. Questioning the man had only brought more continued silence.

Her inability to gain any knowledge angered her, yet fear of the unknown made anxiety swell up inside. It all threatened to spill over and make her lose control. She didn't know if she would scream in rage, or cry in despair. But she couldn't afford to let either happen. Her best chance for survival rested on staying clearheaded.

She had faced the reality it was up to her to find a way out of this. And yet, deep within rested a small glint of hope...maybe *somehow* Walker would find her.

Snow and wind continued to hammer at the vehicle. The car crept over the asphalt now, the man checking every road sign. At last he turned onto a paved, but narrow road. They headed straight toward the forest now and she stared at it with longing.

The forest. I could find safety there.

She watched it grow larger in her vision, while the road became more indistinct, crumbling in places. The man drove cautiously as the pavement gave way to loose gravel and weeds. She studied what she saw in front of her. This looked familiar. Even with snow covering everything she noticed details, the two huge evergreen trees on either side of the road, and the tall grasses bordering the rows of trees farther in. It reminded her of the place Walker had brought her when they'd come to visit the Sacred Circle. If this turned out to be the same place, she would be able to find her way back to her cave home—if she could get away from the man.

By the time they reached the edge of the forest, the road had disappeared under the snow. Her captor pulled the car forward, underneath a huge pine tree, knocking snow loose from the overhanging branches and covering the vehicle.

Perhaps the man planned to leave the car here, which meant they would be walking. He would *have* to cut the rope from her ankles. She would have a chance to break free and run away. She still had no idea why he held her against her will, but the fact he did, made it clear she was in danger.

Without speaking a word, the man turned off the engine and got out of the vehicle. She tried to follow his movements, but the seatbelt held her too tightly. She could hear him open the trunk of the car. Maybe he would be busy for a while. Seizing the opportunity, she feverishly twisted at the rope binding her wrists, and used her teeth to pull at the cords. There—the slightest give in the knot. Just a few more minutes and she could pull it loose.

A shadow passed over her side window and she looked up, saw her captor come to her door and open it.

No. I need more time!

Anger surged in, taking over all her senses. He leaned in the door and she pulled back away from him, but the seat belt held her—trapped. He brought up a handkerchief, pulled taut, in front of her face. She twisted her head away, But he forced the cloth into her mouth. Fear now co-existed with her anger.

Once he had the gag in place, he unfastened the belt, lifted her out of the seat and carried her in his arms. His steps were hurried, panicky. Maybe he knew people were coming for him.

As he carried her off, she twisted her head enough to sneak a look behind. He wore a backpack now, but between it and the man's shoulder she could just make out dim headlights coming their way through the foggy white of the storm. Could help be coming—*Walker?*

Her captor made his way through the snow, pushing past the tall weeds into the forest. Here, huge evergreens stood close together, blocking the snow with their thick boughs, and for now, keeping the forest floor dry. He hurried through the trees, looking often back over his shoulder to where they had been until they came to a small clearing. He sat her down on the thick bed of pine needles under a tree, and leaned her back against the trunk. He took a rope from his backpack and threaded it around the tree trunk and across her body, with her arms held in front of her. His fingers fumbled in the cold and he muttered under his breath. After knotting the rope, he turned and hurried away, leaving her unable to move.

She heard him sprint over the soft dirt back in the direction they had come, and her brief hope of rescue vanished. If someone was coming here, they were now in danger.

Her head snapped up at the muffled sound of a car door closing. She held her breath and prayed it *wasn't* Walker.

The minutes of silence grew more agonizing as she waited, trapped against the tree. When a bird burst from his sheltered spot among the branches and flew off through the snow, the noise startled her, making her heart thump in fear and hope at the same time.

Someone is coming.

She strained at the ropes. Through the trees she could see a uniform come into view, and for once she felt no fear of it.

Good. Maybe this guy caught the bad man.

She tried to yell through the gag, used her bound feet to kick at the brush next to her, rustling the branches. She saw the man stop and crouch, peering in her direction. He furtively glanced all around, then ran from tree to tree until he stood facing her, his gun drawn.

She watched the man's expression turn from surprise to relief, while a wild sense of joy rushed through her—tears springing into her eyes as she tried to talk through the gag. The officer slipped his gun back into the holster and took a step forward.

"It's okay now," he said as he knelt beside her, reaching for the gag.

That's when she saw her captor. Right behind the officer. Her eyes went wide in horror and flicked back to the officer. His gaze locked onto hers, and she saw that split second of knowing. He began to turn, but her captor grabbed him from behind and in one swift movement slit his throat with a large knife, and dropped him to the ground in front of her.

She screamed into the gag, turning her head away from the gruesome sight before her. But nothing could stop the gurgling sound of the man drowning in his own blood. She felt sick...and tried to suck in big gulps of the cold air through the cloth of the gag.

A rustling noise made her turn back, and she saw the killer wipe blood from the knife in the leaves on the ground. He looked down at the dead officer, mumbling. Her mind, numb with shock, at first couldn't make any sense of what he said. But soon she could comprehend that he kept mentioning the word *father*. She could swear it appeared he was arguing with someone—and it wasn't her.

Does he see and hear spirits?

The man reached down then and took the officer's gun from its holster, hefting it in his hand as if uneasy with the weight of it. He leaned down and checked the officer's ankle, found a smaller gun. Discarding the larger gun on the ground, he kept the smaller one, tucking it into the waistband of his pants.

She heard the sound of another car door closing. A look of exasperation crossed the man's face before he turned and walked away. She remembered Walker explaining guns could be used for hunting.

Someone else is out there, maybe Walker. And he will kill him, too.

And she sat here, helpless to warn the person. She twisted at the ropes binding her until she felt them cut into her flesh, then gave up and closed her eyes. How had the lawman known to come here to this place? Was it just coincidence? Or did he know about this bad man? Did that mean Walker would come here as well?

She soon heard footfalls on the leaves and twigs, coming closer. This time she held still, not breathing, hoping whoever came toward her would miss seeing her and turn away and escape this madman.

But she understood now the man had tied her to a tree where she could be easily seen, to lure someone to her. And the dead man still lay at her feet.

A trap.

She spotted the newcomer, smaller in stature and dressed differently than the deputy, moving slowly through the trees.

It's not Walker! Thank the Spirits.

But she feared for the man coming closer. When he saw her and the body, he stopped and knelt behind a tree, watching for a long while. He moved out from the protection in low profile, with a jerking rush of arms and legs. This man did not wear a gun as the deputy had. Head tucked down, he rushed toward her and slid to the ground, landing next to her. He looked up at her in surprise.

She met him with the same startled look.

The reporter from my cave!

He must have wondered at the look of terror that fell over her face, for he spoke in a soothing voice.

"It's me, remember? You're safe now. The police are coming. Let me untie you."

She shook her head furiously and tried to make him see that *he* wasn't safe. She could tell by his changed expression he understood. He crouched beside her, and pulled the gag from her mouth.

"The man who killed *him*..." she said, indicating the body in front of her, "...has his gun."

The reporter looked down at the weapon lying on the ground, back to Nataya.

"He took a different gun. He will hunt you."

The reporter tried to use his foot to slide the abandoned gun closer, so he could pick it up without moving from his position next to her, but it was too far away. They both watched the trees in silence and she wondered if his heart beat as wildly as hers did right now. She could see his hands trembling.

He turned to her with urgency in his voice. "I need to get you out of here, *now*." He leaned over her and reached for the rope binding her wrists.

She saw him jerk in response to a loud thunderclap. His grip tightened on her wrist for a second, his eyes boring into hers. Shock showed on his face and she saw a bloom of red on the front of his jacket before he crumpled against her.

She screamed—couldn't stop screaming. Her whole being cried out against the brutality and the unfairness of this. Two men had died because they tried to save her.

She heard her captor approach as she sat pinned between the fallen man and the tree trunk. Would this be Walker's fate?

Can I live with the thought that he might die trying to save me?

Was her life worth that? Her screams turned to sobs.

The man pushed the body off hers and quickly untied her from the tree trunk, although he left her wrists and ankles tied. He lifted her into his arms again. He didn't even look at the two men. He left them lying where they had fallen as he carried her away through the trees.

Her captor hurried through the evergreens, soon coming to the open woods. Here, many inches of snow had already accumulated, causing him to struggle while carrying her. Now, he began to mumble to himself again. At first she tried to make sense of the words, but soon gave up.

She turned her attention to her own peril. If those men could find her, Walker would too. At this point, the one thing in the world she understood was she did not want Walker to die trying to rescue her. Which meant she had one option. She had to find a way to escape from this man, before Walker found her.

CHAPTER SIXTY-TWO

Country Roads in Colorado

W alker slowed the truck as he spotted the side road ahead. In a few seconds he would know if he was correct. Know if he still had a chance to save Nataya.

He pulled up to the intersection. There—tire tracks turning onto the seldom-used road. He released a sigh, realizing he had been holding his breath. He started turning the truck onto the road.

But wait—three different sets of tracks!

This road never had that much traffic. Snow had already started filling them in. Had Morgan or McClure gotten here first? They *had* been closer to the forest than he when they got his call. Maybe they had time to set a trap for the killer. Maybe Nataya had already been rescued.

He drove slowly, straining to see ahead in the blowing, shifting whiteness. Not until he neared the forest could he see the vehicles. A Jeep Cherokee sat half hidden under an evergreen tree, a sheriff's cruiser near it, and off to the side another vehicle he didn't recognize.

Stopping his truck well back from the cars, he watched for any movement. Nothing. He rolled down his window and listened. Silence met him. The falling snow blanketed everything, muffing down any noise. All of nature had hunkered down somewhere safe, to wait out the storm.

Walker parked and stepped out of his truck, began making his way forward while watching for footprints, listening for any sounds alerting him to danger. He studied the tire tread tracks in the snow from the three vehicles. The Jeep Cherokee's tracks matched the ones he'd seen on the access road next to his cabin. Yes! He allowed a small part of his brain a second to rejoice, while the rest of his mind stayed focused on the task at hand.

Checking the hood of the sheriff's car, he found the engine still warm, as was the second car. He guessed they had arrived within a half hour's time. He found one set of prints coming from each vehicle, leading to the Cherokee parked under the pines.

So the Jeep Cherokee arrived first. Damn.

So, *if* this indeed was the killer's vehicle, he had a head start on the officer on the scene. So much for his hope the law had arrived first and set a trap for the killer. It might be the other way around. He heard Grandfather's soft whisper. *That includes you, too. Be smarter.*

Walker circled the Cherokee and found the lone set of prints the officer had followed. The boot print looked the same as the ones at his place. His heart rate increased. But these prints weren't as clean and precise. The boot toe had dragged into the snow between each step, as if the man struggled. The snow here was much deeper than at the cabin. It could indicate the killer carried Nataya. Which meant she had to be bound and helpless, or already—no—he wouldn't allow that thought.

He followed the trail to the edge of the forest. As he walked, he continued to listen for any sounds from nature…a warning of people moving through the woods. Where the snow ended under the big evergreens, he discovered a trail of disturbed leaves and dirt. The path would be a natural way for anyone to follow…the easiest route through the trees. That's why he wouldn't take it.

Remembering Grandfather's warning, he moved off trail into the trees where he could stay hidden as he followed along next to where someone had walked.

When he spotted legs protruding from some brush, he stopped. The pant legs and boots looked like a deputy's uniform. He crouched, watching for shadows or movement between the trees around him. Dropping to his belly he slithered his way over the forest floor to the body, mentally preparing himself for what he would find.

Two bodies awaited him. The deputy lay the closest to him, on his side in a pool of blood. The second victim, lying face down, wore no uniform, looked to be a civilian. Walker knelt by the deputy and leaned over to see his face.

Morgan. Dammit.

He sucked in his breath. Morgan's throat had been slit. A knot of rage gathered deep within him. He and Morgan hadn't gotten on, but the man didn't deserve to die like this.

Walker started at the sound of a moan nearby. The second man struggled to get up, collapsed again. Walker crawled over to him, noticing the gunshot wound in his back. Looked like a small caliber bullet made it. He gently turned the man over, supporting him in his arms.

The reporter—how the hell did he end up here?

An exit wound bloodied the reporter's side. The shot had hit the man at an angle, hopefully missing vital organs. So the shooter wasn't a marksman.

Still, he has a gun.

But Morgan had been killed with a knife, not a gun. And his revolver lay on the ground next to him. Walker looked over at Morgan again. He could just make out an ankle holster. The killer must have taken the smaller weapon, and shot the reporter with it. Still, why would he leave the larger gun behind?

Walker considered the killer's options. He would be trying to travel fast. Maybe the larger revolver felt too cumbersome. And maybe…just maybe he believed that no one else followed.

Walker looked back down at the reporter. Dammit—he wanted to tell the guy he'd gotten what he deserved, considering all the trouble he'd caused. But the man needed help and quickly.

"You're going to be all right. I'll get you help. Can you tell me what happened?"

The man grimaced, but forced the gravelly words out. "Found that guy already dead. The wild woman was tied to the tree there. I tried to rescue her. A man shot me…and took off with her."

Nataya!

So she still lived! But before he could enjoy any sense of relief, it hit him. The killer had used her as bait. He must have murdered Morgan right in front of her.

Damn the son of a bitch!

The slow boil of rage now pumped through his body. He let it run its course and flow away from him. He couldn't let his emotions be ruled by this.

Every second counted now, but he couldn't leave this guy here to bleed to death.

Shit.

Hands trembling from frustration, Walker laid the reporter on the ground, propping him up to a more comfortable position to breathe. He walked over to Morgan, undid the man's belt and slid it from the trousers. Returning, he opened the reporter's jacket, pulled a clean bandana from his own pocket and applied it to the exit wound on the man's side. Walker then took the long belt and wrapped it around the reporter's slimmer body, holding the bandage tightly, staunching the blood flow. Then he closed the jacket up the best he could over the contraption he'd made.

The man mumbled. Walker leaned over to better hear him.

"Cell phone…in my back pocket…maybe get a signal."

Walker rolled him slowly to his side, just enough to reach the phone.

"Cavalry is on the way," he whispered as Walker tried to figure out the phone.

The reporter tugged at Walker's sleeve and held out his hand for the phone. "Go rescue the woman," he said. "You've got to save her."

Walker resisted the urge to remind the guy it was his story that had put Nataya in this danger. But he didn't want to waste one more minute of time. He grabbed Morgan's hat and hung it on a branch above the wounded man, to catch the attention of the rescue people. He looked over at Morgan's warm coat. Between the frigid temperature and the loss of blood, he knew the reporter would soon go into shock. He figured saving a life would make up for the fact that he had to mess with evidence. Careful not to disturb Morgan's body any more than necessary, he pulled the man's heavy jacket loose, then tucked it in around the reporter to give him added warmth.

"Go! Go!" the man motioned, as he finished his emergency call for help.

Walker nodded and turned to leave. He passed Morgan's body and stared down at the gun. He hated guns. They went against everything he believed.

CHAPTER SIXTY-THREE

Gray's Forest, Colorado

The snow and wind continued to buffet Nataya and the man as he carried her, stumbling his way through the woods, drifts of snow impeding his progress. The longer he struggled, the more he muttered and rambled. She tuned into his words. Again it sounded as if he talked to someone, and the word *father* was spoken often. *Perhaps it is his father's spirit he talks to.*

But this man held evil in his heart. His actions proved it. How could he communicate with spirits—unless he was a demon? She shivered at the notion, decided instead to concentrate on her options for escape. She could feel the man's arms trembling with the effort to carry her now. He would have to rest soon.

As if reading her thoughts, the man stopped walking. And just as suddenly, stood her on the ground. Perhaps he needed her to walk. The snow continued to get deeper as they moved through the trees now.

She stood still, trembling inside, waiting to see if he would cut her bonds. He took out the long rope from his backpack and tied it to her bound wrists. He grabbed the loose end of it and wrapped it around his hand, to use as a tether. He then pulled out the large knife he had used to kill the deputy. She shuddered at the sight of it. But he did not threaten her with it, instead he knelt to cut the rope binding her ankles.

He's going to cut me free so I can walk!

As he began to cut her bonds, she noticed that the tether kept getting in his way. Finally, he tucked the loose end of it into his waistband. Now his left hand firmly held the rope around her ankles in place, making it easier to cut with the knife in his right hand.

She saw her opportunity. Slowly she raised her arms high over her head, hoping he wouldn't notice. She felt the rope fall from her ankles and he moved to stand up.

Now—while he is off balance!

Swinging her arms downward, adrenaline pumping, she slammed her fists into the back of his head with all her strength.

He fell face forward, the momentum knocking off his glasses and causing him to expel his breath as he hit the ground. She grabbed the loose rope and yanked hard, pulling it from under him.

Her heart racing, she tried to take off, found her feet numbed from being bound for so long. A hand grabbed her ankle. Panic gave her the strength to kick back and break free. She lost her hold on the tether rope, but stumbled forward. She rushed through the trees and brush, wildly pushing aside branches with her bound hands, the rope trailing behind her. Moving through the snow, with her wrists tied in front of her, proved more difficult than she had anticipated. Her step faltered, but she regained her balance and continued on. She could hear him curse and begin crashing through the brush behind her. Terror threatened to blind her.

The snow made for slippery footing, so she skirted the drifts of snow, stayed to the windswept flat ground, avoiding rocks and limbs. She weighed far less than her pursuer, and her agility in the woods began to give her the edge as she outmaneuvered him, slowly increasing her distance.

The snow was falling so thick it almost blinded her, stinging her face with its cold wetness. Her lungs burned. She didn't know how she could keep this up much longer. But panic pushed her harder, the blood pounding in her ears, her own breathing so loud she couldn't hear if the man still followed.

As fear drove her onward through the trees, quick flashes of images assaulted her vision—trees all around her, like now, but dark in the night. Trees at a strange angle, as if she saw them from a sideways position...stars in the sky. She faltered, then remembered the man behind her and renewed her effort.

She had to reach the Sacred Circle where Walker had taken her. From there she could get her bearings and know how to get home. She focused on what she remembered of the meadow, picturing the details in her mind as she fled. But when she did, a flash of memory assaulted her—of waking up next to a fire, cut and bleeding. With it came a stab of pain in her head, causing her to stumble, blinding her for a moment. She regained her balance and rushed forward again, but with a new realization.

She could no longer believe these were only nightmares. She had to face the fact they were memories trying to surface. Somewhere in her past these things *did* happen. Someone had done that to her...cut her and left her bleeding. How could anyone be that cruel, hold that much hate in their heart?

The demon man chasing me.

Maybe *he* had been the one. She couldn't remember—didn't *want* to remember, but couldn't dismiss the reality of it. Why else would he bring her here? She gasped.

What if that's his plan—to take me there again?

She began to swerve away from where she knew the meadow lay, suddenly desperate to be as far from it as she could. A sense of dread followed her, compelling her to glance back. She saw nothing. She looked ahead again with new hope that she had lost him.

The wind-driven snow blasted harder, forcing her to slow. She broke through the drifts as quickly as her cold feet and strength allowed. The moccasins were heavy with moisture now, making every step a struggle.

A movement in the forest to her right made her turn. Her breath caught when she saw a shadow moving through the snow and trees.

It's him.

He also struggled through the snow, parallel to her, but he kept pace with her.

Running stride for stride, he began veering toward her, shortening the distance between them. She angled to her left to avoid him, then realized that he'd purposely herded her back toward the meadow. She had to get past him, to go back the other way.

But his headlong rush soon brought him within arm's distance. The moment he could touch her, she slammed to an abrupt halt, darting behind him and to the right. She saw him twist and dive at her, missing.

Free!

Then she felt the tether rope pull taut. He must have managed to grab the loose end of the rope. It jerked her feet out from under her. She fell hard.

She attempted to scramble to her feet, but he threw himself into her, knocking her to the ground again. She fought against him with all her strength, kicking and screaming. She fought out of fear. And she fought out of anger.

He has no right!

⊨ ⊩

Walker stopped in his tracks and listened. He could hear a woman's cries reverberating through the trees.

Nataya!

He started to run, then halted his movements and listened again.

She's screaming in anger. Those aren't the screams of someone being tortured.

But could he reach her before that changed? The echoes made it impossible to tell from which direction they came, while the snow muffled the sounds enough to distort distance.

His heart racing, he sprinted forward, following the snow-covered tracks. Nataya's screams had stopped long before he discovered sign in the snow of a scuffle. Her tracks led off from the man's. She had escaped him.

Good for her.

But, as he followed her footprints, he could see the killer did as well.

CHAPTER SIXTY-FOUR

Gray's Forest, Colorado

Nataya lay in the snow, flat on her back, her captor kneeling over her. One knee pressed into her throat, pinning her head to the ground, half choking her. In this position, with her wrists still bound, she could barely move her arms. She tried kicking, but any struggle brought more pressure to her throat. She could feel him untie the tether rope from her wrist and use it to bind her ankles.

A wave of helplessness washed over her. That had been her chance. He had her now. She choked back a sob of frustration.

So close. I was so close.

He pulled her to a sitting position as he stood up. Nataya raised her head, looked up at him, and gasped. With the glasses missing, she could at last see his face. She was staring into black eyes. The same eyes and face as in her nightmares.

"I saw your face…in dreams," she stammered, while trying to slide backwards over the ground, her feet pushing and slipping in the snow and dirt. She backed into a tree, the trunk stopping her, and stared at him.

"So now you remember...*Jenny*?"

A white-hot blade of pain shot through her head. She closed her eyes to the agony, which brought a flurry of scenes racing through her mind, tumbling in upon her, unbidden, like snapshots in time.

She could see the man kneeling over her. He lifts her in his arms and carries her into the woods...and the dark. Terror surrounds her...fills her mind, until nothing else remains...

"Stop it!" She yelled, and opened her eyes to make the visions go away. The pain slowly subsided as she gasped for breath. What just happened? The man in her nightmares stood before her. And he was real—not a dream. A sickly bile rose in her throat.

He appeared untouched by her agony. The realization pressed in on her chest, making it difficult to breathe. But deep inside a core of rage erupted, and she latched onto it with all her being, letting it expand and fill her with strength. It gave her something solid to cling to in this surreal world.

Using the tree for support, she pushed herself up off the ground and leaned against the trunk, defiantly facing her captor. Inside, she felt none of the confidence she tried to portray. The onslaught of visions had left her confused, except for one thing. This man meant to harm her. *Again.*

"I'm not going anywhere with you," she said, willing her voice not to shake.

He stared at her, not appearing to even hear her as he moved closer. She stretched out her arms in front of her. Her wrists still bound, she pushed at his chest with her hands and struggled against him, trying to keep him away. And still he moved closer. His face filled her vision, the black eyes piercing and cold.

Her mind began to fill with images from her visions. She could not control them.

The bright orange flames in the background, blackness beyond. Then his face before her—and she can't move—cannot get away. The paralyzing sensation of total terror.

Then she saw what had been missing from her visions, until now.

The knife!

No! She didn't want to see it—*couldn't bear* to see it.

Her knees gave way and her eyes rolled back in her head.

Walker had hoped to take a shortcut straight to the meadow, to save time and catch up to Nataya, but when she had escaped and fled from the man, her tracks ran so erratically through the woods, he didn't dare go off trail. He had no idea where they might end up.

To his dismay, he soon found where the man had caught up with her. There had been a struggle and she had put up a fight. That must have been when he heard the yelling.

Now there were only the man's prints, but Walker could tell he carried Nataya. He had to believe she was still alive. There has been no telltale blood in the snow. But she was once again a captive.

At least this will slow the killer's progress.

His own panic bubbled below the surface of his consciousness. He could only imagine what she must be experiencing. He wanted her to know all was not lost, to keep fighting for her life.

She needs hope, came Grandfather's voice in his mind.

Walker stopped and listened to the silence of the woods. On impulse, he cupped his hands to his mouth and called out an imitation of a great-horned owl. He and Nataya had practiced it often. She would know an owl hooting during this time of day would be unusual. If she heard it, she might realize the call came from him. But more importantly, that he followed.

The rocking motion of movement came to her first, as Nataya came to from blacking out. The man carried her again, and she could hear the noise of snow crunching underfoot. She didn't want him to know she was awake, so she kept up the act. Besides, her body swaying as dead weight in his arms made it more difficult for him to carry her through the woods. She would use whatever tactic she could to slow their progress. If her memories were true, her only hope would be to think of a new escape plan before they reached the meadow.

It took her a moment to realize that, through the silence of the forest, she had heard an owl call. It sounded so far away. But there—she heard it again.

It's too early in the day to hear an owl, and in this weather.

She perked up. The third time she heard it, she knew.

Walker! He follows us.

So, the fact those others found her had not been an accident. And Walker had found her as well. But somehow he had managed not to get killed, like the other two did. Then another thought came.

He wants me to know there is hope.

Tears filled her closed eyes and she didn't try to stop them. Energy pumped through her veins, schemes rapidly running through her mind. Walker would want her to stall the man's progress every possible chance she got. She had to give him time to catch up with them.

But he sounded so far away.

CHAPTER SIXTY-FIVE

Gray's Forest, Colorado

Dean glanced sideways and realized everyone in the patrol car leaned forward in their seats, as if doing so would help them to better see through the blowing snow at the windshield.

"This is it," Deputy Harris said, as he turned the car onto a decrepit old side road. He drove slowly, not only due to the snow, but because of the crumbling asphalt. The forest lay directly ahead and Dean could tell they followed more than one set of tire tracks, although the blowing drifts had nearly covered them.

Nearing the end of the road, he saw Walker's truck parked behind a sheriff's car, and another car sitting close by.

"That's Morgan's unit," the deputy said. "Don't recognize that car settin' next to it, though. Could be our killer. I'll call in the plates."

Clay pointed over the back seat toward the forest. "Look. There's another vehicle, under that evergreen."

Dean nodded. "It's a Jeep Cherokee. That would have the wheel base width to match the tracks Walker described out at his cabin."

Deputy Harris parked next to Walker's truck and got out, along with Dean. They checked each car, then Dean returned and told Clay, "Looks like Walker had it right. A lone set of tracks from the Cherokee. The Art Critic would have the woman tied and gagged. That matches what we know of his past abductions. He'd be carrying her at this point. Everyone's prints head to the forest, following the ones from the Cherokee."

Harris jogged over then to join Dean and Clay. "McClure. Just got a call from headquarters. They received a 911 from out here on some guy's cell. Said there's one officer down. And the civilian who called in has a gunshot wound. He asked for paramedics—and no siren."

"Shit." Dean punched the side of the car. "Well, that explains this extra car. Look—Clay, you watch for the paramedics. Harris, you and I can head in and find these guys. Maybe we can do something until the medics arrive."

"Sounds good," Harris said. "The rescue unit will have a hell of a time getting here with these road conditions—and the chopper is still grounded. I'll grab the first aid kit and a bottle of water from the cruiser."

Following the tracks in the snow, Dean and Harris hurried toward the dense trees, holding their voices low as they talked about what might be waiting ahead.

"We've got to be smart, Harris. Sounds like the Art Critic has already gotten two men. He'll kill whoever gets in his way now. *Someone* had to make that 911 call, so maybe Walker arrived after these two guys were attacked. Maybe he's still out there with the victims, or tracking the killer."

"Yeah, but maybe not. We don't know for sure that *he* is even still alive."

"Exactly. We've got to go in with caution."

"Agreed."

Snow had begun to find its way between the thick boughs overhead to the forest floor as they walked into the dense forest. But they could still see where someone had walked through the leaves and pine needles. Dean pulled his gun from his shoulder holster, noting that Harris had already drawn his weapon. They followed the path, moving slowly, each man watching for any movement between the stands of trees, any sign they were not alone. An eerie silence surrounded them.

Harris spotted the hat on the tree limb...nudged Dean and pointed to it. They both sprinted from tree to tree to reach their destination.

Harris reached Morgan first, holstered his gun and knelt by the body. He didn't say a word, but when he stood up, his dark eyes smoldered against the now ashen hue of his face. He shook his head and handed the first aid kit and water bottle to Dean, who hurried over to the civilian lying on the ground.

The young man looked up at Dean and smiled, even as his teeth chattered. Dean eased him up and held the water bottle to his lips.

"What's your name, young man—and what the hell are you doing out here?"

"Jack ...Jack Bailey. I'm a reporter. Heard about the kidnapping on my scanner...tried to save the woman...but he shot me."

"Who shot you?"

"Some guy. I didn't see him. After he shot me, he took the woman. I played dead."

"So, you saw her. She's still alive?"

"Yeah. When I saw her she was."

"Where's Walker?"

"Who's Walker, that Indian guy?"

"Yeah. Did you see him?"

"He helped me...then he went after the kidnaper and the woman. Hope he found her."

Dean and Harris patched Jack up as best as they could, carried him out of the forest and back to the cruiser. If they could keep him warm, they agreed he had a good change until the medics arrived.

They moved Clay up to the front passenger seat and helped Jack stretch out on the full back seat. Harris started the car and turned on the heater, then slid out to let Dean get in. Dean filled Clay in on what little they knew, then asked him. "I need you to keep an eye on Jack here and watch for the paramedics."

"Sure. I take it that means you two are going back in?"

"Yeah," Dean said and nodded. "This snow is quickly covering the tracks. We need to go while we can still see a hint of them. With this storm, who knows how long it will take the others to get here. The roads must be really nasty by now. If we wait, we'll lose him."

Dean exited the cruiser and walked over to where the deputy waited.

"Let's go get this bastard," Harris said.

CHAPTER SIXTY-SIX

Gray's Forest, Colorado

Snowflakes clung to Nataya's lashes as she slowly opened her eyes to see treetops overhead. The snow fell crazily between them, flying straight down toward her, giving her the illusion she floated up toward the sky—and freedom.

But the steady plodding walk of her captor forced her thoughts back to the reality of her peril. She struggled to keep the fear in check.

Somewhere, Walker follows.

Her view above changed and she turned her head to see where they were. They stood at the edge of the forest, the open meadow spread out before them. Even with snow covering everything, she recognized it. The same sense of dread filled her as it had when Walker first brought her here, but now it spread, becoming icy tendrils of horror crawling through her body, paralyzing her.

Her captor carried her across the open space to the centermost tree, stood her on the ground, and leaned her back against the trunk. He held her against it while he stared at her with those black eyes, studying her.

Flashes of memory sliced through her mind. She squeezed her eyes shut to block out the view triggering them. But now they flowed in unbidden, vision after vision, faster and faster, assaulting her without pity. She had no control—could not stop the escalating process as the flashes rolled together until they became one seamless stream of visuals and sound.

The vision played out in excruciating detail through her mind. She relived the agonizing realization that she lay bound, gagged and helpless on the floor of a van, then the sickness in the pit of her stomach while the man carried her through the woods. Every nuance of the memory came clear to her, being bound to the tree, the flames in the darkness, the stark terror rushing through her as it became clear what the madman planned to do to her.

Then the torturous pain of the knife cutting into her flesh… over…and over.

I can't do this again. It must stop!

She screamed. Her knees buckled and the man lost his grip on her as she slid down the tree to the ground.

Walker's head jerked up at the sound of the scream echoing through the trees. The anguish of that cry made him sway with dizziness.

By the spirits above, am I too late?

Panic pumped through his body with the realization that he might have met defeat. He scrambled through the trees and brush, unmindful of the noise he created. He pushed ahead, running blindly, until his carelessness caused him to trip. He fell forward, hard, knocking his breath away.

He lay on the ground gasping for air.

Quietly at first, then more distinctly, he heard Grandfather's voice, calm and full of purpose. *Step outside the emotion. Focus on the task at hand.*

It took all his years of training and experience to store away the panic to a place deep within, and second by second clear his mind, and push his fears aside.

I have to believe she still lives. I have to.

A drunk had robbed him of Haiwi. He damn well wasn't going to let this killer take Nataya, too. He stood up. He would use everything he had learned in life for this one moment in time.

CHAPTER SIXTY-SEVEN

Gray's Forest, Colorado

Nataya awoke shivering, teeth chattering and her head throbbing. Her body sagged against restraints holding her upright. She could feel the bark of a tree against her back. Her coat and sweater had been removed, leaving her torso exposed. She couldn't tell if she shook more from the cold rushing over her skin or from the fear threatening to overwhelm her.

How long was I out?

It took such effort to raise her head. When she did, she stared directly into her captor's face and gasped.

He held a dagger and brought it toward her. Her breath caught.

Where is Walker?

The man studied her body, the blade hovering inches from her skin. She found her voice, even though it came out as more of a choked whisper. "You don't have to do this."

The man didn't look at her face. Kept starting at the scars on her torso. "The ceremony must be done."

She felt the tip of the dagger touch her, the metal cold against her flesh. She trembled and held her breath, preparing for the pain again. But instead, she felt only the tug of sharp metal skimming over her skin as he began to lightly trace the scar lines on her torso with the tip of the blade. When finished, the man slid the dagger into a sheath and stood in silence.

Nataya released her breath in relief.

The man opened his coat and pulled a photo from his shirt pocket. He held it with reverence, and brought it to his lips.

He must love the person in the photo.

It seemed strange to think him capable of that emotion. And why did he look at first the photo and then at her, as if comparing her to it? She watched him tuck the photo away and tried to stall for time, saying, "You can let me go now. I won't tell anyone about you."

He looked at her in such a way that she wasn't sure he even saw her anymore. "Must complete the ceremony...redemption," he muttered. "William must not fail this time."

The blood pounded in her head. What did he mean—must *complete* the ceremony?

What more does he plan to do to me?

Walker crept through the last few trees and stopped at the edge of the meadow, staying hidden in the brush and shadows. He could see Nataya bound to the lone tree in front of the man, her coat removed and torso exposed. But he didn't see any blood, and her head moved ever so slightly.

She still lives!

The realization brought on a dizzy euphoria.

Focus—she is not yet safe.

Walker studied the man...young... athletic-looking. He would no doubt be strong. But his movements revealed he remained absorbed with the woman. The man did not take in his surroundings, or even appear to be worried about someone following him. Walker studied the situation. He could quietly work his way around behind the man, and take him by surprise.

But as he watched, the man opened a backpack sitting on the ground, and pulled a large ornate dagger from it. Walker's hand went to his own knife.

I'm too far away.

And he wouldn't have time to double back behind the guy, to get closer.

A cold sweat of desperation fell over him. Then he heard Grandfather's calm voice. *To outsmart your opponent, you must do the opposite of what is expected of you...even by yourself.*

Nataya watched the glaze slide away from the man's eyes, and a cold, penetrating stare remain. It frightened her even more.

What has happened to Walker?

She made one last desperate attempt to stall the inevitable.

"Your father spirit you talk to...he shouldn't blame you... it wasn't your fault," she said, tears rolling down her cheeks. She hoped he believed the tears were for him, tears that something so ghastly had happened to turn him into this monster. But in truth she wept for her own life. She wasn't ready to give it up.

The man hesitated. He studied her and mumbled. "*He* made her sad. She took her own life because of *him*. Not William's fault..."

"It was not your fault. You did nothing wrong."

"William...I loved her. She loved me. She understood...no one else did." A sob escaped and he choked out the next word. "Mother." His head hung low and swayed as if unbalanced.

But just as quickly his head jerked up, as if hearing someone else speak. He brought his focus back to her and yelled. "No—you will not trick me again. I will not let fear stop me this time. The ceremony must be finished."

He sheathed the knife and strode to her, grabbed the gag that still lay around her neck and pulled it back up into her mouth, so she couldn't speak any more. He pulled out the dagger again, but instead of using it on her, he began to cut her loose from the tree. Nataya's heart pounded in her chest in fear and hope—maybe she had a chance yet to escape.

But he left her wrists and ankles tied and lifted her in his arms only long enough to carry her away from the tree and place her on the ground. The moment her back touched the wet coldness, she began to twist her body and push with her bound feet, sliding in the snow, attempting to put distance between her and this man who called himself William.

Where is Walker? I must stall for time!

But he pressed his knee into her thighs, using his weight to pin her to the ground. With one hand, he pulled her bound wrists above her head and pushed them into the snow until they were trapped against the earth. She couldn't move. In his other hand, he raised the dagger high above her.

She closed her eyes. How could her heart pound so hard and not burst? She found herself cognizant of everything that touched her senses, snowflakes falling on her face, the fresh cleanness of the cool air, wind blowing her hair. Then she caught another sound. Above her, William droned words she did not understand, using a rhythmic cadence.

Part of his ceremony?

A flash of memory sliced through her mind. The flames in the night, searing pain, helplessness. But in the darkness, she heard *herself* speak…weak, mumbling at first, then stronger and stronger, as if drums beat out the rhythm. She could not understand the words, yet even now they were familiar. She sensed strength coming into her body, replacing the fear. In the firelight she saw the man's eyes fill with terror as he looked at her and beyond to the trees behind her. He stood trembling, then dropped the knife, turned and fled in the opposite direction.

What did I say that so frightened him? What did he see behind me?

Now she understood why he had gagged her again.

He's afraid I'll start chanting again.

Hope slid away with the tear running down her cheek. William's droning words filled her mind, until she heard Walker's voice.

"Drop the knife!"

Her eyes flew open and she turned her head toward the sound.

He stepped out from the shadows of the trees, holding a gun leveled at William's chest. He repeated his demand that the man drop his knife. She held her breath as he moved toward them, steadily closing the distance between them, the gun not wavering.

But he doesn't use the gun.

William must have also sensed Walker's reluctance to shoot. He grabbed Nataya and pulled her up against his body as a shield, the blade against her throat.

"No, *you* drop the gun. Or you can watch me cut her."

Walker continued forward, the gun still leveled at them. He was within thirty feet of them now.

William pushed the dagger tip into Nataya's throat. She felt the skin break and a trickle of blood spill down. She held her breath.

"Stop right there! Or you watch her die—now!"

Walker halted. She could read the anger and determination in his stance. The gag stopped her from shouting to him to not give in to the demands. She believed the man wouldn't kill her this way. He kept talking about a ceremony—something important he had to finish.

It pained her to watch Walker's shoulders sag in defeat. She understood what it cost him as he hesitated. He slowly lowered the gun, leaning down to place it on the ground. She watched his hand inch toward his ankle, where he wore a knife.

The moment Walker laid the gun on the snow-covered ground, William shoved her aside and dropped his knife. In one swift move, he stood, pulled the revolver from his waistband and raised the gun toward Walker. She screamed into the gag.

She saw Walker's knife flicker through the air amid the gunshots, as he dove for cover—then fell limply into the snow.

CHAPTER SIXTY-EIGHT

Gray's Forest, Colorado

Dean McClure and Deputy Harris plodded forward through the trees. The falling snow continued to obscure their view. It blanketed everything in sight and muffled their footsteps. Dean likened the silence to having cotton stuffed into his ears. Until he heard the unmistakable sound of gunshots echoing through the trees.

Dean instinctively raised his weapon at the sound of gunfire, heard Harris mutter a curse and do the same. But the way the noise ricocheted through the trees told him the shots weren't close by.

Harris hurriedly called in to report that shots were fired. Then quiet settled in again.

He told Dean, "Our back-up just turned onto the road to the forest. It won't be long before they're here."

"We can't wait for them. Who knows what's going on up ahead."

"Couldn't agree more. Let's go."

CHAPTER SIXTY-NINE

Gray's Forest, Colorado

The reverberating gunshots faded to quiet. Lying on the ground, Nataya turned her head toward an odd moaning next to her. William stared down—at Walker's knife protruding from his thigh. He gave a quick glance out to where Walker lay, and her gaze followed. Her heart jumped in panic at the sight of his still form. She wanted to believe he yet lived. But how could he help her now? She sneaked a look at William, now too occupied with his own situation to notice her. Walker had given her the break she needed, but could she save herself from this madman?

Scanning the ground around her, she saw William's discarded dagger, almost within her reach. With her wrists and ankles still tied, she snaked her body toward the blade. She clasp the dagger handle with her bound hands and slid it to her, all the while slowly rolling her body to the side. She didn't want to attract William's attention.

She turned her head to see him yank Walker's knife from his thigh. He groaned and dropped to his knees. Blood gushed from the wound, saturating the pants material and staining the snow a bright crimson. So much blood. If she could stall long enough maybe the man would die, like the deputy had.

She tucked her knees to her chest in a fetal position to hide the dagger from William's view. Then another idea came to her and she used her bound hands to pull the gag from her mouth. She needed every advantage available now.

Still holding Walker's knife in his hand, he stared up to the sky and began to yell. "See? I passed the test. I'm not afraid!" Then he turned to face her.

The wildness in his eyes frightened her and she struggled to quiet the pounding in her head, to remember what she'd heard the man say during in his ramblings. "Of course you're not afraid. He lied to you, William."

The man stared at her, but didn't speak, so she continued. "Your mother loved you...more than anyone else. She alone understood."

William began to limp closer to her, still holding the knife, remaining silent, but his eyes on her.

"You're father lied to you, William. It was not your fault."

William fell to his knees at her feet. His arm slack, but his hand still grasped the knife.

It had taken immense will power to allow him move close enough to touch her. Adrenaline pulsed through her body as she gathered her courage. She'd need speed and strength to pull this off.

William opened his mouth to speak, but before he could get the words out she flipped to her back and thrust her legs out straight, striking William with her feet—square in his chest—the force knocking him backward. He lost his balance and fell to his side, the knife flying from his outstretched hand.

The momentum of the attack let her rock her body upward onto her knees, William's dagger in her hands. Using her forearms and knees, she scrambled to William's body. She could see his out-stretched hand reaching for Walker's fallen knife. She stabbed his hand with her blade, jerked it out and used the blade to knock the other knife further away. William screamed, rolled onto his back to face her with an expression of pure rage. With both hands, she raised the dagger high above him.

But William snagged her bound wrists with his uninjured hand. He squeezed her wrists together, grinding bone against bone. Moaning, she willed herself not to drop the dagger.

The two of them remained locked in this duel, trembling with tension. But slowly, insidiously, she felt his strength pushing her arms back, pushing her entire body backward. They were both on their knees now, facing each other, his face inches from hers. He pushed out the words between breaths.

"You tried to trick me. Another test. But I will not fail this time."

She braced her toes and knees against the ground and pro-pelled herself into him, surprising him, forcing him back for a second. Surely the loss of blood would soon affect him. She had to hold out a little longer.

But he brought up his injured hand to regain his hold on her and shoved her backwards. Without her arms and hands to stop the momentum backwards, and no match for his strength, she fell back onto the ground, her knees raised to block him.

It only took him a moment to crouch over her, pushing her legs flat and pinning her body to the ground. She focused on keep-ing the blade aimed at his chest. But to her horror, he began to force her hands to tilt the dagger blade away from him and toward herself.

Her arms shook with the effort to stop him, but now the blade pointed straight down, the blood from his wounded hand drip-ping to the spot on her chest where the dagger aimed.

William spoke through clenched teeth. "Now, I finish the cer-emony. Now I find redemption." He straightened his back, pulling his hands up, hers locked in his grasp, and prepared to thrust the knife downward.

A gunshot blast filled the air.

William jerked and stopped struggling, his eyes growing wide in surprise.

With all her remaining strength, Nataya swung her arms to her right, rolling to her side, the knife falling safely on the ground next to her, as well as William. He lay next to her, his eyes staring straight into hers. A spittle of blood formed on his lips when he tried to laugh, instead a gurgling noise came from his throat. She watched him struggle to speak.

"Free...of him..." The breath escaped from his lips in a raspy hiss and stopped.

She pushed herself up, looking away from his open, cold gaze and sucked in the frigid air—trying to quell the rising nausea.

She turned toward where she thought the gunshot had come from and saw Walker on his belly, not more than ten feet away, still holding the revolver. His head lay on the snow. Behind him she could see the disturbed snow trail, speckled with red, where he had crawled closer.

She used the dagger and sawed at the rope tied around her ankles. Once free, she lurched forward, stumbled, then gained her balance and ran to where Walker lay in the snow.

She sucked in a gasp when she saw the dark crimson saturating the back of his coat. She knelt beside him and he stirred, rolling to his side with a grimace.

"It was the only way..." he said, his fingers releasing his hold on the revolver. He nodded toward her wrists. "Let me cut you free."

Only then did she realize she still held the dagger. She let him take the blade. He used only one hand and gritted his teeth in pain, but managed to slice through the rope. When he finished, she rubbed at her wrists and glanced around them, forming a plan.

"I want to get you over to the tree. Can you walk if I support you?"

Walker nodded. "But first, go get your coat. You're shivering."

She hurried back to where her sweater and coat lay on the ground, and slipped them on, snuggling into the warmth against the snow and wind. She rushed back to Walker and helped him to his feet. He leaned on her for support, but still struggled to make much progress. When they passed close to William's body he motioned he wanted to stop. She supported him as he knelt beside the fallen man. Walker checked for a pulse, then reached up to close the man's eyelids, but stopped. He leaned over and stared.

Nataya knelt beside him. "What is it?"

"Contacts. He's wearing black contact lens. That's why his eyes scared you so much in your dreams."

"I don't understand."

"He was only a flesh and blood man, Nataya—an evil man, but no demon."

He picked up his knife from the ground and cleaned the blood off in the white snow using slow, even strokes.

"I hate it that he even held my knife in his hand..."

She supported him as he stood again slowly, weaving slightly, then guided him over to sit down next to the lone tree. She knelt beside him, helping him lean back against the trunk, and winced at the pain she saw in his eyes. She had to stop the bleeding.

Kneeling beside him, she opened his coat and unbuttoned his shirt, surprised to see a small hole just below his shoulder. It made no sense to her, there was so much blood on the back of his coat. She heard Walker speak and leaned in closer.

"Tell me what you see."

"A small hole here." She touched the place on his chest.

"Okay. Look at my back."

She moved to better see where he indicated and peered under the shirt. "There is a bigger hole here. Lots of blood."

"Good. The bullet went all the way through."

She didn't know what this all meant, except she sensed she needed to stop the bleeding. Looking around at the resources at hand, she picked up the dagger again and reached into her open coat to the sweater. She cut off two large sections of the thick material, then remembered the gag, now loose around her neck, and untied it.

She re-buttoned his shirt and carefully pressed one piece of the sweater material against the smaller wound. She had him hold the cloth while she applied the second piece to the larger wound on his back. As she worked, she talked to keep his mind off the pain.

"Thank you, Walker, for coming for me. And for giving me the sign to keep hope."

"You heard the owl call then?"

"Yes." She wrapped the bandana under his arm and over his shoulder, to press the pads of material in place. She knotted it firmly and buttoned his coat back up. "You saved my life."

"I only played a small part. You fought hard and used your wits against that man. I'm so very proud of you."

"I was ready to kill him." Her throat tightened and she choked back the sudden emotion.

Walker's hand squeezed her arm. "He gave you no choice."

"But, you killed him…to save me."

"Yes. It's a burden to live with, taking another's life…for revenge…or even in self-defense. But I'm glad I could take that burden for you."

With his good arm, he pulled her firmly against him. Surprised at this show of affection, she found her own arms encircling him, careful of his injury.

He murmured into her ear, "It's over, Nataya."

She looked again over toward William's body, the snow clinging to it, the earth already claiming it back. All the emotions of the day jumbled together as tears sprang to her eyes.

He whispered. "Let it out, so you can heal."

She turned her face into Walker's coat and let the sobs come, releasing all the pent-up fear, memories of pain, and the relief that she yet lived…and so did he.

When she had gained back control, she looked up at him, saw wetness in his eyes as well and wondered at it.

"Thank you." She leaned against him. He still shivered, so she wrapped her arms around him, holding him tighter and trying to warm his body with hers. But nothing stopped his shaking.

She felt him raise his hand and gently run his fingers through her hair.

"The loss of blood makes me shiver, not the cold. I don't know that help is coming, Nataya…not in time. You need to get me to the hosp—Medicine Lodge."

He spoke with great effort. Her heart pounded in panic as she thought of the two bodies lying at edge of the woods. Maybe no one else knew they were out here.

"Tell me what to do to help."

"We need to walk out…before this weather traps us here," he said.

She didn't want to move him, but knew he spoke the truth. The snow and wind had not let up and drifts continued to accumulate.

With great effort she helped him stand up. With his good arm around her shoulders for support, they began their slow trek across the meadow and into the trees.

Please, mukua…let us make it in time.

⟞╪ ╪⟝

Walker focused every muscle into putting one foot in front of the other. The earth below his feet kept tilting at odd angles, the drifts of snow making him stumble. Wind and snow pushed at him. A vague memory came to him, of his phone call earlier. Had it been only hours ago—or had days passed? He didn't know. He wanted to tell Nataya that one person yet knew where they were, but he couldn't find the breath to speak. And now, even the blinding white snow turned black in his peripheral vision.

CHAPTER SEVENTY

Gray's Forest, Colorado

B etween the cold wind, and deep drifts of snow Dean struggled
through, he questioned more than once why he thought at his
age it was okay to go trudging off into the wilderness.

You're just an old fool.

Movement ahead made him and Deputy Harris quickly take
shelter behind some trees. Weapons ready, they watched the shad-
owy figures emerge through the falling snow.

"Walker!" Harris shouted.

As Dean and Harris hurried toward them, Walker stopped.
His knees buckled and Nataya could no longer support his weight.
Harris grabbed him and helped him to the ground, while Dean
aided Nataya in supporting his back.

"We heard shots," Dean said noticing how Walker struggled for
breath, his face drawn in pain.

"He's hurt...the right shoulder. I've wrapped it the best I could.
But he has lost so much blood."

"We've got to get him some medical attention."

"He's…dead," Walker said, his voice hoarse. "Had to kill him… no choice."

"Save your breath, Walker. Nataya can fill us in."

Nataya looked up at Dean. "How do you know who I am?"

But Walker spoke before Dean could answer.

"Have to…tell you something, Nataya."

"Save your strength," Dean said, but Walker continued.

"This man…and his friend…told me about the killer. I wouldn't have known…where to look for you…"

"Shhhh…enough," she said. "Save your strength now." She looked up at Dean with wide eyes. "Is this true? But how—?"

"I promise to explain everything to you later. Where's the body?"

"Straight through there. In a meadow, next to a lone tree."

Deputy Harris stepped away, and Dean heard him in the background, giving directions over his phone to the officers coming in behind them. He saw the concern for Walker in Nataya's eyes. "Don't worry. Deputy Harris and I will help you get him out of here."

Harris rushed over after ending the call. "McClure, I suppose you want to see the body. You've waited a long time for this."

Dean gazed past Harris to the woods, then back to Walker. "The Art Critic isn't going anywhere—more important to get Walker medical help."

Both men helped Walker to his feet. With one man supporting him on either side, Walker appeared to breathe a little easier.

Nataya fell in step next to Dean and he looked over at her.

"I promised to explain some things to you. I'll tell you about it as we walk. My friend, Clay, and you have quite a bit in common…"

⊨⊨

The exhausted group emerged from the stillness of the forest to where they had first entered, and walked into the midst of chaos. Flashing lights illuminated the driving snow, people and patrol cars and rescue trucks scattered about the area. Nataya halted, but Dean gave her a nod of encouragement. "Just stay with me."

Still, she didn't move.

"Nataya. We have to get Walker medical help." She nodded at that.

Dean shouted to a couple of men who came running over from a rescue unit. "Take good care of this man," he said, releasing Walker to them. "He's lost a lot of blood and is probably in shock. Come get me before you take off with him. I'll be right over there." He gestured toward a car sitting outside the mass of vehicles.

Harris nodded to Dean. "You go ahead. I'll stay behind to answer questions."

⊷ ⊷

Walker struggled to maintain consciousness. He could sense his body trying to shut down the sensory overload. Engines revved, people barked orders, and floodlights lit up the driving snow against the darkening sky. But through the chaos he noticed Nataya being led away. Where were they taking her? He attempted to call out to her, but hands gently pushed him back against the gurney and placed an oxygen mask over his nose and mouth. He turned his head and strained to see around the men attending him. He had to keep her in sight.

⊷ ⊷

Nataya looked back over her shoulder at Walker being strapped to a gurney. The man named Dean held her arm and encouraged her forward.

"Don't worry. They'll take good care of him, and then you can ride with him to the hospital. This will only take a moment. I want you to meet my friend."

He led the way toward a car and she watched in amazement at the sheer number of people scurrying about. Two men emerged from the trees carrying a stretcher. Her eyes filled with tears.

"There were two men. They died trying to save me—"

"Only one…and he died doing his job," Dean interrupted.

Nataya wondered at this new world she had been thrust into. What had happened to the peace and serenity of her life alone in the forest? And at that moment she knew she would never be able to return to such innocence.

As they approached the car, a door flew open and she could see a young man in the passenger seat. He shouted, "Damn good thing you managed to stay alive out there! I didn't want to have to go to hell and drag you back again."

Dean laughed and shook his head. "I take it they've already taken Jack to the hospital?"

"Yeah, sounds like he has a good chance to make it. I heard Walker got our guy, but got shot in the process. Is he going to be okay?"

Nataya stepped up beside Dean, as he replied. "Yeah, he'll get excellent care. We'll make sure of it, won't we?"

Clay nodded and stared at her. "Is this who I think it is?"

"This is Nataya." Dean took her arm and walked her over to the car. He put his hand on Clay's shoulder. "You did it. You saved her from that bastard. She got away, and this time *you* won." Dean stepped back to give the two of them some space.

Nataya watched Clay as he continued to stare at her. As they had carried Walker through the forest, Dean had told her of Clay's tragic past. The murder of his fiancée. As her eyes met his she felt the connection—painful memories—which they both struggled to accept. She leaned into the car and encircled his shoulders in a gentle hug. "Thank you, Clay."

Clay hugged her back. "Is it true you have no memory of your past?"

She released him and sighed. "Seeing that man made me remember what he did to me, but I don't remember anything before that."

"You're so lucky. I wish I could erase my memories—never feel the hurt and anguish ever again—be free of the pain."

"No, you don't."

Clay looked at her with astonishment. "What—?"

"Dean told me about your fiancée. Do you think she would agree? You've experienced what it feels like to love someone, and have that person love you in return. You have wonderful memories of the times you spent together with Stacy. Memories that no one can take from you. I don't have any of that."

"But I also have the nightmares."

"So do I. But I think we need to stop hiding from them, even if we can't make them go away."

Dean watched from a distance as Nataya took Clay's hands in hers. "You loved her. Keep her memory alive, and then maybe you can make the nightmares go away."

Dean looked up as one of the EMT guys shouted, "We're ready to roll with your guy. We've got to leave, *now.*"

He sprinted over to the car. "Clay, she has to go."

Clay looked up at Nataya and smiled. "Thank you. Good luck with what you need to do now, too. Call me if you need someone to talk to."

She squeezed his hand and turned to hurry to the rescue truck with Dean. "He helped save my life—and so did you. How do I repay something like that?"

Dean put his arm across her shoulders, leading her to where Walker waited. He glanced back at Clay in the car and was surprised to see him sobbing.

"You just did," he said.

CHAPTER SEVENTY-ONE

Gray's Forest, Colorado

Dean helped her climb into the back of the rescue unit and
nodded good-bye. "I'll catch up with you at the hospital."

She sat down beside Walker, not sure if he was awake. Her chest
ached to see him lying there so frightfully pale and still. Tubes
were everywhere—attached to his arm, his nose. But when she
carefully reached past them to take his hand, he opened his eyes
and smiled.

"Good...you're back."

"Yes, I'm here."

"You know they're taking me to the Medicine Lodge, right? I
don't want you to be afraid. They will take good care of me. And
they won't try to keep you there—like before."

"It's okay. I'm not afraid."

"Good. I need you to talk to me, Nataya, so I can stay awake."

"About what?"

"Tell me what happened out there, before I found you. Tell me
everything."

She looked away. "I don't think I can..."

"I *need* you to tell me. Then we will never speak of it again... unless you want to."

She swallowed hard, beginning to understand why he insisted on this.

Of course, how wise of him.

She'd been through a horrific ordeal. Talking about it might help her get over the trauma sooner.

She took a deep breath and began...

⊨⊰ ⊱⊨

The rescue truck turned onto the city streets as she neared the end of her story, and Walker struggled to keep his eyes open. She hesitated, but he looked up at her and said, "Keep going, I'm listening."

"When I saw his face, without the sunglasses, I realized my dreams were real. The spirits had tried to warn me. But when he called me *Jenny*, all the details of that night came back to me... when he took me to the meadow and...cut me with the knife. I think I began to chant words. I don't remember them now. But he saw something in the darkness. It frightened him enough to make him run away. And then I awoke by the fire, cut and bleeding."

Walker squeezed her hand. "Thank you for sharing this with me."

He smiled, but his eyes held a sadness she didn't understand.

"But tell me, Nataya. Why do you think he called you *Jenny*? Do you remember anything before that night?"

"No...nothing before that night..."

⊨⊰ ⊱⊨

Walker watched her closely as she looked away. The lights of the rescue unit flashed outside, creating an eerie backdrop. When she spoke again, her voice sounded distant, as if her thoughts were far away.

"I've been having waking dreams, people and places I don't know. Words come to me, names of things. Maybe these dreams are real, from a time before. Dean told me about Clay finding a missing person report. They think it's me. *Her* name was Jenny. I wish I could remember..."

This time Walker let the weariness take over, and he closed his eyes. She was beginning to remember her past, and it would only be fair to give her the opportunity to fully recover her memories.

But as he drifted in and out of the pain and exhaustion, another fear gnawed at him. He had done as the spirits wished, and saved her. But now he didn't want it to end there.

What if she remembered her past, and he no longer fit into her life? Hell, for all he knew she might be married.

Had he saved her...only to lose her?

CHAPTER SEVENTY-TWO

Elk Meadow, Colorado

Nataya sat beside Walker's bedside, holding his hand as he slept. She had grown used to the machines and their noises, the people coming and going to the hospital room. And she'd had time to think about this man and all he had done for her. She had made it difficult for him to gain her trust. But instincts told her their mutual respect had reached a new level. He cared about her wellbeing. And she cared about his.

She heard someone enter the room, turned to see Dean. He crossed the room to stand beside her, put his hand on her shoulder.

"I hear he came through the surgery just fine."

She looked up at Dean. "Yes, he spoke with me a little when he first woke up. He is resting well."

"Excellent news. And what about you? Were you able to get any sleep?"

"Enough."

"Good. It's important you take care of yourself." Dean walked over to a chair and pulled it closer, sat facing her. "I need to ask you...have you had any more dreams?"

"You want to know if any of my memory is returning?" She smiled at the surprise on Dean's face. "I don't completely understand what has happened to me, but I do believe many of my dreams are memories, trying to come back. Words have been coming to me...hospital...doctor. Words I probably once knew...before. So much feels familiar. But nothing more. Maybe I'm not ready for my past to return yet."

"Maybe not. But when you are, let me know, okay? I have someone who wants to talk to you. Speaking of which, there's a patient here in this hospital who is requesting to see you. It seems quite urgent to him."

"Who is it?"

"He asked me not to say—to just bring you to his room. Don't worry, I'll stay right there with you. Come on. Let's do this while Walker is sleeping."

She hesitated, not wanting to leave his side.

"He'll sleep for a while, and we won't be gone long...just down the hall." Dean took her hand and guided her out of the room and down the hallway.

He led her into another room, which looked exactly like Walker's room. A young man reclined in the bed, watching the door.

She stopped and pointed. "You!" But she laughed and rushed to his bedside. She leaned over the bed and gave Jack Bailey a careful hug, making sure to avoid his bandages. "I thought you were dead and I thought it was my fault. I am so happy to see you are alive."

"You have no idea how relieved I am to hear you say that, *Nataya*. I wouldn't blame you if you hated me. That's why I want to apologize to you for—for everything."

"I don't understand."

"Remember when I came to your room at the hospital? And I said I needed to take *x-rays* of your scars?"

She nodded.

"Well, I tricked you then. It wasn't right. I did it to make my boss happy. And I did it to make money. But the worst part is, because of my ambition, I almost got you killed. That's why I want to talk to you. I have something I need to say."

"Okay."

"I think that if I wrote a story about you, it *could* possibly make me famous. But it could, in turn, ruin your life, maybe change who you are. This experience has taught me something about myself. I don't want to hurt people. I want to help people. I'm going on record right here and now—with Dean as my witness—I am not going to bother you anymore. I still want to write, and I want to become famous, but it'll have to be by a different means."

She had no idea what any of this meant, but she could see the sincerity in the man's eyes, so she replied out of politeness. "Thank you, Jack."

Dean spoke up then. "You don't know it, Nataya, but after Jack was shot, he spent time in the patrol car waiting for the paramedics to arrive. Clay talked to him, to keep his mind off the pain and to keep him from drifting into shock. Both men discovered they have the same interests in criminal investigation."

"Yeah, we do. In fact we're going to collaborate on a book together. I want to tell Clay's story of how he has assisted the law with his computer research and investigations."

She could see the excitement in Jack's expression and hear it in his voice. "This sounds like a good thing, for both of you."

"Yeah, it is. But hey, if you ever decide you *do* want someone to write your life story, Nataya, just give me a call." Jack winked at her.

She mirrored his smile, but wondered how her life story could be interesting to anyone.

I don't even know it myself.

She remembered her conversation with Clay.

Maybe it was time to stop hiding from the nightmares…

CHAPTER SEVENTY-THREE

Big Pine, Colorado

F ox Walker shifted his weight in the back seat of Detective Thomas' car, the dull ache in his shoulder a constant reminder to be thankful for his life, and for Nataya's safety. The detective prattled on about how excited he was to reunite her and Mrs. Becker, but Walker couldn't focus on the words.

This could be the trigger that allows her to recall her past.

He accepted the fact she had the right to know her past, to know who she had been before all of this happened to her. But knowing this was the right thing to do didn't make it any easier. He battled his feelings of selfishness, the reality he wanted her to stay just as she was—the woman who loved nature as much as he—the woman who understood his quiet lifestyle.

Would she remember her life as it had been before, and decide to return to it? He turned to look at her and caught her watching him. He saw worry in her eyes.

Maybe she has the same fears.

"Here we are," the detective announced as he turned into a driveway.

Walker studied the house before them. A wide snow-covered lawn separated them from the expansive front porch, but the sidewalk had been neatly shoveled clean. White latticework and railings wrapped around the front and sides of the house, full of wicker furniture and flowerpots, now empty. He turned to Nataya, saw her staring ahead, her hands clenched in her lap.

"Ready?" he asked.

"Yes," she replied, not able to hide the anxiety in her voice.

He winced as he moved to get out of the car, and she leaned over to him.

"Do you need help?"

"I'm fine. Doc says I'll be good as new in a couple of weeks."

The detective led the way up the sidewalk and toward the porch, while Walker watched Nataya for any reaction to her surroundings. Eyes bright with anticipation and apprehension, she took in every detail, but her expression showed no recognition.

Walker climbed the steps to the porch, his attention drawn to the woman standing in the doorway. She reminded him of a Norman Rockwell painting, from her tidy hair and flowered print dress right down to the polished, practical shoes.

Mrs. Becker ushered everyone in from the cold. Then she turned her attention to the young woman in front of her. "Bless us all. It really *is* you!" She wrapped Nataya in an embrace, seemed to sense the woman's confusion and quickly released her. She took Nataya's hands in hers, studied her with a broad smile on her face. "I knew you'd be back. But my goodness, how different you look— not in a bad way, mind you. You look healthier and…happier, I have to say."

Nataya returned the woman's smile. "Thank you." She looked around at the room. "Everything feels familiar, like I've been here before."

"Well, of course you have, dear." Mrs. Becker looked at Walker. "And you must be the man who saved her life. Dear me, what am I thinking, letting you stand there like this! Here, come sit down."

Walker tried to assure her he was fine, but she would have none of it. She fussed over him, and he smiled in resignation.

After they'd all sat down Mrs. Becker again turned to Nataya.

"Detective Thomas here has told me your incredible story, my dear. You've been through so much. It pains me to think of it. I hope seeing the cottage and your belongings helps in some way. But before you do, can I answer any questions you have?"

Walker watched Nataya twist the edge of her jacket as she spoke. "Yes, I have so many questions...like my family. Do I have any brothers or sisters? And what of my mother and father?"

"You were your parents' only child, and they loved you very much."

"Loved?"

"Yes, dear." Mrs. Becker patted Nataya's hand. "They perished in a plane crash when you were just entering junior high."

Nataya swayed and Walker moved toward her, but she motioned him to stay where he was. "I'm fine. Just felt dizzy for a moment. Please tell me more, Mrs. Becker."

"You were very close to your grandfather, Arthur, so he took you in as his own. Made sure you finished school and went on the college. You loved art and science. Arthur loved nature and the Native American culture. He instilled that same passion in you as you grew up. It's your grandfather's legacy."

Walker saw Nataya's eyes grow misty. "I think I've seen visions of him in my dreams."

"Arthur and I were dear friends and I loved watching the two of you together. Don't be sad, you gave him a lot of joy, my dear. After he passed, I thought it only right to offer you the cottage. He had used it as a studio for years."

"So, my family is all gone?"

"I'm sorry—this all sounds so gloomy. But you've done so well since then. It became your ambition to educate the local children about the natural world, as a way to honor your grandfather. You gave art workshops about nature painting, and you took school children on field trips to the woods. You are well loved in this little town of ours."

Walker heard his own voice before he could censor it. "What about someone…else?"

Mrs. Becker smiled at him and gave him a quick wink. "No, she's not married."

Nataya turned to him then, tears on her cheeks, and took his hand. "I'm ready now," she said.

They stood and Mrs. Becker hugged her saying, "You stay out there as long as you need. It's still your home, as far as I'm concerned."

They stepped out the door together, Walker's heart hammering against his chest, making it difficult to breathe. He could well imagine Nataya's anxiety.

Nataya stared at the cottage, just beyond the main house, with a backdrop of deciduous and evergreen trees. But as she walked toward it, her focus shifted and the building appeared to be miles away…at the end of a tunnel. Each step closer brought quick snapshots of images, the cottage in spring rains…then surrounded by multitudes of brilliant flowers in summer sun…gold and red autumn leaves…then drifts of snow, like now.

Everything came into focus and she found herself standing at the door. Walker opened it for her, then stepped aside to let her enter, indicating he would wait outside. She stepped onto the threshold, took a quick intake of breath and entered.

Sunlight streamed into the neat and orderly rooms. Mrs. Becker must have lovingly cared for all the plants in her absence, for they intermingled with the multitude of books that overflowed into every corner and open space, as if they lived and breathed as one. She stood there absorbing the energy of the rooms.

All the green plants gave her a sense of still being outdoors. The comforting, organic environment surrounded her in peace. This, at least, was something she could relate to.

She moved through each room, touching chairs, tables, framed artwork on the walls, marveling at everything within, overwhelmed that all this belonged to her. When she lived in the wilderness she had few possessions, yet wanted for nothing, and felt rich beyond words.

Whatever will I do with all these—things. What did it all mean to me?

She returned full circle to the front room where, amid the stacks of books, she began to notice small objects, rocks, shells, arrowheads, feathers and small carvings. They lay among the plants and books like small, hidden treasures. She smiled as she looked at each one.

So, I've always loved nature.

On a small desk she noticed one particularly worn book, was drawn to it. When she picked it up she *knew* she had read it many times. She turned to the marked page. Open before her was a Native American warrior's song, to be chanted before going into battle. As she began to read the Shoshone words aloud, a flash crossed her eyes. She saw again the flames in the darkness, the man's face. Her gut twisted in fear, but she forced herself to face the visions.

I know you now. And you can't hurt me anymore!

She heard herself in the vision, chanting, her voice gaining strength, louder and stronger. The man before her stared into the darkness behind her, his eyes going wide in terror. He dropped the knife and fled.

The vision faded and she heard only the quiet of the cottage. She flipped to the front of the book and read the inscription written there.

To my brave little warrior. I'm so proud of you. Love, Granpapa.

She hurried to the door and stepped outside. Walker stood as if guarding the cottage and looked up expectantly as she approached him with the book, pointing to the song on the page.

"I remember now. When I was tied to the tree, and sure I would soon die, I chanted this song out loud. I asked for strength, to face the end with courage. And *they* came, Walker, *the ancient ones.* I felt their presence. So did...he. So did William. That's the reason he fled, leaving me alive."

Walker took her face in his hands, leaned in and kissed her forehead. She saw the tension ease in his expression, but he held his silence. She turned to go back into the cottage and realized— *he is waiting for something in particular.*

She walked back over to the desk to put the book down and studied the other items there.

Then she spotted the photo.

An elderly man smiled at her, his eyes creasing mischievously, his handsome face full of kindness. Snippets of images flowed through her mind as she stared at the photo.

Grandfather?

Around the picture frame lay other small articles, as if it were an altar of sorts, a pressed four-leaf clover, a small stone the shape of a robin's egg and the matching earring to the one she wore. She fingered the earring hanging from her ear with one hand, her other hand touching the matching earring. As she did, she saw the old man in her mind. He opened her hand and placed a velvet box on it while he told her, *"A gift from an exotic land far away. It's the Japanese symbol for divine protection—when I can't be with you."*

Nataya picked up the photo, tears flowing freely. "Granpapa...I remember."

The memories cascaded in upon her then, relentless and powerful. Wave after wave crashed over her, overwhelming in their intensity. At first she fought the blackness that threatened to take her, but soon her mind began to sink deep within. She had to know it all now. Had to relive it.

From far away she sensed Walker cradled her in his arms as she clung to the images, voices and smells that permeated her very being. But soon, she lost the feeling of his presence. She experienced the full love of her parents—then the despair of losing them... her Grandfather's tender kindness—and the sorrow of his death. Anguish shook her body.

She tried to cling to the here and now, yet the past pulled her deeper, and she sensed herself sinking below the surface, drowning in the all-consuming images and emotions.

Walker had heard the thump and rushed into the cottage to find Nataya's body crumpled on the floor. He thought her unconscious, but as he eased her body onto his lap, cradling her in his arms, he saw her eyelids flutter and she began to mutter sounds...and occasionally words he could understand. But nothing made sense.

A shudder racked her body and he pulled her closer, kissed her forehead, tried to comfort her, his mind falling into its own turmoil and fear. As she grew quieter and the murmurs disappeared, he swore he could sense her slipping away from him. Fear turned to panic. He struggled to catch his breath.

But then, he heard Grandfather's soothing voice in his ears.
Time to let go of the fear.

At last Walker knew what the words meant—what Grandfather had tried to teach him. After Haiwii's death he had chosen to live without love—to avoid pain.

By doing so, I chose to live in fear.

No more.

He leaned close to Nataya and whispered in her ear. "Please, Nataya, come back to me."

A long sigh escaped her lips and her body relaxed.

"Walker?" she whispered.

He pulled her close. "Yes."

She slowly opened her eyes and gazed at him. He found his own vision going blurry.

"I know who I am now."

Walker held his breath.

"I'm glad I know. And Jenny will always live inside of me, and all her memories. But I can never go back." She held his gaze. "I remain Nataya."

His chest tight and eyes burning, he pushed through his own fears, and forced out the words. "Will you come home with me, Nataya?"

Her arms pulled him to her.

The End

AUTHOR BIO

 Indy Quillen has always loved to write but took many side adventures along the path to publication, including raising a family while organic gardening and learning self-reliance skills, owning and running a natural food store, training and competing in martial arts, creating and selling nature-themed watercolors and greeting card illustrations, as well as designing gemstone jewelry. She grew up in Indiana, lived in Colorado and the San Diego area, and now resides with her husband in the Pacific Northwest. When she's not writing (or camping and practicing her survival skills) she enjoys reading, gardening, traveling, hiking, bike riding and swimming.

ACKNOWLEDGEMENTS

I am fortunate to be surrounded by supportive family members and friends who believe in me. They keep me going when I struggle with frustration. It's a solid base to work from and I don't take it for granted. Thank you—every one of you!

My writing friends have a special understanding of the pain and joys experienced during the creation process. They cheer me on even as they strive to find their own way. The Gorilla Writers group played an important part in my writing life—thanks to all! I want to give a special shout-out to my writing buddies, Kathy Paulek, Suad Campbell, Rick Landin, Lynne Kennedy, Anita Knowles, John Mullen, Kevin Smith, Michele Scott, Dot Caffrey and Annoushka Lyvers, for their unwavering friendship and support. It has kept me going, especially during some dark times.

But writing is like any other skill. It has to be learned, and I have had many teachers, editors, and organizations along the way that helped me find my path. For these people and groups I am forever grateful: my agent, Paul Fedorko with N.S Bienstock, my writing mentor Mark Clements, my editors Aviva Layton, Mike Sirota, Laura Taylor and Jennifer Silva Redmond. I would like to thank the following authors for their support and inspiration: Jonathan Maberry, Matt Pallamary, Alan Russell, Judy Reeves, Jill G. Hall, Larry Edwards and Carolyn Wheat. And for guidance along the way: David Hough with Houghton Mifflin Harcourt, Jill Marr with Dijkstra Agency, Michael Homler with St. Martin's Press, the San Diego Writers, Ink and all of the great staff at Southern California Writers Conference, led by Michael Steven Gregory and Wes Albers.

Through it all, one person has been there for me, encouraged me when it all looked so bleak, and believed in me without fail, Michael, my husband.

To you I say, "To the moon and back, Babe."

Made in the USA
Columbia, SC
18 May 2020